# Norty

# Norty

## GUILD WARS

# Charlotte Bishop

Order this book online at www.trafford.com
or email orders@trafford.com

Most Trafford titles are also available at major online book retailers.

Printed in the United States of America.

ISBN: 978-1-4907-4768-2 (sc)
ISBN: 978-1-4907-4769-9 (e)

*Trafford rev. 10/02/2014*

 www.trafford.com

**North America & international**
toll-free: 1 888 232 4444 (USA & Canada)
fax: 812 355 4082

Dedicated to those who have purchased my other books; in whatever format.

With the death of Caspo Kwil a new leader of the enchanters was to be chosen; yet the council were against his wishes when he spoke Norty was to be his heir. They refused her right to lead yet the guild was solidly behind her. Leaving the great hall with her as un-inaugurated leader a rift had been caused between the elves.

Lore stated if the elves fought amongst themselves then all the elves would perish. It was why her carefully laid plans ensured there was to be fighting.

# Guild Wars

Barthic watched the intricate wooden carving of the dwarf walk across the triangular checkerboard on the table in front of him; with sword drawn it struck the elf on the chest, "Nevertheless, it will happen."

Her elf moved two spaces as Blyth beckoned, "We force the issue."

"Your elf is challenged. The Chosen Ones are quested, this you know."

At her gesture the elf returned to his original position, "We speak always of the same subject, it wearies me. I saw not your move."

"Each time we play you lose and always the same excuse. All debated this and it will happen, their quest has yet to finish."

"We ask much of them, too much I believe. Let them live their lives in peace."

"Your voice was heard at the debate, with two more choosing your side."

"The Chosen Ones believe their quest to be won."

"The quest will come at the appointed time."

"We should leave them in peace; they live but five hundred years."

"A quest has been set and must continue to its end."

"To right the wrongs done by us; it is much to ask of them."

"There were mistakes, this is agreed by all."

"Yet we expect mortals to correct our mistakes?"

"The future is not yet scribed in the book of history. We erred and may not change what is passed, yet you may plan what is still to come."

"And it is they who must ensure our plans come to fruition? Unforgivable! The Chosen Ones must have the help I insist upon and as promised. Pose was born to help heal those first wounds and will be instrumental in this part of the quest. Norty begins to realise and, when the truth is finally seen, they may triumph."

He yawned, "*If* I let such happen. Remember, I rule and no others."

"I remember only too clearly! It is much to ask; the odds stack well against them."

"The odds will be greater afore the year is old. You take not the skeletons into account."

"I take all into account; as is my role in the Gods. You have summoned them from the void to which they were banished so long ago."

"It is time they saw the world again and the elves will make an interesting fight for them. You know well they hate the elves; or any who have skin."

"The quest you place in danger if the elves fight the skeletons. It is too much!"

"*I care not if they defeat your elves or no. I wish to see the fight.* The Chosen ones will live to continue the quest, this I will ensure!"

"My planning was given to Norty and should she give thought to this they will defeat your skeletons. Others now see this and wish to join them."

"I am unsure if I will allow this to happen."

As her elf finally gained the upper hand the dwarf fell, "We are sworn not to intervene yet I would give them aid."

"It is not aid they need, Blyth, but the courage to face their foes."

"In truth I believe their foe to be us."

Barthic grunted as his finger beckoned to another piece on the board, "We are the foe? Hmmm, I see your meaning yet disagree."

"We test them time and time again and it is in this way we are the foe. Norty suffered much anguish when she believed her calling to be wrong, and great pain from you for her doubts when mana was gifted to her. You gave the thought to Arabella to take Elesee and Juin to the dungeon, causing yet more pain; yours the plan to have Norty follow many years later. If not for the intervention of Messenger she would have survived not to lead her sisters on this quest. Our plans would have been in disarray for your acts."

He waved her to silence, "My decision alone; she survived."

"She survived through no help from us. Think not to intimidate me! Few will speak against you yet I will always do so when you are wrong."

"Think not to push me; I suffer it not! Messenger gave her the thought which saved her, he likes the sisters."

Blyth blew on the board and the remains of the dwarf turned to smoke, "I would speak with them. I wish only to offer advice, counselling on the fight to come. It was I who named the sisters, my planning ability given to Norty, as Aronath and Trenth gave their gifts to her sisters. Always it is I who feels closest to them; I it was who made their kind, they are *my* children, *my elfin*."

"What is it you hide from me? A form I see at your side though it is blurred."

"It is for you to know not. As to our discussion what are you thoughts?"

Barthic shook his head, "Denied. All agreed they must fight alone. If you are allowed to council them others may demand they guide their foes."

"Others need not know of this."

"They would know. Why is the form a blur and I see it not?"

2

She tried to keep his thoughts away from the one at her side, "There are ways to ensure they know not. I would strike a bargain with you. Should you lose this game I am to be allowed to council them for ten minutes of their time."

"Your position is too weak to win this game."

It had worked, he was looking at her once more, the thoughts on his face obvious, "My position is poor yet still I offer the challenge. Are you not sure of your prowess?"

"The game must be worth the fight; what reward would you offer?"

"I have seen the way your eyes watch me, know the thoughts you hold for me. I will be your reward for one night; should I lose."

"Then I agree to the challenge."

"There are to be no others to advise their foes. Agreed?"

"Agreed. Your dark elf is under attack from my giant, the game is lost to you once more, Blyth."

## Favours

Elesee glanced at her daughters sitting crossed legged on the floor before blowing on the still wet ink as she finished scribing in the large brown book. Closing it she smiled at them, it was not often they were with her since Icee had finally joined in wedlock to Kare E'Thelt, the first marriage between elf and dark elf. Yet she knew this was a more than just a visit from them, they were planning a strategy as only they could, their minds were linked, a gift from the Gods. Sitting with their backs straight, shoulders back and eyes lightly closed, they looked the very picture of elfin ladies. The posture and ways of meditation she had taught them from birth, now seeming so many years ago, sent her mind drifting slowly back to the days when she was younger.

In one way she had been unlike any before her. Her parents had taught her elfin Lore and ways and, as her parents had been, she was one with the rivers and trees, one with the animals of the forest for none would harm a druid. Yet she had a curiosity in her for the glade near her home others shunned. To her it was a place of peace and tranquillity, to others it was to be avoided at all costs, no matter how many trees they planted in the glade none would grow. For hundreds of years they had tried, only the twenty-four growing there would survive.

She had taken to visiting the glade most afternoons from late childhood to her coming of age, to ponder its meaning. Yet another elf would sit and watch her from a distance, and at first she resented his intrusion into her private world. It was then she began to realise how different she was to other wood elves, her hatred of him began to change to one of liking as he slowly, day by day, drew nearer, and her mind began to change once more, to thoughts of love for him; and it frightened her. It had convinced her she was different, elves fell in love the instant they saw the one destined to be theirs; she had fallen in love over time.

At first it worried her to speak of her feelings to him, even if she could she was bound by Lore to wait until the male spoke first of love.

When he did she remained quiet, unable to believe he also had fallen in love slowly with her and not instantly as it should have been. When she joined in wedlock to Juin only one other knew their secret, Dreth, a gnome and lifelong friend to both.

4

Her eyes closed and her thoughts grew lighter as she remembered speaking of a child for them. As with all elves she could have a child at will, when she consented in her mind during love. She had planned where she would consent, in the glade where they had first met. She had planned it all so carefully, even the name of her daughter for, somehow, she knew her first child would be female and had decided her name was to be Aleathia.

Elfin Lore was biased towards the male, as well she knew, yet one point of Lore she loved above all others, the right of the female to name their child. The name she had chosen was to be different; never before used in elfin history.

Yet she had consented so many times with her husband and still no child was conceived. She began to wonder what was wrong; her body felt no different and her mind was clear, there was no reason why they could not have the child of their dreams. Eventually a thought crossed her mind, she was too different from other elves, and began to curse the Gods for her very being, for denying her the right of a child.

Finally her wish had been granted yet in a way she could never have foreseen. The Gods gave to her three children, born on the same day, when in elfin history no female had born twins, and never had more than two been gifted to an elfin couple.
Her head shook a little as she thought of how she had never been able to name her children. The sweet voice of the Goddess Blyth spoke to all in the forest of their homeland on the day of their birth, of a quest they were born for, and had named them also.
Blyth had named her first-born Norty, an enchantress with a mind unlike any other. Icee was named second, a wizard of incredible power. Malinna was last named; a cleric with healing powers far above all others.

Yet her daughters were never to train with her, for her to teach them the druid ways. Each had chosen a profession different to which they were born, one never open to wood elves, and it was to different races they had turned to begin their training.
Norty sought training with the high elves, Icee turned to the gnomes and the dwarves welcomed Malinna with open arms.

"Mother, are you well? Fear not, Malinna is here."

"I am well. My mind turns to thoughts of many years ago."

"Never do you fail to hear your daughters as they speak."

Malinna ran her fingers swiftly over her mother waiting to feel the tingling in them she always had as she felt the pain of the one she was to heal.

"I am well, concern yourself with duties to those who have need of you."

"You are my concern, mother. Be still and let me ensure you are well."

Elesee sat back knowing it would be useless to argue with them.

"I feel nothing wrong with you, mother."

"When my daughters worry I have learned to let them have their way."

"I must return home, Sha'Dal is to take the second druid test on the morrow and Finglas is to be amongst those who track him."

Norty laughed, "My husband will ensure they try all the harder to track your son."

"I would be disappointed if he did not, yet Flight has taught him a few tricks he has learned also."

"I pray to the Mother of All it will go well for him."

Icee stood, "I also, Kare and Finglas still disagree which ale is stronger, ogre or troll. I fear I know the way they will settle the argument. They know my feelings of ale; I care not to see any drunk."

"I believe he will feel the sharp edge of your tongue, sister."

Icee giggled, "Not only my husband, sister, yours also."

As they left she turned to her mother, "You scribe in the book once more and still I know not of its contents, will I ever know of them?"

"As I have spoken to you since your birth, the scribing is not for now. Always it is you who speaks of the book, Norty, never your sisters."

"They have little interest it seems yet the more the book is withheld from me the more my curiosity grows."

"It seems the curiosity of the race of man is infectious, the longer you spend with them the more you become as them."

"Mother, there is little need to insult me!"

"Your tongue should not be sharp to those who would tease, Norty."

"Forgive me; much is on my mind."

"There is no need of forgiveness. Speak your mind to me."

"I would ask from you a favour. The death of Caspo Kwil leaves the enchanters leaderless. On the new moon the enchanters stand before the council for a leader to be appointed. I wish for you to take Nortee to the land of man during this time."

"She will object most strongly."

"There will be an excuse to have her with you."

"How is it you know this?"

"Take her with you, I ask of you."

"How long should she be away?"

"Seven days, mother. She is to return not before this time."

"I hear the king is ill yet still will they hold the festival as he demands. As it will begin on the new moon it would seem a suitable time I believe."

"Thank you."

"It seems a strange coincidence it is to be held when you have the need of her to be away; I had thought you would wish this yet the reason eludes me."

"It is better she is away, she would refuse to remain silent at the ceremony, her actions have always been those of impatience. She would stand, give voice to her thoughts and bring shame to herself. Time is needed to ensure our plans come to fruition, or friends may turn against us."

"Those who would turn against you are not friends."

"They will be afraid and it is this fear which will turn them, and turn them back to the path they must follow."

"Why it is you must always speak in riddles?"

"If thought is given you would see it is not a riddle."

"I have not the time. Nortee will need a new robe and must learn to dance."

"I have asked Myra to place aside a silk Nortee will like and I feel she will like the dancing more than I."

"Always you ensure plans are flawless yet I know not how you do so. You were unhappy to learn to dance yet with Finglas in your arms you seem happy to do so."

"He is elfin kind, not mankind."

"One day your thoughts of man may change."

"No, mother, my thoughts of them could never change."

# For A Child's Sake

Finishing the last steps she bowed, "Would it be the elves had such customs."

"It's hard to believe this is your first dance, Lady Nortee."

"I have watched others and wondered why they smile; now I see. Grandmother teaches much yet fails to mention there would be pleasure."

"You dance like a feather. I'll demand no others dance with you."

"You seek to flatter me, grandmother speaks you are your father's son."

"So, I'm talked about?"

From the corner of her eyes she saw her grandmother beckon to her, "It seems duties call. Mayhap we will dance another time?"

"Grandmother, always it seems you call when I have need of you."

Taking her by the arm Elesee lead her along the hall towards the doors, "It is obvious he has feelings for you. The king has called and we must see him, Ventil will be here on our return."

"I attend these meetings at your request and mothers insistence yet I should be with her, she has need of me this day."

"You are passed the coming of age; it would be your right to take no heed of her requests; as well you know."

"To have refused would not be appropriate, as well both know."

"As my replacement she seeks assurance you are well instructed."

"Mother should be the one you instruct, not I."

"She feels not towards them as do you, a true ambassador must love the people to whom she serves in the role."

"Tonight she has need of me at her side, I worry for her. She must see this, grandmother, she must."

"Your worries are groundless. I have duties to attend and would ensure you see the ways in which man must be sometimes handled."

"You conspired with mother to have me here yet I fail to see why, she has a need of me as never before."

"Her needs are many. Today she has her guild to tend and to keep you from harm's way so she may deal with the council."

"I should be at her side, as Lore demands."

"Her guild is on her mind and she must be with them. She will be rejected, this you must know."

"Mother speaks little of her plans, she is often frustrating."

"I also have need of you. Do you know with whom you danced tonight?"

"Ventil, grandmother, he is the king's son."

"He is heir to the throne, one it is hoped may reign in peace."

"I believe not such is possible, they have a long history of wars."

"As we once had, and they trust to the elves to help them once more."

"As you have spoken, we have oft helped them in their wars."

"And we have fought against them also."

"Who would they fight this time?"

"In all your talks with them you have no answer to such a question?"

"I have not."

"Your mother is correct, you have much to learn."

Tapping lightly on the door Elesee waited for an answer, "Never must you enter until bid, it is considered impolite to do so."

"To wait for an invite seems rude to me. They have strange ways."

"Nevertheless the ways of others must be respected."

"Grandmother, how long must I train?"

Turning she smiled warmly to her, "I am still learning of them, Nortee."

As a small door to the anteroom opened she bowed to the unkempt man, "The king wishes to speak with me."

His head jerked backwards, "Come in, Elesee, come in."

Entering the room she smiled, "If you will lead the way?"

"He wants to see you; he didn't mention anyone else."

"I introduce Nortee, my grandchild and replacement should it become necessary. Without her I will enter not. If you would be so kind to instruct the king we will await in my room for further instructions."

"If she's your grandchild I suppose it'll be alright, I trust you as much as he does. He's in the bedchamber and his strength fails; don't tire him or you'll have me to deal with."

"Thank you, Laric, the visit will be brief; I have no wish to tire him. Please lead on."

Following him along the room Nortee whispered, "Never have I met another so distasteful."

"You see only with your eyes, Nortee, look past the man to see the truth. He loves his king above all and seeks to protect him, as he will protect Ventil should he become king."

"There is doubt he will become king?"

"He has spoken nothing of his elder brother?"

"Not a word has been spoken of him, and the elder should reign."

"He has been missing many years, the patrol never returned from the boarders, each patrol searching for them failed to return. You must now learn to see who is friend and who would harm the peace hanging so tentatively over this land."

"Yet I thought this man's words for his king meaningless, used to show he has power over any who wished to enter."

"Such are the ways of these people; he spoke the words in jest. It will take many years for you to realise how they think and act."

"This lesson has been learned."


Bowing as she entered the bedchamber she walked over to the king, "My friend, it is good to see you once more."

"My fair Lady Elesee, I would die in no prettier company."

"Always you are the one to flatter."

"With you I don't flatter, I speak the truth."

"You are weak and must tire yourself not. How may I help?"

Waving Laric from the room he sat up in bed, "There're those who want war, I don't."

"They say your strength will soon be gone, yet you move not as one suffering, though your skin is pale as in illness."

"I fain the illness and use flour on my face to give it credence. I'll live a few more years and this way gets me my needs."

"In which way?"

"When the king's on his death bed he soon finds who are friend and enemy. Now, who's this at your side?"

Her hand, palm up, gestured, "Forgive my inattentiveness. I introduce to you my granddaughter Nortee; I train her to be my replacement."

His head shook, "None could replace my Elesee. Ah yes, the image of her mother. Beauty runs in the family, handed down from the grandmother."

She laughed, "Is there no end to your charming?"

"Grandmother, Laric listens at the door."

"It is expected of him, Nortee."

"Their ways are so strange. Never will I understand them."

"You underestimate them also."

"In which way do I do so?"

"We have spent many years together as friends; do you believe the king would understand not our language?"

She felt her cheeks redden a little, "Once more I am remiss."

"There's much for you to learn about us, child."

Stepping back she bowed, "Thrice I have erred this day and trice is enough. I will be more attentive. I believe I may enjoy the challenge of an ambassador."

Elesee smiled, Nortee was all she had hoped her daughter would be should she have followed in her footsteps. Nortee would become an ambassador, one to be proud of. Yet it still caused pain her eldest had failed to follow in her stead. It had been an elfin tradition for thousands of years; first-born daughter followed her mother on her chosen path, as first-born son followed his father.

Norty had broken the tradition claiming she had other, more important, duties and knew her daughter was right; their quest was more important than any other part of her life. They had won and the world had not been destroyed, as the Gods had vowed it would should they lose.

Yet the cost to her daughters had been great, and she knew it. As their leader Norty had born the weight outwardly, yet she knew it was only a facade to all she met. She would not let the world see how the weight and fear of failure had taken its toll, yet she saw it in her eldest.

Icee knew little of the weight her sister bore; always eager for battle to commence she had taken to training as a wizard with all her will and skills. She was better than any other in her chosen profession, only she could cast with such fury all her mana could be used in one lethal blast against a more powerful foe, and such might had saved them on more than one occasion. Icee was so different to her sisters; she had a power few other wizards would ever match, and had not yet realised her true strengths. She was the power of her daughters yet since the battle to save the halflings had used her power more wisely.

With a slight shake of her head her thoughts turned to her youngest daughter. Malinna had been gifted in ways she did not yet realise. As their spiritual guide and healer she was the envy of other clerics and druids, none could heal as she did, only she could feel the pain within the people brought to her for healing. She could heal the pain and mend the wounds of those brought to her when all who tried had failed.

Now Nortee had bowed before the king to make amends for her mistakes, she would make an excellent ambassador, she would ensure it. She had so much of her mother in her it seemed she was watching her and not her granddaughter. With an inward sigh she realised Norty would never feel towards man as she did. Reluctantly she let her mind return to their troubles.

"How may we help you, my friend?"
"By calling me by name, never once have you used it."
"One day I may, your majesty."
"I give up with you, Elesee. I was talked into holding the festival."
"May I have a guess who spoke the suggestion to you?"
"You'll not guess if you live all your five hundred years."
"Norty has spoken to you and, knowing my daughter, mayhap offered a promise in return?"
"I never could fool you, Elesee, though I've tried many times, and failed all of them."
"Mother arranged the festival? When was this?"
"She called to see me more than a month ago."
"Mother has been busy these last months, speaking with many peoples. Now I see why she knew I would be needed here. She plans well though I know not them all."
"You mean more to her than your realise. She gave a promise she hates to ensure you are safe."
"My daughter...."
"Elesee, I know her true feeling, she hides them but not well enough. I've known you for so long how could I not see through the faces your daughter presents to us?"
"Few see my daughter's feelings."
"It's not her manners which betray her, it's her unspoken words."
"I will speak with her on our return. Oft I have asked she use her ways and she fails me in this."
"You'll say nothing, Elesee. I agreed to the festival for other reasons, I needed you here to ask a favour."
"It would seem many ask favours of me these last days. What is it you wish of me?"
His voice lowered ensuring Laric could not overhear, "Take Ventil to your lands, teach him the ways of love. Do this for me it's all I ask, for our friendship these last fifty years."
"I would be honoured to do so yet there are problems in other cities I must deal with. Nortee has need to know your people more and I believe she will be most suited for the task. Each may learn from the other to mutual advantage."

12

"I trust you, Elesee. He'll be in safe hands."

Elesee turned to Nortee, "There are those who would harm him."

"And those who would bend him to their will. If he were strong he's still too young so they would kill him and place a puppet on the throne. He needs time to grow and become wise to the ways of the world. To know who is friend and who is a foe. I want him to lead our people in peace, not the ways of war and hatred; there's been enough of it in my time."

"I have hope he will reign in peace."

"My eldest son, Barac, is the one who would have war; war with everyone he sees."

"Yet he has been seen not for many years."

"For me to say this seems hard but I'm glad he's dead. He would lead my people to war and to the death of us all."

"There is strangeness in this. The Gods took your son yet left the lands of man in a peace."

"Always they strike a bargain to their favour."

"Their ways are unknown to us."

"I know their ways. They took him so when I die I'll leave someone who wants to live in peace; others will attack us to take our lands thinking it an easy victory. I won't have it! I want him to see peace and live it as long as he can. But your people know the art of war; never have you been defeated. They can instruct him."

"You wish we train him to fight us?"

"No, Elesee. I want you to teach him to be one with all things like your people. But I want him to be able to see who is planning to attack us and how to prevent it; without the use of war if possible but with its full use if not."

"I am unsure over this. I will teach not someone to attack us."

"I want you to show him the ways of peace. I've taught him how to fight and win battles."

"It shall be as you ask. Yet not in the way you believe."

"I know the look on your face, you have plans."

"I had surmised I would be asked and have made arrangements. Nortee and Ventil will accompany me to Kalona, yet not as the man he now is."

## Strange Meetings


Waving goodbye to friends Aurorai opened the door to her mother's inn and closed it behind her before leaning on it. It had been a good day. Norty had summoned her to her study and informed her she was not to attend class but, after midday break, was return to the study for Pose and herself to train her in methods of entering a mind seemingly blank.

It had puzzled her why such training was needed yet they knew things of the mind so far past her own understanding she was in awe of them. The next day she was to attend for yet more tuition and then seek out Jenay for introduction to the next class. She had been instructed her progress was excellent and this was to be her reward; though she may find the class hard to cope with. She had only been in the previous class for three months and when she arrived home she was in a good mood.

Her training had begun with Nortee yet their paths had diverged quickly, she had thought they would be together throughout their training but worried she would never make the profession to which she was born; no matter how hard she tried she could not make her mind leave her body. Her parents had been so patient with her yet she knew she would fail the test when the enchanters called her to the guild on her coming of age. Once she was tested and found lacking she would be banished. Her only recourse would be to have her parents banish her and not suffer the humiliation of watching their guild banish her before all those assembled. Whichever way she chose she would become an Undesirable Elf.

Her mind recalled the time she sat behind the enchanters' guild hall sobbing softly and knowing she would never enter its doors. Eventually she wiped her eyes and became aware of someone sat in front of her wearing a green black robe.

'Why the tears, young one?'

Almost without realising she answered the female, 'I will be an Undesirable; never will I enter the enchanters guild.'

'Why is it you think this way?'

'My mind will leave not my body. So hard I try. So hard, so hard.'

'Mayhap it is the problem. May I try with you?'

Before she could refuse a voice was in her mind.

'Follow me, young one.'

'How may I do so, I know not where you are?'

'Follow my voice as you would a friend who calls you.'

Nervously she began to follow the voice as it led her slowly forward. With each step she became unsure; still the voice in her head coaxed her ever forward and she could do little to refuse. Suddenly a glass wall prevented further movement.

'Why is you stop, young one? Not far is there to go. A little further is all I ask.'

'A glass wall stands before me. I see no way around it.'

'In your hand is a hammer; strike the wall.'

Looking down she saw the hammer and wondered how she had not noticed it before.

'Strike the wall, young one.'

Mentally she raised the hammer and struck the wall, to no avail, 'It moves not.'

'Strike all the harder.'

With all her mental force she struck once more, 'It budges not.'

'You strike not the wall of your fears. Speak of the trouble within your mind.'

'I may not.'

'To know your troubles you must speak of your fears. Speak to me of them.'

Without realising why she began to tell her, 'If my mind were to leave me I would be afraid it would return not; it would be lost to me; lost forever. I would be a body with no mind. Well you know what will happen if I am found in such a way.'

'You listen to whispers and fears which are not true. It is not the way of our people to put to death any whose mind is lost.'

'I have heard this happens.'

'Never has it happened; we care for our own.'

'Yet if my mind were to be lost....'

'Your mind is your own, how may it be lost to you; it must always return to you for do you not own your mind?'

'It is mine alone. Yes it is mine.'

'Banish your fears.'

'I know not how.'

'Think of your fears, control them and let them not control you.'

'How would I know my fears?'

'Your fear presents itself to you, you see it as a wall; impenetrable by you yet you see through it for it is clear to you what it is. The hammer is there to aid you, to strike your fear and end it. Strike your fear.'

'I cannot!'

'Is it fear who owns you?'

'I am myself, none may own me!'

'Then strike, show fear who is the mistress.'

'I am the one who commands?'

'Strike, young one, Strike! Show to fear he may not own you!'

Mentally she raised the hammer and struck the wall, 'I am the one who commands. I.'

'Strike all the harder!'

'It cracks, it cracks!'

'Once more, strike once more. Destroy fear before it destroys you.'

'May I do this?'

'You are the one who commands; always remember this.'

A mental scream rang out as she raised the hammer and struck with all her fury. The glass wall shattered to spin away in a glittering display of shards catching the light. Then her mind was out of her body and could look around, 'So different it is. Never had I thought it to be like this. I see so much and all is so different.'

'Look around you and see what all enchanters see. Linger here and enjoy, as so many before you have done.'

So much was revealed to her. The female in front of her seemed to have a light shimmer around her head and she could see the minds of creatures such as birds all around her. Carefully she stared at each of the creatures and could see a glow around the heads of each of them. Her mind darted around eager for more as she soaked up the new experience in her life.

'It is beautiful, so beautiful.'

'It is time to let your mind return to you.'

'Must I? I have seen so little. Never did I know....'

'Your mind has been out of your body twenty minutes and you begin to tire. Call your mind back to you.'

Suddenly her mind was once more in her body and a feeling of sadness took her.

'The feeling is normal for a first time. As you train it will become easier for you to do this, and more enjoyable. When you enter the guild seek me out.'

When she opened her eyes they were wet once more, but with tears of joy. At last she knew the world of the enchanter and so much was now open to her. She must seek out her parents and speak to them of the new found skill; the one they had tried so desperately to show her. Jumping up she suddenly realised she must thank the one who gave her this blessing yet the female had gone, 'Your name, I know it not. How may I seek you out?'

"Aurorai, we are busy this day. You are early and help is needed."
Her mother's voice brought her out of her thoughts and she looked around. It had become a game to her as she entered the inn after training and see the customers, to wonder what they would order.

Two old dwarves with beards of pure white down to their stomachs sat in the table in the middle of the room playing the game their entire race seemed to enjoy. A coin would be tossed and the other would call the face. If they lost they bought the next round. Already there were sixteen mugs stacked in two heaps on the table and probably thirty before the game ended. They would be here until asked to leave, and do so begrudgingly, yet would buy enough ale to ensure more barrels could be bought.
Close by two high elves watched the dwarves with a smile on their faces they tried in vain to hide. They seemed to be playing a game also, on who would win the toss of the coin. The look on one of their faces deemed he had lost; yet what the forfeit was for loosing she could not decide.

Close by two gnomes sat with their backs towards her yet she knew them by name; Grismor and his brother Herden. They were hard to tell apart yet she had, after she had served them so many times, realised it was always Herden who paid and, when he thought she was not looking, Grismor who paid his share to his brother.
The other tables had the usual customers, some already eating and some obviously waiting. Most were there to drink and socialise after the day's events or to purchase food for travelling. Her mother made the best elfin travel cake, as most of her people knew.

To one side she recognised a young dark elf. She had seen her around a few times and wondered why she was here. Shadow knight by birth she was the dark elf version of a paladin but where the paladins put to death any un-dead they found the shadow knights used them; mainly in battle. During the day she was escorted to several places but had never seen where she went. It took some moments to remember her name; Jennka. Today a ranger was the escort but he also seemed more interested in the dwarfs' game than the girl at his side. From the look on his face he was

obviously unhappy with the role in life he now had, and unhappy he had
to sit there and not drink.

Her attention was taken as several voices called her; some asking for
drinks or food whilst others called out greetings. Her mother's inn was
bustling with activity; it would be a very busy night. Moving forward
to heed her mother's call she stopped as the table in the corner became
visible to her, sat around it were four customers. Since the elves had begun
to let other races enter their lands, over one thousand years previously,
if they did so in small parties, she had become familiar with most of the
races.

Two sat there were easy, one high elf and one wood elf. The others were
from the race of man yet were different from most of them. These were
from the land of permanent snow. All races insisted on wearing the
clothes from the land of their birth; to these men it was seal skins, and it
was misplaced here. All too soon she would be asked to serve them and
knew the stench of their sweat in those clothes would be repugnant. More
distasteful was the seal clothing; the thought of animal skin on her body
revolted her. She preferred the silk robe she wore.

Large black beards hid their faces and when she removed the plates and
mugs she would be drawn to look at their beards, and see remnants of
food and drink in them. With a shudder she hoped her mother would
serve them; she usually served the Undesirables, and both of the elves sat
at the table were outcasts.

Her attention turned to the two elves with them. It was unusual for elves
to be friendly to this race of man. They were considered as cold and
heartless as the lands from which they came. Most of these men were
hunters, but hunters of man, and merciless in their task. If cash were to be
paid for the return of someone, for whatever reason, these men were rarely
known to fail.

If the reward was offered for the return of the person in any condition
they always returned a severed head.

More surprisingly one elf with them was dressed in black and it was
obvious there were friends; the laughter they shared from time to time
confirmed it. The elves were Undesirables yet normally such elves wore
silver grey as their chosen colour. As they did not enter a guild, for
whatever reason, they continued to wear the colour all elves wore until
entering their guild.

18

For the men to wear such a colour was understandable. They were a little darker of skin than most men and the seal skins were black. Yet for an elf to wear black was almost inconceivable. No elf she had seen had ever chosen to wear such a colour; and no high elf had hair as black as her clothes. Black hair had never before been seen on a high elf so it was plain to all she had used a dye. But she could see no reason she would do it.

Her eyes were drawn to the cloaks each had placed over their weapons as they lay at their sides; and another surprise found her. Four bows were leaning against the stonework close to the log fire. Two, obviously those of the men, were standard bows, or so she believed in her brief encounter with such weapons. One was better made, obviously belonging to the wood elf. It was typical of the bow most wood elves carried and bore a personal mark near the tip of the bow, in this case twin vertical marks. The last bow was of outstanding quality; made by someone with a great love of their craft.

It had long since been an understanding, any entering the inn would leave their weapons on the floor beside their table; her father always insisted upon it yet she had never found out why. The only reason she could think of was they were not easily grabbed if a fight was to start, thereby offering less chance of a fight. There was no chance of seeing what arrows they carried, whether for hunting four footed of two footed prey. She had heard, though the use of a bow never interested her, some arrows were designed to whistle as they flew towards their target, mesmerising them to ensure the kill. Looking towards the quivers she was disappointed, the cloaks covered them.

"Make haste, Aurorai."

"I am here, mother."

"Take these to the men and the Undesirables, too long have they been waiting."

"Always it is you who insist you serve Undesirables, mother."

Her father interjected, "Your mother is busy, Aurorai. Do as she asks."

Taking the tray she headed to the table, she would take a look at the quivers given an opportunity. If they contained arrows for hunting two legged quarry she knew they would be mercenaries. The thought somehow pleased her even though she knew it to be wrong.

Balancing the try with practised ease she began placing the drinks on the table. Two mugs of ale for the men and a glass of wine for the high elf; she placed the light beer in front of the wood elf. Turning round she cast a glance at the quivers, disappointed to find the cloaks still hid them.

"Your service is flawed, elf."

Looking closely at the high elf she wondered why she had called her elf. She had never heard the term used by one elf to another, "I apologise for any mistake. Where am I amiss?"

"I drink beer; Kessy is the one who likes wine."

Swapping the drinks she apologised once more, "An unusual twist. I hope the drinks are to your liking."

A hand clasped on her wrist, "Sing us a song, little elf."

She looked at the hand and back to the man, "You travel with my kind. I had thought they would have instructed to touch without permission is not permitted."

"I'll remove it after the song and when you take me to your room."

Her voice became threatening, "Remove your hand or I will be forced to act."

"Think a little elf can best me, do ya?"

In a blur of movement Aurorai saw the high elf's hand move to her shoulder to grab at something and a dagger seemed to just appear at the throat of the man, "Leave her be, Rolf."

"I want a song! And then a room with her for the night; I can do a lot for an elf as pretty as her."

Purposely she pressed the dagger harder, "You want her as my blade wants your blood."

"I want her. *Now!*"

The knife twisted and blood began to trickle down the blade, "She is not for you. Leave her be."

His hand released her and Aurorai turned to walk back to her mother.

Wiping the blood from his throat he turned to her, anger in his voice, "You never stop me having anyone! Why now?"

"She is not for you, not this one."

"I want her!"

Her voice hissed at him, "Touch her once more and my dagger will stop not with just a little of your blood. *My promise on this!*"

"I know elves and their promises. She's a high elf; one of your kind; one of those who threw you out; why protect her?"

Looking towards the bar where Aurorai stood with her mother she whispered, "The ones who cast me out to be an Undesirable; you are closer the truth than you realise, Rolf."

His eyes had followed the girl, watching the sway of her hips as she walked; admired the soft curves of her body as the robe clung to her figure. Spitting on his hand he rubbed it into the stinging wound on his neck. The girl had heightened his sense of lust and he would have her soon; no matter what had been promised. His mind returned to how graceful and swift his friend moved; and the years he had wanted her.

After he had finished with the little elf they would move on to another town, hopefully before her body was found, and he would have his friend there. If she objected it would heighten the lust for her and the pleasure would be all the more. He liked them to fight back a little; it meant he could hurt them. Finishing the ale in one gulp his mind began to think of her once more as he left the table; he had plans to make.

The ringing of the enchanter bell awoke her, 'Once more you are late, Aurorai. Why is it all awake before the bell sounds and seem to do so easily?'

Removing her purple and red robe from the drawer she slipped it over her shoulders revelling as the mana with her robe made it cling to every part of her body it touched; after years the sensations still sent pleasure coursing through her. At times like these she knew the pleasure of being able to cast spells and of silken robes soaked with her mana.

When the mana was first gifted to her, shortly after her coming of age, her parents had spoken of how the mana would slowly seep into any robe she wore. They did not, however, speak of the pure pleasure as the robe of soft silk begins to become one with the wearer. The more her mana seeped into the robe the more it clung to her, and the more pleasure it gave her. There was a limit to the mana the robe could absorb and she found she could remove the robe by mere thought. She had only to think of the robe opening and it did so, falling from her shoulders into her hand as if it were a living thing; and to a point it was.

Anyone else wearing her robe would feel the same, and it would obey their thoughts as it did hers, yet only if the other wearer was a caster. Those unable to cast could never feel a robe as casters did, and each time she thought of them not feeling the life in a robe she was saddened.

Pausing only to take an apple from a bowl she opened the door of the inn. She would at least have something to eat before training began. The walk to the guild of enchanters was one of the longest she had to make. The guild of guards was the nearer and she had often taken food to the hall when they trained late into the evening. She could run all the way to the guild but it had been instilled in her since birth; an enchanter never ran, no matter what the reason. If she ran she could, with luck, be there on time but if anyone saw her running she would be in trouble. She resigned herself to being late yet again and to the, sometimes, caustic comments of the class mentor.

There was no one else about this early in the morning; most except the enchanters' content to let the sun warm the land a little before rising. Once more the thought of running entered her mind but it was dismissed. Her mood was still high and she did not want to start the day with comments from the new class mentor, Ralis. He was known for ensuring the ways of the enchanters was adhered to strictly. It would be foolish to upset him on her first day as his student. Passing the shop of Jess the shoemaker she tried to bite the apple just as a cloth bag was pulled hard over her head.

He watched her as she left the inn knowing the enchanters always answered the summons of the bell, and she must pass the shop on her way to the hall. His years of hunting all the races would come in useful once more.
He knew all the professions and the way they fought. In most cases the best way of taking a prisoner was to surprise them; she would be no exception. He had caught several enchanters over the years, most had been dark elves. Man would pay a large amount for a female enchanter, most preferring the dark elves, for the pleasure they could bring; yet they were the hardest of all to capture. An enchanter was not only a caster of spells but could use their minds to attack and even change the thoughts of the attacker to one of benevolence. To catch this female he needed to be quick and do so in a set order or he would be enchanted and turned over to the guards; they hated everyone who tried to harm an elf. They were not too careful with prisoners who tried to harm any of their kind; many met with nasty accidents.

As she passed the corner of the shop he stepped out behind her and threw a cloth bag over her head. Their first method of attack would be to use their minds but if they could not see the attacker their mind was useless to them. Her mind must be stopped from being used against him. As he slipped the bag over her head he threw the weighted rope in his other hand to spin out and round her, pinning both her arms to her side.

With ease he caught the end of the rope and flicked it over the other ball attached to the rope. She would be unable to cast a spell if her arms could not move.

His hand now free he slipped it into his pocket to bring out a pear shaped piece of wood. As her mouth opened to call for help the wood was pushed into her mouth. Another cloth was wrapped over her mouth and tied at the back of her head to keep her from spitting it out. She could not use her mind, her spells or call for help. The only thing remaining was to have his pleasure with her.

Had she been away from the city he would have used her until he become bored, and he usually do so quickly, then sell her on to someone out of the way where she would never be seen again. When they had used her and become tired of her she would be sold on yet again or killed; as the whim of her new owner dictated.

He was in their city and once she was free she would raise the alarm and a hunt would begin; and he knew enough of the rangers and druids to know they would track him no matter where he went.

They were even capable of following his footprints from here, in the middle of their city. There was only one option open to him. After he was satisfied he would slit her throat. Late last night it had been arranged for a druid to take them to their next stop and no one would know who had killed the little elf.

The building close to the shop was ideal for his needs and it was there he dragged her. She was putting up little resistance, the attack had been swift and efficient and there was no way she could recover her wits fast enough to be of use to her. Opening the door he threw her inside and onto her back.

"You weren't so good to me last night, little elf, but I'll make you a deal. Make me really happy and I'll spare your life."

His hands began to enjoy the curves of her body and caress her breasts but he knew he could not linger too long; he wanted to enjoy the moment and make it last but realised he could spare a little time to enjoy her.

Aurorai was in a state of confusion; not from what was happening to her but her mind seemed to go blank and then darkness began to grow in her mind. It demanded his life in a way she had never thought possible.

It seemed she had given in to his promise, her body was accepting his lies and he knew she could do nothing except believe his promise to spare her.

His heavy hands on her body revolted her, he was not only touching without permission, the fact alone caused her to heave, but he was getting firmer with her. His hands squeezed places giving her more than a little pain. Her mind could stand no more, thoughts of what she wanted to do to him became darker and revolted her almost as much as his hands on her. She fought the dark thoughts with all her will yet succeeded only a little in controlling them.

They were screaming, screaming this was so wrong in so many ways. They wanted his life, in a most painful way, yet deeper down in her mind the dark thoughts were enjoying the firm caresses of her body, relishing in them.

He had enjoyed her curves enough; he must hurry, someone may come past at any moment. His hands strayed once more over her breasts to enjoy their ample size and firmness. Now he would rip open the robe and see them.

He never knew who it was who lifted his chin a little, as he never saw who it was who pushed the stiletto into his jugular vein and down his throat. As he dropped to all fours his blood flowed into his throat stopping him from calling out for help. His last thought was his attacker knew what to do; he would either bleed to death or choke to death in his own blood. Yet most of all he would never get to enjoy the little elf beneath him.

Aurorai finally began to control her own mind and now it was racing. His position between her legs left him a little vulnerable. If he tried to open her robe she could bring up a knee and twist over to bring him to the ground. If she could get her arms free and remove her blindfold she could use her mind to attack him. Laying on the floor it would be hard to cast a spell to harm him but she wanted to hurt him more than anything else in the world at this moment. He was going to defile her, use her as if she was a slave to do with as he liked. It raised anger in her she never knew she had; dark thoughts once more crossed her mind and she liked the way they ran.

Then she felt wetness seep through her robe and onto her chest and squirmed at the thought. Then he was across her, his weight heavy and the wetness was on her face. She had never known such fury and revulsion as she did now. She must have his life, *she must*!

The blade of a knife against her robe heightened the feelings of revulsion in her; he would have his way and kill her. If she could appear to accept her fate he may spare her life, if she was lucky. Then the knife began to cut the rope pinning her arms so tightly and she wondered what he was about to do. Was it to give her hope, or so she might respond to his ways with her?

Once more the dark thoughts entered her mind and she knew she would not accept his ways. The knife would be used for its true purpose, to kill her. Rather a death in agony of a slit throat than to be humiliated by another. Then the dark thoughts screamed at her and she knew she would never submit to a death such as this. Her arms fought against the rope and felt them gradually weaken. He had cut the rope just a little too much. She had suffered enough of his ways and would show him an elf could never be taken and used in such a way.
Her mind screamed in anger, demanded revenge, and her knee came up as she twisted over and felt him drop to one side, unmoving. Pulling her right arm she felt the rope slacken and finally snap. It was all she needed to have her revenge. She wanted his life no matter the cost, her mind was screaming for revenge and she would have it. Something in her seemed to be taking control, to demand his life in a way which revolted, yet pleased, her.

As she ripped the bag from her head she saw him at her side and her new robe was covered in blood, his blood. Now she had more reasons to kill him. She had stitched the new robe only weeks before and only wore it at home in the privacy of her bedroom. She was saving it for when she was instructed to change classes; a gift to herself for all the hard work she had placed into training. He had ruined it; never would it be used again. Each time she wore it she would be reminded of this day. She would burn it, destroy it!

The slight sound caused her head to turn and see a shadow in the early morning sun slip away. She screamed in anger, hating the one who had saved her from such a terrible ordeal; she wanted the pleasure of killing him in a slow and torturous way.

Slowly he mind began to calm once more as she saw the body at her side. He had little blood on him; most of it was on her. She screamed aloud once more. She had been robbed of the revenge she so desperately wanted, 'This is not you, Aurorai; never do you want such vengeance. Something is wrong within you yet what?' Then the dark thoughts in her mind were gone, as forgotten as if they had never existed.

As she collapsed to the floor in mental exhaustion a guard came to the doorway and, seeing her slumped to the floor, gently lifted her in his arms, "Fear not, mistress Aurorai, he will harm not others. Come, I take you home; you have need of your mother I believe."
She only had the strength to nod her head on his shoulder.

# High Council

Ilsto Ventrel cast a glance right and down, from his slightly elevated position behind the bench at the end of the hall, to the high elves sitting behind the long bench. Eight of them, as Lore demanded, sat with arms resting on the highly polished top, wearing a look he knew they had practised over the years, one of indifference. It did not fool him, they were worried, this situation had never happened before and it had fallen to him, on the death of the leader of the elfin communities, to remedy the situation.

When the runner had informed him of the death of the enchanters' guild leader he was with friends fishing downstream of the Great Waterfall of Sahera; close to the city of the wood elves. The summons had been simple in nature, and direct. With the death of his oldest friend he had been elected as leader of the elfin communities. He was to return immediately and take his place for the ceremony of the inauguration of the next leader of the enchanters and thereby, he knew, his troubles had begun. He wished he was back at the waterfall, resting and no cares to worry over, but it was not to be and he realised it.

He knew each of the elves on the council, their names, professions, likes and dislikes and the task at hand was to push forward their decision with as little fuss as possible, it was not going to be easy. Rumours had reached his ears, and he did not like them. Neither did he like being chosen, in his absence, to lead the two peoples; especially when it was he who would take the brunt of the words, which were bound to fly, in this meeting.

As his eyes swept over the elves gathering in the great hall he realised the rumours had reached other ears. He missed nothing as he watched them sitting before him, each and every profession was in attendance, and for once all the guild leaders had arrived for the inauguration, sat in the sixteen honoured places on the front benches; he could not remember the last time all the seats had been taken. The great hall had been built twelve thousand years ago, at a time when all could enter, for never had more than a few thousand attended a ceremony.

Now the balconies were filled to bursting, as were the seats before him, with more waiting in the aisles. With a glance at those still filing through the massive doors he realised not all would be able to attend.

He swallowed hard, and sometimes smiled in amusement, as he heard the murmurs rise as rumours circulated the hall yet tried to keep his face as impassive as those to his right, hoping he looked much calmer then he felt.

His eyes continued their sweep and came to rest on the enchanters, and received his biggest shock. Only a handful, some twenty in all, were in attendance. Suddenly he realised, so few enchanters were now seen in the city. He could not believe it. A new leader was about to be chosen for them and so few were here to see who it would be. Yet there they sat, only the occasional smirk at a rumour betrayed the fact they were not as aloof as they would like to think. Not a single purple covered seat, the colour of the enchanters, had been taken by an elf of another guild, it did not surprise him; none would besmirch their name, or their guilds, by doing so.

His gaze finally settled on the wood elves seated left and below him, once more eight in all. Here was something he could almost touch, they were talking feverously amongst themselves and he wished he were with them, instead of sitting in the centre of the benches feeling vulnerable. Such was not to be and he knew it.

The thought of peace and quiet with so many fish to catch made the task at hand all the harder but it could put it off no longer. Reaching for the gavel he tapped it lightly on the desk, and there was instant silence. He had begun and now he must conduct the inauguration with reverence.

"It falls upon me to begin this ceremony and I thank each for their attendance. Before I continue I would speak of Caspo Kwil, of our friendship and of the enchanters. He was my dearest, my oldest friend, when I heard of his death I was saddened, I shall miss him. He served as mentor to many and friend to all. So few enchanters attend the ceremony, I find this offensive."
He allowed himself a small smile at the nodding of heads, before realising his words had little effect on the enchanters, their faces remained impassive.

His gavel struck the desk once more, "The ceremony will begin. Caspo Kwil sits with the Gods and the council has debated his wishes and chosen a new leader. Dolat of the enchanters, I bid you stand before this council." All eyes turned in the direction of the enchanters. No one stood.

Once more, and with firmness, his gavel struck the desk, "Dolat of the enchanters. I bid you stand before this council."

Once more no one stood.

"Dolat of the enchanters. I bid you stand before this council!"

With eyes closed he breathed deep, he could feel it was going to get worse, "Dolat of the enchanters honours us not with his presence it would seem. Permission is given for another to speak as to his whereabouts."

"Ilsto Ventrel, I am Jenay of the enchanters. I would speak on his behalf."

"Permission is given."

"It has been surmised the council's choice for Dolat to be our leader. For this reason he has no wish to attend for in his absence he will be unable accept the honour bestowed upon him."

"He has been duly chosen. His honour it will be to wear the twin gems of leadership."

"He does not accept, as his absence proves, the leadership of the enchanters. It should now pass to Norty, as was the request of Caspo Kwil."

Now the words were out he knew he had a fight on his hands. The wishes of his friend for Norty to become leader of the enchanters was known to him, he had spoken often to him of his choice but knew it would never be allowed. No matter how hard he tried Caspo Kwil would only shake his head and repeat the same words, 'the elves must change both ways and direction; she alone will know path to follow, soon it will become obvious to her.'

He had hoped there would be no troubles for the ceremony, but knew there would be. Norty had a reputation, a good one amongst all the elves, and if Caspo Kwil has singled her out to be his successor he knew she must be capable of leading them. But the council had spoken; they did not wish her to lead the enchanters.

"The council understands your wishes, Jenay, yet they decide who is to lead a guild on the death of a leader. It is not for any other to say and not for the enchanters to choose who will lead them."

"Caspo Kwil had decided; his wish was for Norty to be our leader, as it is also the wish of all enchanters. Lore demands you accept her as our leader for he had no heir to his position."

"Alas his wishes will remain unfulfilled."

"She is the one chosen by him, the one we would have lead us."

"The council thanks you for your words, Jenay."

"I have more to speak on this."

"Your words have been heard. Take your seat."

"As is your wish, yet I do so without all my thoughts voiced."

"I believe all here know of your thoughts, they have been voiced most eloquently."

Norty allowed a slight smile to cross her face; Jenay had handled the situation perfectly, as they had rehearsed. The few enchanters in the city had remained behind to attend the ceremony. Over the past weeks the others had departed for their pre-arranged destination, but slowly so as to cause no concern to the guards still on duty.

Although she would never have admitted it to anyone she had looked forward to this day. The guild of enchanters had asked her to lead them, not a single voice had been raised in protest when Jenay had proposed they defy the council and demand she lead them. The mentors of each class had voiced their support and discussed strategy into the early hours of the morning. With the first rays of sunlight touching the highest towers of the city they had left her and Jenay to plan the details; and they would have only three months in which to ensure they were perfect.

Caspo Kwil, her oldest and closest friend, was near to death. He had spoken of his wish for her to lead the guild and offered advice on matters she would face, and she had listened very carefully to his words. She was with him when he died, holding his hand as he left life behind to join the Gods, to take his seat with them. He was in the old chair he loved, and where she had learned so much from him when first she came to train as an enchantress. Those first few months and his teachings had been strange to her, even baffling, as she had sat in study at his side; it had been long and hard work before she been allowed to enter the enchanters' guild.

It was only then she had found out why he had trained her in secret for so long, they had hated her. She was a wood elf in the realm of the high elf and they would not tolerate it.

Finally, after she had had enough of the way they treated her, she fought back, casting spell after spell and using her mind on those in her class. She was hopelessly outnumbered but her determination had risen and there was no stopping her. The fighting had ceased only when the council intervened, it was then she discovered she had been accepted; each in her class had tried to explain it was a training session somehow out of hand. She realised once she had fought them to prove her worth they were ready to receive her to their ranks. During the night she had time to think about their actions and, for the first time since she had started her training, had cried for joy.

With a shake of the head she thought of elfin history. Their ways were set in stone and never had an elf changed the profession to which they were born. Druid offspring became druids as the children of warriors became warriors. It had been decreed by the Gods many thousands of years ago. Yet she and her sisters had been born of the Gods demand to fight a quest. They also decreed they should defy both elves and elfin Lore; each had followed the path chosen by the Gods. Yet their decisions not to follow their parents' druid ways had caused a rift in the elfin ranks, becoming larger when she and her sisters had killed the druid elder in battle, and later the son who had taken his father's position.

Her smile returned a little as she realised she could not leave all her forebears traditions behind. Their training had been the same undertaken by all wood elves, except in the way of the bow; they had refused to use one, disappointing their parents once again.

Her home, once she had joined in wedlock with Finglas, was also to be different, at ground level and not high in the tops of the massive trees where most liked to be. Her eyes closed momentarily as thoughts of her joining in wedlock to Finglas at the druid Stones of Life returned to her. Once more she had broken elfin Lore to join out of guild and bear them a child, Nortee. The thought of her daughter with the king brought little relief.

She was safe with her mother and the king yet Nortee had a spark in her she always found hard to control, she would have stood in the great hall and given voice to her thoughts, for her daughters sake it could not be allowed. A shudder ran through her at the prospect of the price the king demand from her, but elfin ways did not allow the breaking of promises.

However hard she tried she could not understand why her daughter found man so fascinating, it was they who had tried to kill her when she was newly born. Yet she was grateful at this moment she was with them. There would be no trouble yet, but within days there would be rumour and fear, and she had wanted Nortee away from harm for those few days. Her mother would keep to her carefully laid plans; Nortee would be safe for seven days.

Her mind could feel her sisters sat behind her; their professions never available to wood elves they sat in the aisle to watch the proceedings. Turning she smiled at them, so few outside of the enchanters knew the plans they had made, and so few would ever forget them. It was with difficulty she forced her mind back to listen to the problems in hand.

"....Lore states 'on the death of a guild leader with no heir to take their place any nominated by them may stand for the open position'. It is not for conjecture and only one stands for this position. However, a wood elf has never been an enchanter, or the leader of the enchanters, we see no reason for this to change. With this in mind I ask for an enchanter to step forward and take their place as leader, should the council approve them."
He waited a full minute, no one stood.
"The council waits."
Finally Jenay rose, "The wishes of Caspo Kwil are not to be taken lightly."
"Jenay, I believe the council will support not your stand for leadership."
"You misunderstand me; I stand not for leadership but to speak for all enchanters if permission is given?"
He sighed, "Your words we have heard; permission is given yet if you would be brief."
"Caspo Kwil has spoken of whom he wished to lead the guild, we stand firm behind his words. As one voice we speak, Norty is to be our leader. She was chosen by him, by *all* enchanters."
"Impossible! She is wood elf not high elf born."
"Her parentage is not in question. We have spoken and wish it to be."
"There are other reasons why she should be not your leader."
"To turn from the last wishes of our leader would be to besmirch his name and reputation. We followed Caspo Kwil and will do nothing to mar his name. Norty is to be our leader, as it was *his* wish it also is *our* wish."
"It is plain he was not of clear mind when his wishes were spoken. She is too young, maturity is needed in leadership."
"She has a mind unlike any and maturity does not always come with age."
"A female has never led the guild of enchanters."
"Pose trains with us and leads her guild, an enchantress also."

"Yet she is dark elf and we care not for the ways of our mortal enemies."

"Care enough was within Caspo Kwil for her to train with us; she is a friend to this guild."

"You do naught but prove my words. Dark elves are our enemies and he consented to instruct her in our ways. He was not of sound mind."

"Your beliefs are not important. Our own enchanters' train in their city and many dark elves now train here, none have caused concern; indeed they are well respected by the enchanters and others within this and wood elf city. They move freely and are greeted as friend by many."

"Who brought the enemy to our midst? Norty! Clearly she should not be the leader of the enchanters."

"Pose sits here with us and never has she caused concern to any. All respect her and many ask to travel to her city to be further instructed. The joining of our guilds should show to all the dark ones wish to be our friends."

"Pose has not the right to sit here, this all should know!"

"She is enchantress born; her right is plain for all to see."

"An enemy has no right in this hall! Think of the tales she will speak of when she returns to her city, speaking of our ways, our training!"

She had heard enough; the council of sixteen had nodded in agreement with Ilsto Ventrel, as they knew it would happen. It was time to finish the debate.

"We leave with our chosen leader, with or without the council's permission."

*"The council decides who will be the leader for all the guilds!"*

"The council merely give consent to an issue as a point of Lore, to have it seem they have power when in fact they have none."

"You dare to question the council?"

"We question not the council, merely refuse to abide by rules it would break at the slightest whim. Our Lore is our law and must be followed. We leave this hall."

*"You are refused permission to leave until this matter is settled!"*

"This matter *is* settled."

*"This matter is settled not.* Never has any defied the council as do the enchanters. It cannot be allowed to happen. *All* will abide by our word; there is no room for doubt in this."

"Doubt there is not in our minds. The council wish to demonstrate the powers it thinks it has."

"The council has all the power it needs! Think not to act against us, Jenay of the enchanters."

"The council's demands are to remain demands, we listen not to them."

"How dare you ...."

"We dare for we are right. Look to yourself; you are red with anger towards us yet for a reason which should not be. When calmness takes your mind once more we may be found in our guild hall; with our leader."

"Never will she be a leader of the enchanters; this the council speaks!"

"Look to those before you and not to those at your side. See the way most agree with us and not with the council."

"We care not for their thoughts ...."

He realised the trap he had been led into too late; and he had been an easy victim losing his temper so easily; he had to make amends, "We sit and debate this in a polite and sensible way. All here will listen as you voice your thoughts."

"Our thoughts have been voiced and ignored. It would seem debate is not for today's agenda."

With a stiff bow she turned to leave, the enchanters following her lead.

He could take no more, "Norty of the enchanters, stand your ground before this council! See the trouble you cause this day?"

"I cause none, Ilsto Ventrel. You turn against the will of Caspo Kwil and our Lore. You insult all here and believe you sit on the council with power over all. This can never be so. You do an injustice to the enchanters and repercussions must surely follow."

His fist struck the desk as his temper flared once again, "You would threaten me? Threaten the council?"

"On the contrary, I feel sorry for you; you have but spoken the wishes of the council and thought not of this. Your actions may cause the end of elfin kind."

It was too much, his fist slammed once more onto the desk, "*Explain your words!*"

"It has been known in Lore throughout the ages, we are dependent on all guilds for our survival. If one guild should fail then all elfin kind will perish. The enchanters wish to move forward and the council's thoughts are to have them remain in ways unbecoming of us. We would join with the dark elf enchanters to become strong once more; yet you would have us retain old ways which will lead to the elves ceasing to be in this world. You bring forth war between the guilds and this day you may have begun the downfall of our people. You and the council deem yourselves above all and care not if fighting will ensue between the guilds. I suggest you debate this when next the council meets."

Turning back she continued towards the exit, following behind the rest of her guild, the shouts of the elves around her echoing in her head. She had spoken correctly, so much was obvious. Most of the elves were voicing their fears to the council members while some supported them; the fighting between the guilds had started.

# Gem-less Leader

Jenay raised her arm and there was quiet, "This day we have little to celebrate. True a new leader takes her place at our head, yet it is without the twin gems of leadership to adorn her left sleeve. When first she came to us we would have nothing to do with her, fighting her as if she were an enemy. Yet she has won our hearts and minds with her skill and prowess. The wishes of Caspo Kwil are known to all, for her to lead this guild to a new future. His wishes will be granted; in the next few days those remaining will leave the city as planned and move to the ruins above the gnome city of Gronich where our temporary home will be formed."
Turning back she winked at her, "Worry not."

She smiled back; it had been obvious what would happen in the meeting with the council, they were too set in their ways; only a severe shock would change them. It was at times like these she was saddened she could plan so well. Sat with her sisters their thoughts joined as they let the countless variations of the way the meeting would turn out run through her mind. With her sisters to guide her she had planned every eventuality and this was but one of them. Now she needed to continue with the plan before the situation could become worse.

".... So it is with regret I ask none sing morning song but to assemble here and join as one voice."
Aizil stood, "Three hundred years have I lived and in my life I have been asked but once to join in morning song."
"For what occasion, Aizil?"
"When leadership passed to Caspo Kwil, it seems fitting my second time is to mourn him."

Finglas listened to the enchanters as they spoke amongst themselves. It was not the first time he had been in their guildhall and was greeted as a friend whenever he entered. He had doubted his yet to be wife, when he had first taken her to high elf city, could ever be an enchantress.
She had proven him wrong and he was happy to be so.

He knew of her plans and was unhappy with them; nowhere in them did she seem to take into account the footprints of the skeletons as they started in Whisper Valley and head towards high elf city. Trouble was coming, fast. He knew her skills as a planner; the battle with the goblins years ago had taught him she was never wrong, the Gods had given her the gift. Eventually he caught her eyes and she came over to him.

"It happened as you have said yet I am unsure of the move to the ruins. It is no longer a defensible site and offers little in the ways of comfort."

"From what is there to defend? There is fresh water and food aplenty. It will make a place of safety for all, and has one other very enviable quality."

"I have been there with Xandorian; I see nothing in its favour."

"It is not homely, the very reason it was chosen."

From her birth he knew she had always spoken in riddles and, after so many years with her, some he could understand easily but others like this one baffled him. No elf would wish to move out of the city to which they were born and live in the ruins, "Ack, more riddles. I had thought to hear the last of them."

"The explanation is before you, where is the last place any would look for a guild of enchanters who vanish from sight?"

"They would think not to look in the ruins above Gronich."

"The few remaining here will leave yet slowly in numbers, for all to walk away would bring only hatred towards us. If it seemed all disappeared slowly others would become unsettled and demand the council find and return us immediately."

"It will be obvious; travellers will see you and the news will spread quickly."

"For weeks we have observed if any pass by the ruins. Few do so and less will do so when the news abounds the enchanters have all but vanished."

"They will search all over."

"They will search the forest of the uplands and its caves; it is there they believe we may hide. Items have been left in the caves to confuse those who search for us. Few would think to look in a place not homely to us."

"If you have done such and watched the ruins you have planned this for so long."

"For almost three months now, Nortee does not know all the plans."

"She is linked with you, how may she not know?"

"Mother has taken care of her side of this and has taken her away often when we had the need to set about our plans. As ambassador she takes her often to their cities, yet I fail to see her liking for them."

"Never have you liked them, it is as if they bring out hatred in you."

"There is no hatred in me, they bring out in me feelings of.... shame."

"You speak little of your feelings towards them; it is a strange time you choose to explain."

"When the Gods made man they made them arrogant and warlike. It is this which causes me the shame I feel."

"The Gods made all the races; it is not for us to judge them for their ways."

"I judge not the Gods yet question their reasons. Why is it they make a race which brings shame to others for their very existence?"

Aurorai Minlets bowed, "Leader, Nortee left with no word, she is well?"

"She is well, Aurorai."

"Yet she speaks to me of all, never has she disappeared as she does now."

"My daughter has parts to play in this yet is not a part of all the plans. You also have your role to play. I have need of you to join her in the land of man."

"Never have I been to their cities, mother shops for drink always alone."

"Now you will see for yourself their ways. Finglas will take you as near as the stones allow. I wish you to give her a message."

"Leader, I would be honoured."

"I thank you for the use of the word Leader, Aurorai, yet until the council place on my sleeve the twin gems of leadership I ask you use not the term. Ask my daughter to visit with Kyna and take this message for her. Accompany her; I feel the journey will be of benefit to both."

"I wish to walk the path Nortee treads."

"Her path must leave yours once in a while and her path may oft be dangerous."

"Danger shared is a danger halved, Leader."

She smiled, "Once more the word you use; I begin to believe my daughter take her stubbornness from you."

"I have respect for this guild and for its leader; the word should be used."

"Thank you, Aurorai. Now go and see my daughter; and walk if you please."


"Ilsto Ventrel, have you opened not your eyes in so long you are blind? None have seen an enchanter for three days. There are none to patrol with the guards."

"They patrol with them to see through the illusions dark elves may cast to fool our guards. They now come and go freely, of what need is there for the enchanters to patrol?"

"It has always been such for us to see the patrols and is a source of comfort. Now the city is in unrest, they demand an explanation from the council."

"Give them one, Herth."

"I have none to give."

"Then best you discover their whereabouts, I suggest you start with the husband."

"He will speak not of where they are; this you know."

"There are ways to ask and there are ways to ask."

"I would not use force; it may be deemed I attacked another."

"It would be for the good of all."

"Not for my good if Norty decides to take this as an attack on her husband. I spoke with Pose and heard how she fought dark elves and won."

"Speculation, and from a dark elf only."

"Pose has no reason to lie and was with them during the fight. I believe her."

"Then you are foolish! She is a friend of Norty and wishes only for us to worry; I refuse to bow to her ways."

"The fight has been known of for ages, yet not before Caspo Kwil may have conceived of the idea for Norty to lead them on his death."

"Yet it is still their word only."

"Well you know she hates to lie."

"There are other ways to speak an untruth and lie not. She has only to leave out a few details of the fight and you believe they won."

"She was not alone; many were with her during the fight."

"Friends and family alone; none are independent."

"There was one whose voice I have listened to and speaks of how the battle was won. She I believe. Her life was spared after the battle and she has reason to be here. She wishes to speak to the council and for matters to change. For seven days she has been escorted around our cities as she waits to speak to the council."

"Who was there?"

"I have asked you speak to her and always you refuse. Speak and listen well. Her name is Jennka, a shadow knight from dark elf city."

"Send her to me. Send me this Jennka."

"She waits outside."

"Send her in then go to wood elf city and seek out Finglas, demand he speak."

"You must do this yourself. Consider me as stepped down from the council. Good day to you."

As she entered the room he did nothing to hide his distain to her kind, "Sit."

"Greetings. I thank you. It seems there is trouble in the city."

"Nothing to speak of."

"You hide not your fears as easily as you would believe. There is fear in all I see in the city. Your enchanters leave you and this is shown in your faces."

"How did you get here? You should have been killed the moment you set foot on our lands."

"I set foot on your lands as a guest."

"Impossible! Your kind are unwelcome here."

"All is possible should you know the way to ensure your needs are met."

"How is it we met your needs? You intrigue me."

"To the south east of your lands is an old wooden bridge. We call it the bridge of Idgur."

"I know it well. We call it the bridge of songs. Should you sit and listen the wind sweeps though it and gives the bridge a song."

"I have heard its song. For two days I sat in the middle of the bridge, my sword point buried deep in the plank nearest your lands."

"A sign you wished to talk. It is an old way yet still recognised."

"I thought your land patrolled yet still I was there two days."

"You were seen within hours. The patrol waited to ensure you were as you seemed."

"It is why I am here. I have information you require."

"You sat on the bridge two days. It was dangerous; the bridge is in danger of collapse. It has been decided it must be rebuilt."

"To remain still ensured I was in no danger."

"Enough of this talk. What news do you bring?"

"I would speak of the fight in my city, and the part Norty played within it."

"You bring more lies?"

"I bring none. I see your people different from what I once did. My life has been spared and a debt I must repay although Norty spoke none was owed. She caused not the fight to start but ensured it was won. Never have I seen I fight so well planned, so well executed. All may have been killed yet she spared those who wished to surrender, I was amongst those who did so."

"Then you will speak in her favour no matter the truth."

Removing her breast plate she indicated to his dagger, "Place it here, should you believe I speak and untruth you have but to press hard on the hilt."

"You think me a fool? I would be accused of attacking you."

"You have but to speak I attacked and you defended yourself."

Rubbing his chin he thought a few moments. This could be used to his advantage, "I will listen to you and believe you speak only the truth."

Clipping the plate back in place she smiled, "I speak only the truth. Where would you wish me to begin?"

"From when your kind entered the room would seem a proper place."

"I was not the first to arrive so may speak not of such happenings. I admit to some surprise when a white elf appeared; I knew not who she was. Many reached for weapons yet her ways ensured no hand grasped one, no spell voiced. She spoke....."

## Reds and Blues

Almost exhausted Malinna sank into the chair; another year and dozens more injuries, she was beginning to dislike the week of the reds and blues. Once a year the dwarves would divide in two; the blues marching out of their city deep in the mountains would stalk the reds. It was a test of skill, to get closer to the other, to surprise them and inflict damage with little loss to the attackers. Each year was the same as far as she could see. Those chosen to be blues would attack along the paths leading to one of the entrances to the city. The reds would lay in wait to surprise them somewhere along the way. A light tap from the sticks they carried deemed the other dead and they should withdraw; many claimed they were not tapped and fights would erupt.

She had, finally, convinced them to make a waiting room outside of the treatment room she used. Thinking they would build it out of stone next to the room she used she received a shock, they had started to hew it out of the rock close by and with an interconnecting passageway Within a short time it was ready, and the walls were as smooth as if they had been polished. The dwarfs' skill on working with stone never ceased to amaze her.

Now another year of fights was drawing to an end and the waiting room was full to bursting point yet again. By the fifth year she had tried to end the game pointing out an enemy knowing of the games would choose such a time to attack. The response she could have guessed. "The reds hate the blues, the blues hate the reds. The reds and the blues hate the enemy more."

Garat turned to her, "No time to rest, Mistress Malinna, more wait in the outer room."
Wearily she stood, "How many are injured?"
"Thirty wait now, maybe fifty before the day ends."
"Each year more are injured in this folly and the clerics pay dearly to heal them. Has their armour been removed, Garat?"
"They grumble when asked but know you will refuse to see them while they wear it."
"How may I treat them when I see not their injuries? Never have I known a people so stubborn; yet not one do I hear complain of their wounds."

The door opened and an old dwarf looked in, "Mistress Malinna, a terrible accident; come quickly."

Racing along the narrow corridor she asked, "What has happened?"

"Three hundred young ones tried the old quarry path. The rocks have collapsed on them."

"All know it is a dangerous place, so dangerous no guards keep watch."

"The reason they chose the path."

"Have them brought to the clearing before the quarry."

"I gave orders for all clerics to come but they will be hard pressed, the injured are many."

The tenth dwarf was brought to her, his left arm crushed, yet no moans passed his lips.

"Mistress Malinna herself tends me, I will live."

Through the dust and grime on his face she recognised him, "Brut Stonehouse, how many times must I treat you for accidents? Six times must this be."

"The seventh time, Mistress Malinna; accidents seems to like me."

As she cast she laughed, "This time Lady Fortune favours you."

His face showed the pain, "My arm is crushed and you call it a favour?"

"What else may it be called? Had you been a caster of spells you would never cast again yet as a warrior you may still use a weapon in your right hand."

His voice trailed off as he began to argue.

"You are becoming my best aid, Garat; your sleep spell was cast when needed and almost as I thought of it."

"I will ensure he attends you for healing on the morrow."

The linking with her son became strong once again, "Sha'Dal has need of us, come."

Kneeling beside her son her fingers ran over the dwarf, "So many injuries, so many. This will be hard."

Sha'Dal whistled and a dwarf was at his side instantly. Together they worked, casting to heal the breaks and wounds as Krall held him steady.

Looking at her son she frowned, he was trying too hard; she could see the strain on his face.

"Mother, this is Krall, he has enormous strength but tends not to hear as people call him, I found a whistle always brings him to me. He fades from us, mother, he fades!"

As the dwarf stopped shaking she touched her son's arm, "Not all may we save; oft the Gods call them and there is little we may do."

"Too poor I am in the ways of healing, I must train all the harder, study all the more."

"You work hard, Sha'Dal, make not yourself so ill you are no longer able to help those around you."

"I will be careful, mother."

"Many more need our help; Garat will ensure all who need more help come to us on the morrow."

Still tired from the last few days she woke; with all her will dressing to continue the day's work. Casting so often during the day drained her not only of mana but of her strength. Each morning was the same, dozens of dwarves would be waiting; most with heavy bruising but many with more serious injuries, it seemed as if more than just the touching sticks were being used. With reluctance she checked once more in the mirror before breathing deep and opening the door to the treatment room.

"Days of endless healing and I tire so. Were it possible I would sleep all of the morrow."

"So many have you treated this day, Mistress Malinna, only one remains unseen in the outer room. I have refused his entrance."

"I see all, Garat, this you know."

"He refuses to remove his armour."

"Show him in, I will have strong words on this!"

As the dwarf entered she glared at him, "So Brut Stonehouse believes my rule applies not to him?"

"Mistress Malinna, my arm is the trouble not other parts of me."

"Is your arm not a part of you? I set but one rule and all will abide by it! Think not to challenge me on this."

"There are times when rules...."

"You will remove your armour now! Or is it a challenge you wish; to test your skills against me?"

"None can beat you with the staff, we know your skill. I have only one arm but I'll try."

Throwing a staff to him she put her right hand in her pocket as she took her staff, "I use my right hand yet will fight with my left. Honour must be seen."

With a grin he started to circle her waiting for any sign of attack. He had been offered good payment should he follow his plan and have Malinna come to him. He had planned this carefully, to refuse to remove armour normally made Malinna angry, and she had learned to deal with problems as the dwarves would, by force.

He had watched her every fight in the arena since he was eight and knew her weakness, now he would prove to all he was the greatest with a staff, even if it would be with only one arm.

His staff swung round to her head but dropped as it changed direction to attack her legs. He could not believe he had been blocked so easily, or the way in which the sharp movement of her staff plucked his own from his grasp to send to the corner of the room; or how fast her staff was under his chin as it pushed him back to the wall. He had been disarmed as if he had never used a staff in his life, yet he was easily the better of any in his class.

"Never do any enter wearing armour, remove it now!"

"Mistress Malinna you took my staff with ease yet I saw your weakness each time you fought."

"To display a weakness beckons others to place their effort there; it means I am more ready to stop such attacks. You are half my height, where would be the obvious place to attack?"

"Your legs would be the easier, Mistress Malinna."

"As most have thought and seem to believe. You attack the easiest place to reach, a weakness you place in yourself, not one of my doing. Remove the armour faster and none will know of this."

"One day I will best you."

"The day is still so far off. This armour is light, who makes it and where may I find him?"

"The old one makes them; it's training armour only."

"Lay on the bed. What pieces may be purchased?"

"All pieces yet they are light and offer little protection, they dent so easily."

"Mine is so heavy, mayhap lighter pieces would serve me more."

He felt his face redden a little, "He will have none in your size, especially a chest piece for a female of your....build."

As her fingers once more tingled she cast her spell, "Move your arm for me."

Very slowly he managed to lift it, "It moves, Mistress Malinna, it moves!"

"Never will it be as before yet will become easier as time heals also."

"I'll work it hard until it can hold a shield for me."

"Take your armour with you and enter not with it again."

"Yes, Mistress Malinna. Will you thank Sha'Dal for me?"

"He has tended you?"

"He tended one dear to me, I look on Silis Slate and my heart quickens."

"I will pass to him your thoughts. Before you leave where may I find this old dwarf and what his name?"

Closing the door behind him he hid his grin; he needed to test her, to ensure she was all he hoped she would be, "I'm not ill so don't need your services, no, I'm not ill."

"You know not how pleased I am you are well, Grad Flintforge."

"You know me, how is it you know me?"

"It is the seven days of the reds and the blues and many wear your armour. Brut Stonehouse spoke of you and where you may be found."

"I have not made it for years, for years I have not made it."

"You make armour lighter than any I have seen, more suited for my strength."

"Elves are not as strong as dwarves, dwarves are stronger than elves."

"It seems you are not yourself, should I return another time?"

"Not myself? Who else might I be? I have always been myself."

Becoming confused by his ways she decided to ask directly for her needs, "I come with an offer of payment for your light armour, yet if you are unwilling to accept?"

"Armour she wants, she wants armour."

Removing her chest piece she placed it on the floor, "My armour is not as part payment but may be used if needed."

"A strange one you are, always willing to help the dwarves. Put the armour back on, strange one."

"You refuse my offer?"

"They are idiots, yes, idiots they are."

"Who are idiots?"

"The others who work the forges; all the others are idiots."

"Why are they idiots?"

"Old ways of many generations, they use old ways."

"What old ways do they use?"

"Armour must be heavy they say, protect only with heavy armour."

"Armour must be heavy to protect yet it is why I speak to you; I need light armour. The Gods decree I wear armour for I am a cleric."

46

"They show to me a new way, only to me they show the new way."

"What new way?"

"Ale, I need ale; a mug and ale."

"Make me light armour and I will ensure a barrel is yours."

"A mug of ale for each piece; for each piece a mug of ale."

"There are many mugs in a barrel and I know of the best ale."

As she watched he turned towards her, his once dull eyes suddenly shining bright as he smiled at her. It was as if the old dwarf no longer existed and a new one stood in his place.

"Not many stand my ways; I have them running for the door almost before they enter. I'll make the armour for you."

"You use this way of speaking to have them leave you alone?"

"Idiots set in their ways; even the God's powers could not budge them when their mind is set."

"They are known for their stubbornness. There is a saying amongst others when they refuse to change their mind, 'as stubborn as a dwarf'."

"I understand their frustration. Many years ago, when I was but a young one, father taught me the furnace and, as I grew, I began to drink ale."

"As all do I believe?"

"I drank to keep cool, I don't like the taste, father had the furnace hotter than most. While he was away I was instructed to look after the chest plate he was forging. I had a thirst and reached for the ale; I'm not as nimble as an elf and knocked it over the chest plate. When father returned the armour was dull in colour; ruined he called it."

"Well can I imagine his anger."

"Humph. We are a race quick to anger. He threw it away but I was fascinated and began to work on it. My best chisels could only mark it yet the only difference was the ale I has spilled on it. Through my life I worked to find the secrets."

"A life times work? The loneliness must have been hard to bear. How is it you managed this"

"I paid little heed to it. Each time I failed I tried again. The heat was too little, the heat was too much; the ale was used to temper the armour at the wrong time. I worked hard and slowly extracted the secrets; I was able to make it thinner and lighter as more was revealed to me."

"Then all should know of this, your people may wear it to protect them."

Feverously he started searching a draw, "Bah! Once it is known we have better armour my people will be attacked, the armour stolen as they search for the secrets. Each time they fail they will kill more of us. They will form alliances to attack us and wipe us from the face of the land. Then the alliance will be broken as they fight the others to keep the secret."

"Yet you offer me the better armour?"

"You are one of the Chosen, the Gods protect you and no thought will be given to your armour, believing it to be a gift from the Gods."

"I see your thinking. You are right."

"I know it's in here, it's where I put it."

"For what do you search?"

"Seven days to make the armour if you agree the price."

"Name the price for each piece."

"Payment will be the replacement of the ore I use in the making but a little more would be appreciated."

"I offer the extra. Agreed."

"A barrel of ale for each piece."

"Half a barrel for each piece."

"A full barrel I say; I need to drink and temper the armour."

"Heth Stonehouse brews ale; all say his is far the better. Agreed."

"None come to see old Grad."

"I am here."

"A night of talking for each piece would be agreeable; though not forced."

"You make it not part of the bargain?"

"Not forced."

"Then this I say. Two nights of talks for each piece and the price is agreed." Stopping the search he gave her a wry smile. "For an elf you know how to strike a bargain."

"Long have I lived amongst you, to live as a dwarf you must act as a dwarf."

"My people are hard to live with, all say so. You live with us and I hear you act as us. You gave Brut Stonehouse a hard lesson."

"I set but one rule; he chose to break it."

"As I say; you act like us."

"I admit to some surprise he spoke to you."

"I spoke to him. I needed you here to see you. Where do you hide; where?" Triumphantly he threw the ball of twine he had been searching for to her, "Make the measurements for each piece and knot the twine to show me. Take the old stuff with you; I've no need of it to make real armour."

"I will return on the morrow night for the first of our talks. I have a feeling they may be very interesting."

"In what way?"

"Your beard is almost pure white; I guess your age to be over one hundred."

"One hundred and twelve."

"I know few of such an age. I would speak with you of the old times when a boy you were."

"Boy? Don't call any boy! We were called chidups. The word hasn't been used in years."

Opening the door she turned back, "Never have I heard the word. The talks will be fun; it seems I have the better of the deal."

As she closed the door she heard him laugh.

# And Then There Were Two

Olva bid her daughter to sit, "A decision has been made; you will journey to the lands of the river elves and replenish stocks of wines for the inn."

"We have more than enough, mother."

"Uncertain times approach and I feel more wine will be required. However, you will shop only for wine on this occasion."

"You wish for me to buy ale and beer another time?"

"We may send you other times to buy our needs. War comes."

"War is not a time to drink I believe."

"Mayhap you are correct yet should the battle be won there will be much celebrating and we are the only inn within the city."

"Then ale and beer should be purchased. Sweet treats also I believe. Many buy them I have noticed."

"Never have you seen the victors after a battle; it is a sight I wish you to see not. Two peoples there are after a battle; one who would drink and boast of their deeds; these are harmless yet there is one who is much the worse."

"I have seen many drunken peoples and may imagine not how they may be worse."

"Many would drink alone and think of lost friends. With each drink their sorrow would mount and the merriment of others serves to anger them until no more would they take. It is a pitiful sight; grown they may be yet they act in childish ways. Many a fight would ensue and more would needlessly die."

"This I have never seen I admit."

"Think not of it. If only a little ale is to be had the fights grow less, or so it is hoped."

"Yet if we have not enough ale ...."

"They would leave without the fights. When many have left the city the ale should be delivered. True friends will stay longer and it is these who should be rewarded with ale."

"I had thought not of such things. How is it you know of these things when no battle has been fought on our lands?"

"You believe your father and I never travel? Not always did we live in the inn."

"It is the only place I have known you to be and little you speak of the past."

"I followed in mothers footsteps and became one who travelled and brought to our people items not made by us."

"Though I have asked never have you spoken of your younger days. I wish to know all of them; it is my heritage, my birthright."

She had opened the door to her past just a little and Aurorai had pushed it wide in asking her to speak. It would do little harm to explain of those days, "I would travel with mother when she left on her journeys and many a night we would stay at the inns. They became a second home to me and found I began to like the stays."

Aurorai found so many questions springing to mind but said nothing. At last her mother had begun to open the secret world of her past; to ask any question now might place her mother back on guard and she would never know of her past. Almost not daring to breathe she listened intently.

"Forty six summers, from my coming of age, I travelled with her and knew so many of those who sold to us; many I still call friend. On one such travel we stayed at an inn too long for we enjoyed the company. In the early evening men entered and were bloodied. A battle had been fought not an hour's walk from the inn and they had become lost as the battle moved back and forth. Soon they were drinking heavily and became violent to others there. Before the fighting could become too hard to control mother intervened and they softened, soon all was pleasant once again. There was laughter once more and it is then I learned to be wary of the quiet ones who drink. He came to mother and she greeted him thinking naught was amiss as he had caused not any trouble but sat quietly alone. A knife he plunged into her stomach several times before any could stop him. As they held him he looked to me and in a voice I remember to this day swore at me and my people. It was an elf who had taken the life of his friend yet only a few of our people had fought in the battle. Anger flared in me, anger unknown before. I ripped his throat out with my hands until others held me firm. It was the first time I had killed; *it is the last time I will kill!*"

With tears running down her mother's face Aurorai could be still no longer and held her mother. It was obvious she was too upset to continue but knew she had only a peek at her past.

It would be insensitive of her to ask questions, she would remain quiet. Her mind had filled with so many unanswered questions and foremost of these was why her mother would choose to spend her time in an inn; the very type of building in which her mother had died. Hopefully her mother would continue to speak of those days.

"I am composed again, Aurorai."

"You would speak more of your younger days?"

Her head shook, "You see why I speak not of them?"

"Not all the days would have been sad. Speak of a happy one."

With a light smile she nodded, "For most of the year I grieved the passing of mother until I found one who took sad thoughts from me."

"You speak of father?"

"I do. This inn is all to those of our city and I had neglected its use, much to my chagrin. I had heard the whispers of the customers and decided enough was enough. I travelled once more to places I knew and there I saw the one who was to be my husband. When we spoke I found he loved the inns as did I and a promise we made to the other; upon wedlock we would ensure none would see thirst in our city and ales from all lands would be served."

"Oft have I wondered why so many are sold in our inn."

"The promise to ourselves has been kept; when it was decided I was to be with child it was he who travelled alone to buy ale. I believe he was afraid a fate similar to mother would befall me."

She tried desperately to sound as if she was asking out of curiosity and not desperation, "When was it the first born arrived; was it summer or snow fall? What your thought when your first child was born?"

"Mayhap another time, Aurorai. One day I will speak of B.... I promise."

All her life she had known she was second born and was desperate to know who had come before her. Each and every time she had mentioned the first born she had been scalded into speaking no more. Now there was a faint glimmer of hope she may find out more. She had no idea if she had a sister or a brother or if they were alive or dead. A step had been taken towards finding out and she realised the rest of the steps must be trodden carefully. Now she had a clue to the one born before her, their name began with a B.

Unwilling to change back to the original conversation she knew it must be; her mother had started to speak and she was sure she would do so once again; meanwhile she would wait.

"When the enchanters have left I believe many will come here and drink; and to ask you and father where they have gone."

"I asked Norty to speak not where they go; in this way we will lie not when asked. We will be the only enchanters in the city; it is obvious others will come here to ask. You will do as instructed and make this journey."

"This father ensures is his task, mother."

"You must learn the ways of dealing with those who supply our needs. You may make any deal you feel may benefit us."

"The enchanters have left the city and I would be with them."

"I spoke with Norty; she consented to have you remain here."

"I am enchantress born, I must be with them!"

"There are other duties to tend and I admit to send you to trade so early in your life is not the way I would have this. I wished to be as my mother before me and take you with me to learn the ways of trade. Yet I worry; I would have not my past repeated."

"Then send me not."

"It was agreed with Norty you would be the one to take her any news and to bring instructions back to us."

"It may become dangerous for an enchanter who remains in the city. Mother I worry for your safety."

"There are reasons we stay and reasons you must leave. You are correct; it may be dangerous to remain. It is one of the reasons we send you away, with you gone there will be little danger for you."

"I fear not danger."

"Then you are foolish! Argue not and do as asked. The journey will take but a few days and it will be all the safer on your return."

"I like this not; my duty ...."

"Your duty is to your parents and your guild! We instruct you to make this journey and here your education in dealing with others begins. Ensure you make a deal benefiting both parties. A sour deal will ensure those who supply our needs will sell it at a higher price the next time. Mark well my words, Aurorai."

"Yes, mother. When is it I leave?"

"A travel pack is placed next to your bed; ensure you rise early on the morrow."

"I am not known for my early rises."

"You will do so. The journey is safe yet you must keep your wits about you and follow the directions given. Worry not, you will be safe. If you fail to return in four days others will find you."

"You sound as if you are unsure of me or the path I will take."

"The path is safe yet cannot always be guaranteed free of troubles once our lands are left. The river elves guard not their lands as do we."

"Never have I been to their lands and four days away is long enough."

"Finglas has agreed to take you to the druid rings close to their city. At noon on the fifth day he will wait where he leaves you. Be not late; others are in this also."

"Any would do so, mother."

"He will speak not if questioned by others."

"I see why he is chosen."

"Heed well his instructions. Rumours abound other eyes turn to our lands; it seems many have heard skeleton tracks are found."

"They would dare attack not."

"If we were to win we would be fewer in numbers and give them an easier victory."

"Norty must be informed she ...."

"Be assured she has thought of this, worry not."

"She has a mind to think of all. Would it be my mind was the same."

"Dawn breaks soon, Norty, yet no enchanters' bell will sound this day."

"The enchanters return from patrol with the guards, also for the last time."

"'Tis a sad day for all."

"It must be, Jenay, yet in truth I also feel saddened. We must be away from here before the day breaks. The only enchanters to remain will be the Minlets; they will act as we discussed. Indeed, they are essential to our plans."

"Our ears in unfriendly lands."

"They have the ears of many in the city and those who speak not directly to them are heard in other ways. We must know what others believe and to have whispers enter the city. They alone will whisper."

"Aurorai is still young; it places an unnecessary burden on her to be the one to bring us news the city."

"Olva will instruct her in the ways she must be and when to take word to us. Twice each week Finglas will enter the inn and order a drink. Should Olva have news he will know and bring Aurorai to us."

Jenay laughed, "Asked to enter an inn and drink is a task he will well like."

"Yet great danger there will be also if others drink into the night."

"He will be safe, worry not."

"This I know. Most of our people will wish to move little from the comfort of their homes when the enchanters have left. They need us, or so they believe, to protect us from the dark elves yet still they trust us not as friends. We must change their thoughts of us else we may not move forward to new times."

"The enchanters who patrolled with the guards come this way. It will be strange to train in our new home, many will be unsettled."

"It is how it must be and all know this. Many ways must be left behind as we train until we return to our only home."

"The battle is still so far away?"

"Whilst our lands are patrolled where the skeleton tracks abound we will be safe. It cannot, must not, be forever this way. One day we may become careless and forget the skeletons and it is then they will attack and we will be ill prepared. Only by removing ourselves from the city may we open the eyes of our people to the plight we face and the threat of the skeletons." With the enchanters now gathered around her she nodded to her husband, within moments he had taken them from high elf city yet a deep sadness remained in them. It would be some time before they would see their beloved city once again.

## Black Arrow

Walking down the rickety old stairs of the inn Aurorai stretched a little; a night sleeping on open ground followed by a day's hard walking before she found the inn had left her stiff. Twisting her body left and right in slow easy movements she felt the stiffness of her muscles easing. She realised she had not listened to the instructions Finglas had given her and had become lost quiet early on her travels. At last she had found the inn, and at last a comfortable bed. The man's voice startled her.

"Me bed's not to ya liking?"

She had failed to notice him in the dark corner under the stairs. With a bow she answered, "The bed was comfortable, thank you. A night in the open has left me a little stiff. I realised not how fast you must travel to ensure the safety of an inn such as this."

Leaning forward from the darkness he picked up an old clay pipe, "It ain't far from the druid circle; no needs to run. You'll be wantin' a warm breakfast?"

"Thank you no. If you have a little fruit...."

Lighting the pipe from a candle he used the stem to point, "On the table. Eat what you want. Where ya headin'?"

"The land of the river elves, I have business there and only a little travel cake. May I take some for the journey?"

"Ya won't need the stuff it's only a few hours from the left fork in the road. Have what you want the others won't eat it."

"I heard voices in the night."

"Three men and a dwarf arrived late; still managed to drink all night."

"Others stay here?"

"Nope."

"I have a feeling someone follows me. I saw them not so my parents ask a druid or ranger to follow me."

"You's done somethin' wrong?"

"To my knowledge I have not."

"Then why hunt you?"

"To be hunted would mean capture. Other reasons they must have."

"What reasons?"

"To ensure I am safe; to keep me from harm mayhap."

"Party of goblins stayed here couple o' nights ago. Watch for them thieves."

"They harmed you not?"

"Don't travel much do ya?"

"This is my first time alone."

"None harm an inn keep. If they did there be no places for them to stay. It's a sort of unwritten law. All can stay and none can harm us."

"Then you are probably the safest of all people. We have not the luxury of such safety."

"You live in trees, be hard for them to kill ya."

"I am high elf born not wood elf born."

"I dont's know the difference."

"The ears of a wood elf are pointed a little upwards; those of a high elf point a little backwards. It is easy to see."

"Up or back I don't care. Hide and surprise them."

"Clearly you know them not. All will be known to me in time."

"If'n you need water the well's outside."

"My water skin is dry, thank you."

A smoke ring blew towards her as the man leaned back once more; it seemed her conversation was over.

Almost exhausted Aurorai sat down, the sun way too hot for further travel and the water in the skin sack hung by her side too warm to quench her thirst. Leaning back against the tree for the little shade it offered her thoughts turned to her best friend. 'What is it you would do, Nortee, how do I survive in lands as hostile as these? What is you would do for cool water?' As if in answer to her thoughts she felt the stiletto at her side and withdrew it from its sheath. Digging at the soft earth for a few minutes she placed the water skin in the hole and covered it with the soil. 'It seems I learn more than I thought, Nortee, this is the way you would ensure cool water I believe. Now I must find the path to the river elves; how is it you do this so easily? I wish not another night on the hard ground.'

Shielding her eyes she looked up at the sun as she tried to judge her position, 'Druid I was born not yet I believe I took the wrong turn at the fork in the road; he spoke go right, I am sure of this. Should I return to the inn or continue this path; which would be better?

So little water do I have for a mistake. I am thankful mother sends me only to the rive elves; their city is close and should have been easy to find.'

In the cool of the shade she let herself relax and think of which way to go. It was obvious the road was little used so finding help or the river elves would be small. It seemed best to return to the inn and try once more come the morrow. Nortee would think little of spending a night in the open, she would love it. She was not as her friend, she needed a comfortable bed.

Opening her eyes she was shocked; the sun, once high in the sky, had sunk low, 'Aurorai, you sleep when you should be doing. It seems two nights you will now spend under the stars.'
Taking the now cool water from the earth she took a sip, 'It seems I do something right at last. Friend Nortee you would be proud of me.'
Taking a small bite from the travel cake she set off, "Sing, Aurorai, sing. Make the most of the day and hurry whilst you may."

Ahead of her a green hand was raised and the goblin band stopped.
"Elfin voice! Bah, I can smell her stench. We set a trap for her tomorrow."
"We can kill her tonight, there's still time."
"Darkness will fall soon and their eyes are good at night. Tomorrow we capture her and feast, or take her back as a prize."
"Silly elf takes the north road; we take her at the rocks."

The sun had risen by at least an hour when she awoke, stiff once more from yet another night on hard ground, 'I must pay more attention to the maps and listen as others instruct. The sun is high and I wake late yet again. Which way to go?'
Looking down to the ground she saw the arrow-shaped mark she had scratched in the ground, 'Nortee would know the way without thought; this is the way I would remember. Though you feel not like singing it will lift your spirit and make the aches in your muscles ease. Sing, Aurorai, sing.'

Approaching the steep cliffs to the right she paused, "Nortee would chastise you for being not careful, Aurorai. The cliffs would be a place of bandits. Mayhap you should walk around them; to step in to a trap you know could be there would be foolish.'
Checking the rise of the land her head shook, "Too steep it is and I ache so after another night on hard ground. The road is little used, it will be safe."

Two hundred paces later a small rock falling behind her span her around as she dropped into a defensive posture, ready to cast a spell as her eyes

searched the rock face, ears strained to catch the slightest of sounds. With nothing happening she turned to continue her journey.
'Too nervous you are, Aurorai. Continue with confidence."

Twenty steps later the rock falling caused her to turn yet again; and this time ten goblins were headed her way. There were too many to fight, it would be an impossible task. There was only one option, to run. Casting her pet spell she commanded it to stay; it would obey her and attack anyone who came close and, hopefully, hold them at bay while she made good her escape. Turning her heart sank. Ten more were standing to block the way to safety.

Her options were getting small; to slide down the shale of the slope to the left in hope of escape would only result in serious injury, or death. It would be impossible to dodge round them; to surrender to them would lead to a slow death and she had heard tales of what they did to captives, she would die first. There was only one choice, if it could be called such.

The need to gain height became paramount in her. If she could reach the small ledge some distance above her they would have to come at her one at a time, she would stand a small chance of surviving. Preying to the Mother she began to climb as she called to her pet, "Give me the time I need, pet, attack!"
The shield of living glass formed around her as the fur ball unrolled to attack those threatening his mistress.

It was an impossible fight, as well she knew, but she would die and rob them of the chance to take her, in which ever way they wished to do, 'Fool, Aurorai, well would Nortee scold you for such thoughts. She would fight and she would win. Fight, Aurorai, fight!
Be proud you will take so many of the green enemy with you this day. Hope someone finds your body and see you died taking many of the green ones with you. Make your parents proud!'

Then she was on the ledge as she saw her pet turn to dust and blow away on the breeze. Without a moment to catch her breath she saw the first goblin scrambling up the rock.

"Great Mother help me, I am not proficient to charm them, to have them fight amongst themselves. Give to me power in my spells; your blessing is all I ask."

Her force bolt hit the goblin half way towards her, and he screamed in agony. A second spell stuck his shoulder and he fell. No scream was heard; she knew he was dead before he let go of the rocks. It encouraged her in the fight, if they died so easily she may have a chance in the battle. 'Thank you, Great Mother. You grant my pleas.'

Looking down she realised she had thanked her too early; the end looked certain, five more were climbing and the looks on their faces showed they wanted vengeance for the death of a friend.

Her aim changed, as did the spell type she cast. Fire was, she thought, the way to stop them, if they were burned they would be unable to climb. The first cast was off the mark; she was aiming at their hands and missed. A second cast sent the small overhang above them crashing down, to take two of them on its slide to the pathway below. A moments struggle from one and he stopped all movement; another would never attack her kind again.

Her voice hissed at them, "Enough of your ways; leave before you anger me."

"Smelly elf! Your stench sickens us, soon no more stench; soon you dead!"

She had bought a few more seconds, time for a little of her strength and mana to build up inside of her. She was casting fast, the mana used also took strength and it was beginning to tire her.

The goblin who had called to her screamed and fell as she watched. She did not know how it had happened but she was happy it did. If more fell it would help to even the odds, and perhaps live to tell the tale.

As the goblin hit the ground she was casting once more, and failed to see the black arrow protruding from his back. Her overriding concern was to fend off the others attacking her, to keep them from reaching the ledge at all costs. Once they did the fight would be over and, if she were still alive, it would be a very unpleasant way to die.

Her spell changed yet again, this time she cast a blinding flash of light, and another goblin fell as he tried to cover his eyes; his fall taking two others with him as they climbed just below. It brought a smile to her face; she was winning against all the odds. The smile faded as fast as it appeared, a hand was on her ankle and was pulling at her. Then his arm was almost severed from the shoulder and he fell.

Unable to believe her luck she glanced down to see a wide tipped black arrow laying at her feet. Somewhere she had a friend, and they were need. She called out as loud as she could, "Friend I have need of you here; come to my side and fight with me! Apart we may both fall to these foul creatures!"

There was no time to look who had aided her; a goblin was standing in front of her. Almost in a panic she did not realise the training she had undergone take over and she entered his mind. This time she was successful, she charmed him into doing her bidding. She has never known such sweet relief.
Spinning round he struck the first to stand on the ledge, "Die, you won't harm her. Die in the dust where you belong!"

Within minutes a strange feeling entered her mind as she lost the link with him. She needed him for the duration of the fight; the link had been only brief. The shock of losing the link not only stunned her it caused dark thoughts to rear up in her mind; to take control of her.

She was out of his mind and anger rushed into him he had never known before. She had charmed him, defiled his mind and he wanted her dead at any cost. With sword raised high he would cut her many times and the wounds would be deep, but not enough to kill her, yet. He would slice her into pieces, cut her as she screamed in pain but he would not stop, she would die in as much pain as he could give her.
With sword raised high he would strike her arm first, and she would be unable to cast again. It was his last thought as an arrow took his life.

Green blood covered her; the arrow had a thin point and passed almost through its victim. As he fell at her feet the dark thoughts in her mind screamed she should push him over the edge of the ledge and on to another enemy. She had delayed too long, another goblin was standing by her and instinctively she moved backwards. It saved her life; the dagger piercing her side caused a pain she had never known before. She passed out as she saw him raise the weapon once more to strike the final blow.

Consciousness returned slowly and painfully and, as she remembered the ledge, tried not to roll over. Opening her eyes she closed them quickly, opening them slowly as relief took her. Gone was the rock ledge and in its place a soft comfortable bed. Gone was the dark cliff face and in its place a window through which the early evening sun shone warmly. Her left hand moved to feel the wound and discovered tight bandaging; her robe was missing.

"Best you lay still you got some broken ribs and a deep wound."
The man's voice startled her causing pain as she moved sharply, "Who are you and where am I? How did I get here?"
"None ever remembers an innkeeper's name. You was here before. Names Jassy and I owns this inn. Ya robe's at the bottom o' the bed."
"How did I get here? And thank you for the bandaging."
"I didn't do it; some elf brings ya here and bandages ya. She's no healer so went to get somebody who is."
"She removed my robe?"
"Yep, and washed and mended it, pretty good job she's done at sewing it while she watched over you till she was sure you'd be alright. Then she goes to the druids circle and another of your kind comes here. She's down stairs waiting for me to tell her it's time to see ya."
"I have a need to thank her, where is she?"
"Left yesterday she did."
"I have been here overnight?"
"Ya been here two days."
She was stunned, "Two? Where did she go?"
"Don'ts tells me anything."
"Would you be so kind as to ask the one down stairs to see me, she will do the healing."
"Not her; she's one o' them druids. I refused to let her near ya till ya opened yer eyes."
"A druid may heal me, thank you. I grow hungry; may I have some food and drink?"
"I'll get you some if ya promises not to move."
"You have my promise."
"Ya wants me to send the girl up?"
"If you would be so kind, yes."
"Only if you don'ts leave. I know you sneaky elves. A good night's sleep and I thinks you be well enough to go home."

"Thank you, my parents will be most worried."
"The first elf sends a message you's be alright. Gets a message to them the moment she could be sure."


The door opening brought recognition to her face, "Rinini; if memory fails me not? Oft have I served you."
"Greeting, Aurorai. May I see the wounds?"
Pulling the sheets back she waited as the wounds were examined, grimacing once or twice, "They are still somewhat painful."
"The bruising I may help yet a cleric is needed for the wound. If not for another travelling the road you would be dead I hear. You have been lucky, Aurorai of Minlet's inn."
"An archer came to aid me. I saw them not so may thank them not."
"Jassy spoke a high elf archer was the one."
"He is wrong; high elves use not a bow."
"He says you spoke of how to tell us apart. I think he knows who he saw. She did spend time here, never leaving your room except to wash your robe and her tunic and pants."
"Did Jassy speak of the colour she wore?"
"You have an idea as to who aided you?"
"I do. The arrows used were black, war arrows, and I have an idea who shot them; an elf who drank in our inn but a few days ago."
"Black he said, black as the night."
"Once have I seen a high elf dressed as such, and in the company of men dressed the same; I saw not the arrows as their cloaks covered the quivers."
"You have an idea as to which it was?"
She felt her face glow a little red as she answered, "One tried to take me on the way to training. He was slain...."
"You took his life? I would do the same also!"
"I did not, no time did I have. I freed myself and saw the shadow of someone as they left the building to which he had taken me. Sure I am it was the shadow of a female and my thoughts turn to the high elf; she was most upset when the male with her took my wrist and wanted me. Thinking of such actions I begin to wonder why she was upset so."
"To do such you would be in your rights to slay him if he listened not to you."
"The one in black, I know not her name, pressed a dagger to his throat and he let me go."

"You are right, it could well be the same female yet why would she do this?"

"I know not. Take me home, my parents will be distraught."

"They know all is well."

"Finglas was to take me home."

"I spoke with him and he continues his duties; he asked I be the one to care for you."

"What duties does he attend?"

"He would speak nothing of them. We go now, put on your robe."

"Wait; first I must thank Jassy."."

"He climbs the stairs; be quick, your parents worry and I would know something before we leave?"

"What is it you wish to know?"

"All enchanters have vanished, where may we find them?"

"I know not."

"yet you are enchantress born; you would know where they are."

"It seems not all is spoken to me. I know not where they are."

"You will speak to me when you are told?"

"I cannot. Had they wished others to know they would have been told; I may speak not."

"Speak to me when you are told."

"It is not my duty. I am to pass messages only; I believe I will be told not of where they are."

"Yet enchanter you are."

"It seems I am trusted not. If I may walk not to another town without being lost on the way how is it they would trust me with taking to them information?"

"The way to the river elves is easy; follow the path and take the left fork in the road."

"Jassy spoke the right fork, I am sure."

The door opening stopped their conversation.

"Elves! Canny trust them ta listen. Left fork I told ya, left."

"I apologise, Jassy. Now, as to the matter of payment for my care."

"Its bin sorted; the other elf says I was to looks after ya good. Three elfin jewels she gives me. I don't need any more."

"It is a lot for such care."

"Ya askin' I gives ya some back?"

"I do not. Keep the jewels and I thank you once again."

"Fer an elf ya's not bad. If'n you come this way again the room and foods free."

The bow brought a pain to her side but she could not leave without showing her appreciation and had an idea Rinini would speak to her parents of her poor manners had she not bowed."

## Battle Zone

Dodging right and rolling twice Finglas saw the fiery ball of mana explode against the wall behind him. Still crouched he threw himself left as another hurled at him, once more suffering the same fate as those previous. He had dodged most the spells thrown at him but was getting tired and had used most of his mana in fending off attacks, the chances to cast offensive spells had been few and far between. Those he cast had been, for the most part, deflected; his attacker showing no sign of weakening; if anything the spells seemed to have a greater ferocity about them than the first few.

Most of his tricks had failed, the few spells he had managed to cast had barely taken hold, and so few had a reasonable effect. His attacker had been slowed, if only a little, to a walking speed, and he knew he was being toyed with, there was more to come; he was being teased.

As he stood a spell found its mark, hurling him backwards a few feet, his natural agility managing to land him in a crouch. Turning he faced his attacker once more, in time to see the next spell was already on its way to him. His leap upwards took him to top of the low wall, and a ledge to hide him from sight.

Keeping low he breathed deep, needing a few moments to catch his breath, to think how to stop the attacks, or at least to find a defence against them. No matter where he went his attacker was there, for each trick he tried there seemed to be a counter move for it. He longed for the forest and the opportunities they would offer; he was more at home in the forest and could show a very different fight.

Above him the old ceiling shattered into fragments as yet another spell hit it, showering him with tiny sharp pieces. He would get no rest here, he knew it, the spells had been changed to heat the rock and cause them to explode into pieces. Dropping to the ground he dived left as yet another spell hit the wall, showering him with more splinters. At last his attacker has made a mistake by moving close to the bushes; he saw an opening, too good an opportunity to miss.

His spell cast he watched as roots of the bushes broke the surface to grab at his attackers shoes. Now he could move around the wall and rest, to regain mana lost in the fight while the roots held his attacker steadfast. He needed an hour for all the mana to build back within him, but he knew the root spell would last only a few minutes, five if he was very lucky. He had to change his attack strategy, all of his tricks had been met with a defence seemingly impregnable, but he knew there had to be a way around them, everyone had a weakness, no matter who they were.

Leaning back against the wall he breathed heavily as he slid down to a sitting position, his eyes closing to start his meditation and, therefore, the mana regeneration he needed so badly. Almost the moment he closed his eyes he was under attack once more, the mana ball hitting the wall above and behind him, showing him with splinters yet again.

"Desist! I yield to you."
"You are not in the position of surrender!"
As another spell shattered the rocks around him and he dropped to one knee, "I surrender."
"There is a cost when one surrenders."
"Name your price."
"I would have your kiss."
"A price I gladly pay."

Enjoying the kiss she eventually pulled away from him, "Well, my Finglas?"
"You are cunning."
"You evade the question."
"I found it hard to pass your defences. You knew each move I would make and which spells I would use."
Sitting she patted the ground at her side, "Enchanters are physically the weakest of all elves so we study each of the classes. I have studied you, watched as you fought in battles. Others study the ways druids fight and, one day, it maybe you are hurt or killed because of those ways. It is time to learn to fight differently; to surprise an enemy is the only way to ensure you defeat them."
"I am a druid so must fight as one."
"All have surprises hidden deep, you must find and use those ways."
"If they are not hidden but missing?"
"They are there, waiting to be discovered."
"When I am recovered I wish to fight again and this time I will be the attacker."

Pose stood, "I will be your adversary, yet how was it Norty knew where you where and when you rested?"

"I saw her pet, he was everywhere."

"My pet is my eyes, through him I knew where you where."

"If I had killed your pet you would have been blind?"

"I would have only my eyes to use and not those of my pet. Your position was known through the linking of my mind to yours. The battle balanced in my favour."

"This time I fight Pose, she is not linked; I have ideas of my own to try."

"I wish you well; I know the forfeit she would extract from you."

"If you would have a kiss for your victory then I have a mind to make the same demand."

With a slight nod of the head and a smile towards Pose she turned and walked towards the spire in the middle of the ruins, her ears picking up the sounds of battle.

Pose was in love with her husband and had cared for his injuries after his fight with a giant. She was the same as any other elf, falling in love the instant they see the one to be theirs. Yet the Gods had given her love to Finglas, for years she had thought it impossible for a dark elf to love an elf, for more than one elf to love the same male, yet Pose loved him. Her head shook as she ducked to enter the spire, Pose would play her part to train Finglas, and she knew his life was in danger, yet not from where the danger would come. She would ensure his chances of surviving any fight would be great, even at the risk of Pose claiming her forfeit.

Nodding to the dark elf enchanters gathered at the practice session she took a seat to watch as they trained. It had pleased her so many of them had wished to follow Pose and train with the elves, more than she had dared dream asked for the opportunity. Over thirty had originally asked, all of different abilities, to join them, most enchanters welcoming then with open arms.

As they trained they returned home and spoke with others of their guild and yet more asked to attend. One such was Hetyial, a young dark elf enchantress of just fourteen summers, had shown promise and Pose had taken to instructing her personally.

Eventually others had greeted the dark ones; even hold conversations, yet only the enchanters trusted them completely.

The elves still distrusted their own enchanters, her mother's words rang once again in her mind, 'the enchantress may control the mind of any, yet it also makes them the most feared and hated of all the professions. None like to have their minds played with, use your power wisely.'

"Your mind is troubled once more, may I help?"
"Many things are yet to happen, Jenay, I worry over them."
"Word from the Minlets speak of unrest within the cities."
"It was known such would happen."
"They speak also of the rangers finding tracks in the forest."
"Skeletons still walk the lands. The paladins know of them also."
"Never have they been seen in such number and the council show concern. Why is it they walk our land?"
"They seek a weakness within the elves, a place where they may attack and be victorious."
"How is it you know of their plans?"
"Place your mind in theirs. If you were to decide to attack would you not look for a weakness?"
"Yet if they choose to attack...."
"Not if they attack, Jenay, when. It will happen. The tracks start high in Whisper Valley and each night finish ever nearer high elf city. When the rangers wait to see the skeletons none appear. They will attack and our plans must be finished before the day comes."
"Yet why attack high elf city?"
"Wood elf city is built high in the trees; they would be hard pressed to climb them. We would destroy so many before they could fight."
"Mine is on the ground and no walls afford protection."
"Once more your mind must be in theirs. If you were to plan the attack which of the cities would you choose?"
"I fear mine would be overrun so easily."
"It is why our plans must come to fruition before the attack. If the council will listen not to the rangers warning the lives of many will be lost, lives we can ill afford to lose."
"Lives are always lost in battles."
"Always the elves fight in battles we should not. Should we win this battle still shall we lose."
"I follow you not."
"Alone we have little chance; any victory will be at a cost too terrible to count. With so many lives lost we would perish; too few would there be to recover."

"The Gods give us the right to have a child when we wish. All must bear children, through duty if not through love."

"Yet we may have two only, Jenay. Others races soon replace losses of war, we have not such a luxury."

"Then we must fight no wars?"

"Ours are the largest of all lands and many view them with envy. Never could we hope to keep them free."

"None would dare attack if alliances were made."

"Alliances would show us to be weak and unable to protect our lands. It would bring others to us looking for an easy victory, and we would be honour bound to help if others were attacked; yet more would die in battles. It is not the way."

"Then how are we to protect ourselves and our lands?"

"Through strength and unity, Jenay."

"It is easy to see why Caspo Kwil chose you to lead us. I pray the Great Mother protects you."

"Leader, forgive my interruption."

"Aurorai, of what use is a mentor if they are not there to listen?"

"Two days pass and I leave to see Nortee; are there other tasks for me?"

"Your wound heals well?"

"Malinna insisted she help and the scar bleeds no more. It is a painful reminder I must listen well to others."

"A lesson you do well to remember; ensure you strain not the wound. I have no tasks for you at this time yet I would ask from you two favours. Look to my daughter, ensure no harm befalls her."

"She and I have been close friends for many years. I will protect her life as if it were my own."

"I speak not of her body. When the danger comes it will be obvious to you."

"The second favour you would ask?"

Standing she smiled, "On your return she will ask a question, mayhap even demand you speak. You will not do so."

As she left she whispered, "You spoke not of the question."

70

# High Priestess

"Your father brought me to the druid rings, Nortee, yet still it took an hour of running hard to find you. Where is Elesee, I believed her to be with you?"

"She spoke I should continue the journey yet not of the reason. How is mother?"

"She speaks she is well yet I know she worries. The message from her was strange. How may you know her meaning?"

Warming her hands by the fire she shook her head; "I know not her meaning, Aurorai, it is for another to know."

"Then how may you know what is needed of you?"

"She asks I seek out Kyna, a friend of many years, this is easy to understand. It is the message I must speak which is a mystery."

"Her words were 'Punish not the elves for the thoughts of one. Be a friend to save my life once more.' She spoke not of what she wishes from Kyna."

"Mother spoke of no threat to her life yet Kyna will know her meaning, of this I am sure."

"Her words were repeated to me often, she spoke I must say them to you as she had done."

"You touch your side often, Aurorai. What troubles you?"

Careful to not let Ventil see any part of her she opened the robe enough for Nortee to see the scar.

"Aurorai! How did this happen, are you well to travel?"

Her face grinned, "I have a tale to tell, my first adventure."

"So close it seems you came to your last adventure. Aurorai, how may you be left alone; how may I leave you alone?"

"I have an adventure to speak. Would you scold me as a child or wish to listen to my tale?"

"Sit, if you move with the telling of the tale I will tie you to a tree and gag you till you see reason!"

She grinned at Ventil, "She is the younger yet thinks she may command me."

"Sit, Aurorai. I would hear this tale."

Sitting on the small log she stretched, "Mother instructed I visit the river elves. It is there my tale begins."

Listening as Aurorai recited her tale she twice tried to speak yet was told to hold her tongue in a sharp way. As her tale finished she sighed at her,

"Aurorai, well should you know the way to the river elves. How is it you became so lost?"

"I listened not to your father as he spoke to me the way to travel."

"Your life may have been lost through inattentiveness! Why did you listen not?"

"Long have I thought of this. I was happy mother trusted me to buy wine and happy she begins to speak of her early days. These thoughts distracted me."

"The world is dangerous if your attention wanders, Aurorai. So many times it is spoken to us to be watchful as we journey."

"The lesson is well learned, Nortee."

She fell quite, watching as Nortee slipped quietly into the woods, "Someone comes."

Ventil narrowed his eyes, "How could she know?"

"She hears them, as do I."

"I forgot about elfin ears. Why let her go alone?"

"She is at home in the trees and will call should help be needed."

"By then it might be too late."

"You worry without cause; she will be safe and will attack them not, unless it is needed."

"There's more than one? She'll need help."

"Sit. You must remain here."

"If they harm her...."

The words of her mentor became clear at last, "Your feelings for her are obvious yet not returned."

"I know the elfin ways. She'll love only when she sees the one destined to be hers."

"You are not the one, Ventil."

"It doesn't alter my feelings."

"She has been asked to help in your teaching, you are a friend only."

"I follow my father. He loves Elesee and I love Nortee."

"Dismiss the love, it can never be returned to you."

"Can an elf choose who she falls in love with?"

"It is not a choice to us, it is instant, the moment we see the one to be ours."

"I love her and can't change my feelings."

"The voices fade. Be silent on our talk or you will regret this."

"You dare threaten me!"

"I am sworn to watch over her. I make only a promise."

"I know elves and their promises."

Nortee crouched once more beside the fire, "Three men hunting a dear."

"She evaded them?"

She giggled, "With a little help."

"The druid in you shines past the enchantress at times."

"Think not to distract me with words, Aurorai; the look on your faces is plain for all to see."

"We have spoken of you."

"You think I may speak not for myself?"

"I seek to protect my sister, is this so wrong?"

"Your sister?"

"I think of you as a sister."

"Long have I wished for a sister yet it is not mother's wish."

"I also yet it seems not to be."

"When first we met you spoke of being the second born. Where is the first born?"

"Ventil, I have a need to speak alone to Nortee. If you would but give me the time to speak a debt I will owe you."

"I don't know which I hate the most."

"I follow you not."

It was hard to keep the sarcasm out of his voice, "Women always want to talk together and elves are always secretive. I'll be back in a few minutes."

Aurorai shook her head, "So much he has to learn of the female and of us."

"What is on your mind to speak to me in private?"

"I ask you speak not my words to another."

"Nothing will I speak."

"Second I was born and hope to hear who came before me. Many summers ago I demand my parents speak yet they would not, chastising me hard."

"I find it hard to believe their actions. I see how they adore you."

"As I adore them also. So long have I wished to know if I have a sister or a brother and if they are they alive or dead."

"Mayhap one day they will speak of it."

"Upon the coming of my third year I became resolute, I would find my sister or brother and set a plan. Those who frequent our inn know me and many speak freely to me. I became friendlier towards them, smiling and on occasion would sit for moments with them. As I grew a little bolder I would ask them of my parents."

"I begin to see why you ask I speak not your words."

"This was so hard for me and it tormented my mind so much, I am known not for my friendliness; most deem me as shy."

"This I saw when first we met."

"I asked in a casual way how long they had known my parents and if they had always been happy. I smiled and laughed with them yet little did I gain from my exploits. One must have spoken to mother or father about my ways and questions for they summoned me to them one night when the inn was not busy. Never have I seen my parents in such distress or anger. Father grew so angry he left the room and returned not until the next day. Mother's tears were enough to flood the room and I began to hate myself for my unthinking ways. On father's return he asked I promise never to ask others of the first born and promise to mention it no more to them. I gave a promise I would ask not others in the inn yet refused to promise never to mention the first born to them speaking I have a sibling and it was my right to know. Father grew angry once more yet mother hushed him to calmness saying one day, when all was right once more, they would speak."

"Never have I seen your parents' anger. Indeed it seems they endure so much from those who drink at the inn and are always pleasant. I think of the race of dwarves and man; oft I find myself frustrated by them."

"I grew ever shyer; oft speaking not to those I served with drink or food. I began to wonder who it was who spoke to my parents. Each one would smile to me and I wondered is this the one who betrayed me. With each I saw I grew angrier. At times I had to excuse myself as I calmed outside the inn."

"Think of it not as betrayal. They were worried as to you."

"To me it was a betrayal though much later in my life I saw it differently. It has left within me heartache, no, a torture I find at times hard to bear. Yet at times it leaves in me fear of meeting my sibling. What would be my first words; how would I feel? So many worries I hold in my heart."

"When the time comes you will know the words, the way to be. I know this."

"I know not if I wish for a brother or a sister. I think and find I know not which I would rather have."

With a light laugh she touched her arm, "The choice is not yours; it has been made for you."

"Deep within my mind this I know. Mother spoke a little of her past to me but a few days ago and became upset. Mayhap the time will come when she is less upset and I will know more. So much do I wish to know."

"Do not push her, Aurorai; let her speak when she feels the time has come. Look to me as a sister and think of the way you would speak had you met me but moments ago."

Ventil dropped beside them, "I've waited long enough. I'm used to others waiting for me!"

Ignoring him Aurorai reached out, her finger resting on Nortee a little above her heart, "Sisters?"

She followed the same movements, "Sisters."

Ventil looked annoyed, "What's all this mean?"

Together they answered, "Forever sworn in sisterhood; forever sworn in friendship; forever sworn to protect the other."

"Sleep all; tomorrow we travel and have far to go."

Trying her best to keep a sorrowful face she turned to them, "Nortee, I like not another night on hard ground; is it you have a spell to bring to me a bed?"


"Never have I seen the cities of man, Ventil, they are so different to what I thought they would be."

"Use not his name, Aurorai, we wish not others to know who he is."

"I'll use grandfather's name; Jorin."

"You have visited this city before?"

"Not this one."

"Then we must ask where Kyna might be found."

"After we eat; I want meat and bread, and mead to wash it down."


Sitting at the table he stabbed the meat with his dagger, "Boar, my favourite."

"I would be ill if I were to taste it."

"Aurorai, each have their tastes and must be left to be as they should. Many meats are palatable."

"I know you have tasted meats."

"Xandorian would ask I try his recipes."

"Nortee! Meat is not the food of elves."

"The ways of others must be learned, oft Pose eats white meats and fish."

"Many times have I severed her such foods; the thought alone revolts me."

Nortee grinned, "Smell the meat; is not the aroma pleasant?"

"You seek to have me become ill?"

"I seek to instruct the ways of others, to mayhap save your life one day."

She sniffed the meat, "Not unpleasant."

"Now try a piece."

"You ask I eat meat?"

She laughed, "As your sister instructs so you will do."

"I am the elder, you would be the one instructed."

"Then try a piece for your sister."

Pulling the piece he offered from the knife she looked at it, "I do this for you; while I am ill you will care for me."

"Aurorai, if you eat not how will you know if the taste is to your liking?"

"The taste is odd yet not unpleasant."

"The mead will help the taste, enhance the flavour."

"I touch mead not! The smell alone turns my stomach."

"You would argue with me on this?"

"I would."

"Then it is for the good I ordered wine to complement the boar."

"Never have I met one who teases as do you. I had thought you to ask me to try meat when we reached a town of man. I have prepared."

"Aurorai seeks to outwit me?"

"I have already done so. Oft I visit my friends the gnomes and Xandorian spoke of your love for meat, with his guidance I tried many, and enjoyed some. I hope mother will know not I have done so, she will be displeased."

"It would seem only you know not your mothers ways. Why is it you have never accompanied her to buy wine? In the towns she visits she is oft found in a tavern eating meat."

"Never have I seen her eat meat; it is hard to believe."

"Yet she does so. Finish the wine; time to seek out Kyna."

Her head shook slowly, "I begin to see."

"What is it you see?"

"Mother spoke of journeying with her mother to many places and all the taverns and inns she stayed at. In all such places meat is served each night and mother must have tried many a piece."

She laughed, "And still has a taste for meat it seems. Come, I long to see Kyna once more."

"Nortee it's wonderful to see you again, is your mother with you?"

"She is not, friend Kyna, yet I would introduce friends to you."

"A friend of yours is one of mine."

Her hand, palm up, gestured, "Aurorai; enchantress and as a sister to me."

"Greeting, Aurorai."

"Greeting, Kyna. Nortee speaks often of you, with pride always in her voice."

Once more her upturned palm gestured, "Jorin, friend and travelling companion."

Her hand clasped his wrist in greeting, "Odd to see one of ours travelling with elves."

"I want to learn their ways, they offer to teach."

"Learn well, but Nortee reads the way the body reacts, taught by her mother, she's not easy to fool."

"I've no wish to fool her."

Walking round her she admired the red cloak, "Kyna, the cloak of a high priestess adorns your back. I am happy you are accepted into the ranks."

"Thank you, but don't speak of it to your mother."

"She would be happy for you."

"I want to surprise her. If not for her I wouldn't be wearing it."

"Mother spoke not of helping you."

"When you were a child in danger she came to see me in the Woods of Faith where I was reaching for the Gods. Later I spoke of my fears to her, I was not the only one who had doubts as to my calling; she has suffered the same anguish. She gave me back my beliefs; what is a paladin without her faith?"

"She owes to you her life and would do anything to help. I also thank you."

"Each time we meet you thank me, it's too much."

"If not for you I would be born not, I have much to thank you for."

"Where is she, I've not seen her for ages?"

"The enchanters were summoned before the council; a new leader to be chosen from them."

"Then Caspo Kwil has died. He was a good friend to your mother."

"His wish was for her to lead the enchanters."

"Never have I been so happy for her."

"She will be chosen not."

"She's born to lead them, you elves have strange ways."

"A message she sends yet I know not the meaning."

"What message?"

"Her words were 'Punish not the elves for the thoughts of one. Be a friend to save my life once more'. What is the meaning of the message?"

"She's not told you?"

"I know some of her plans, nothing of the message."

"When is the fight?"

"She seeks only to lead the enchanters, not to fight the council."

"No, who attacks the elves?"

"There is no threat."

"There's always a threat from someone. Tell me of her plans."

As she had once done for Norty she sat in silence, listening as Nortee spoke in detail of all she knew.

"I see why she has need of my people."

"You know of what she speaks?"

"Of war; a dreadful war not fought for a thousand years."

"I spoke to mother her actions may bring fighting amongst us."

"She'd do nothing to harm her people. The fight is against another foe."

"None threaten us."

"Why would she ask you seek me and not her mother to speak to the king?"

"You are a friend."

"He would do anything for Elesee, think again."

"Ack, you are so like mother, she would have me think and explain not the thoughts in her mind."

"The only way to ensure you grow is to make you think."

"The king may reject her pleadings?"

"Not if she were to ask Elesee to do it."

"I am unsure; I believe you hold not the power to persuade your people."

"Some will listen to me."

"You are a paladin, if you ask it would mean...."

"Continue."

"Mother believes the un-dead are the threat?"

"The signs are there, I've heard tell of them. What have you heard? Think Nortee."

"Skeleton tracks are found in Whisper Valley, with each passing night they draw ever nearer to high elf city."

"What do the elves do about it?"

"Rangers and druids keep watch yet never is a skeleton seen whilst they do so; only when the watching ceases."

"They can't keep watch forever. When they leave the skeletons will come back. Your mother would never ignore such an obvious threat. Why would she ask our help?"

"Paladins are the slayers of the un-dead, so much now makes sense. What is the meaning of the message?"

"Once, a long time ago, I helped your mother as a lion attacked her."

"This I have known for many summers. Oft she relates the tale to me and I have heard as you once spoke through the night of it to father."

"If the lion had killed her I would have been next. She thinks she owes me her life."

"This she is sure of, as am I."

"The time has come to think about it from my side."

"I see a lion and two people. They kill the lion and become friends; there is little to think of."

"There is so much more. When you cast a spell what happens to you?"

"A little of the mana within me is used."

"Yet is also costs your strength to cast."

"With each cast we become all the weaker. Mana also gives us strength yet takes it from us also."

"Your mother is gifted, this you know."

"The Gods gave to her their blessings."

"It means she casts with a greater fury than others."

"Yet her mind is the greater gift."

"She could not control the lion with her mind; she was too weak from its attack and had the bird in her charm. I know you can only charm a single person at a time."

"This I agree."

"Her cast was powerful and could have killed her in her weakened state yet still she did so to save me. We both killed the lion, not her and not I. Both! She owes me nothing but says she does. No matter what I say I can't convince her otherwise. The message asks I save her, and her people, once more. I can't speak for others."

"Your paladins will ride not with you?"

"We don't want war but the skeletons are why we are trained so hard."

"You would risk our people for *them*?"

Kyna spun round on him, "Them!? These are our friends and have helped us in so many wars, more than the years you've been alive! Watch your tongue!"

His anger rose, he was not used to being spoken to in such a way. Remembering what he was really trying to learn he held back his words. Turning back to Nortee she apologised, "He doesn't know your people like I do; or how much we owe you."

"There is little to forgive; what of the skeletons?"

"They must be returned to the grave."

"I agree with your thoughts. I have thought on your words also; I believed it was we who held the debt to you now I know; there may be little doubt about it. Mother owes to you her life as I do also."

Kyna laughed, "Bah, I finally get a chance to tell my side of the story and still can't get it through to stubborn elves."

"Stubborn we are when we know we are right. Who rides with you?"

She laughed, "Should none ride with me I will be there; this, it seems, I owe to your family."

"As I speak, nothing is owed."

Taking the bow and quiver from the shelf she stroked it, almost lovingly, as she spoke in elfish, "I owe more than you might imagine. Three years after I met your mother I was attacked by bandits and cornered. If not for this bow and enchanted quiver and the training from Elesee I would be dead. I ride for the elves; to death or to glory!"

# Homeward Bound

Spreading a small cloth on the ground Aurorai cut three small pieces off the cake and turned to place the remainder in her backpack. She did not have to see him to realise what was happening, "The food is not yet offered, Jorin."

"I'm hungry; we've walked all day and not stopped to rest."

"Never would we take food not offered, it is not our way."

Reluctantly he placed the cake back.

"You have tasted not elfin travel cake?"

"No, I've never heard of it."

"Without water you would find the taste not to your liking."

"We have water."

"The skin we carry the water in has been in the warm sun; it will no longer be sweet to the taste. It is why Nortee will bring fresh water."

Glancing at the tall sparse grass he grunted, "Scrub land as far as the eyes can see. She'll find no fresh water here."

"When I was small, not two summers in age, father spoke of a journey he made with a ranger. They travelled in land such as this and father worried as to where food and water could be found. Each day the ranger would set forth and return quickly with both. Father spoke he would survive but a few days yet to the ranger there was little worry."

"The last time we saw fresh water was the stream passing through the village where we stayed the other night."

"The water in the skins will be for naught but the hardest of times. With Nortee to forage for us it is unlikely it will be needed."

Pushing himself deeper into the sparse shade of the grass he tried to relax, "How will she know where to find us?"

"You see not the tracks we leave?"

"Yes I see them but they're not easy."

"To a druid and ranger they are as easy to see as words on a scroll. Here is a place with some shade and she knows it is where I will wait for her."

"I'm hungry, I want to eat."

"You can wait not?"

"I'm used to doing what I want when I want to and I want to eat now."

"You would wait not for friends to arrive?"

"I eat when I want so pass the water."

"It would seem the first thing you must be taught are manners."

"You are refreshed, Jorin?"

"I ate only a little but feel full."

"The water swells the cake to fill you and will give strength enough to face another day."

He muttered more to himself than anyone, "If we knew how to make this we could feed an army as we marched."

"It is not for such purposes, Jorin."

He changed the subject, "I don't see why we have to walk. Elesee could have taken us to your city."

"You are here to learn the elfin ways. To stay where you are will ensure you do so most painfully."

"Why?"

Her spell sent the scorpion scuttling away, "The grass is home to many who like not the sun, and to those who hunt them. Nortee will be her in minutes I believe."

"Looks like you're right, I can see her now."

With a smug smile she lay back against the tree.


Reaching them at last Nortee sat down, "It seems you learn well my teachings, Aurorai, and you were safe, Jorin, only with the coming of night will large predators roam the land. You have little cause to worry."

"We should build a big fire to keep them away."

"There is little here which may burn and a fire may attract others."

"Then we should take turns at watching through the night."

"It is needed not. Four elfin ears would hear the sound of danger."

"I feel stiff, we walked hard today."

Slipping the stiletto from its sheath Nortee dug near the grass before handing him a large bulbous root. "Slit the root with your knife and rub the sap where you ache; it will ease you for the walk tomorrow. By nightfall we will be once again near a village and you may rest in a bed."

"How do you know we'll be near a village?"

"The tracks around head the same way, so a village must be close."

"You can't go by one set of tracks."

"So many I saw as I searched for water; all lead the same way."

Suddenly he held his stomach, "I feel ill, the pain!"

"I asked he wait and eat not the cake, Nortee. He drank warm water also."

"You explained not to him?"

"He would listen not."

"Stand, Jorin."

"It hurts so much!"

"Stand and I may ease the pain."

Reluctantly he stood as Nortee moved behind him and placed her arms around his middle.

"Breathe out, Jorin."

As he did as he was told he felt Nortee pull hard and sharp around his middle and wind exited in a large belch.

"A lesson, Jorin. Eat the cake slow and with cool water."

After a day's travel the inn of the village was a welcome stop. It was small but seemed comfortable as the mug in his hand banished the thirst. With a sigh of pleasure he put the mug back on the table; his knife finding the remains of the meat.

After a few moments he put the knife down and picked up the meat.

Aurorai giggled, "You expect to learn our ways when you cannot defeat a piece of meat?"

"My knife is blunt."

"You would ask an enemy to wait whilst you sharpen your weapon? Always should it be ready to use."

He grumbled, "Another lesson?"

"A lesson which should be taught not; surely you know this?"

The loud roar of laughter at the bar made him look round, "There's a blacksmith next door; I'll get a sharpening stone in the morning. Nortee takes her time speaking to him."

"He is cousin to Keitun, many questions he will have."

"Dwarves, I hate them! They live in caves like wild animals. They don't deserve life!"

"Nortee lives high in the trees of our homeland; would you call her an ape? Each has their own way; dwarves have little use for open spaces."

"It would be difficult to attack them in their city; the tunnels are not wide enough to fight in. They should fight in the open like men!"

"Yet men they are not, dwarves they are. You would attack them?"

"I've heard talk we should but I'm not sure. Their lands are in the mountains and we can't grow food there."

"They trade little with other people yet still feed themselves and never hunger. You would attack only those on whose land you may grow food?"

"I'm in a difficult position. We need room to grow."

"Your lands are large and so little is used as it should be. Use your own lands and think not to take those of others."

"Others want war so we can have the room to grow."

"War would serve to reduce your numbers also. If you lose then your lands may be taken by the victors."

"I've watched father fight wars and battles; I know how to win them."

"If war were to be waged then to whom would you turn to ensure victory?"

"The dark ones would be easier. They don't guard the lands as they should. We could be at the city before they knew we were there. I hate them."

"Why so?"

"We fought them once, long ago. We entered the city and they tricked us; they came from behind, from everywhere and slaughtered us."

"You attacked them; did you think they should protect not themselves?"

"They had no right to slaughter us; only a few returned from the war."

"Never does it cease to amaze me. The losers of a war speak they are slaughtered, the victors speak of a great battles."

A hand on her shoulder spun her around, "Elf, we're in the mood for a dance."

"Remove your hand. To touch without permission is allowed not."

Thoughts of the last time this happened returned to her and she felt the dark thoughts running through her mind once more, "Your hand remains on my shoulder. Remove it if you would."

"After you dance for us."

"Remove your hand if you would. I ask no more."

His hand slipped down her arm and gripped her wrist, "Dance, elf."

Only with difficulty did she hold back the dark thoughts once more as they fought their way to the forefront of her mind, "To the elfin people dancing is strange. It is not a custom we practice."

As Jorin tried to stand hands held him down, "Let her be or answer to me!"

With effort she banished the dark thoughts, "There is little need to worry, Jorin; these men wish only a little fun."

"Dance elf. Entertain us."

Her eyes looked towards his hand as, with great effort; she once more held the dark thoughts in check.

His free hand moved forward, "Dance good and I'll buy you a drink."

Her hand moved up his arm to come to rest on his cheek as a smile lit her face up, "If you would remove your hand you may find a mug of ale the entertainment you need."

The idea pleased him, "You'll drink with us?"

Casually she placed a jewel in his hand, "I have duties to attend yet the cost of a few drinks is not beyond my means."

Watching them walk away Jorin scowled, "If they had tried to harm you...."

"Too fast do you think of the fight, a smile and a few words may change the mind of many."

"You used your enchantress ways to charm him?"

"Had I done so I would have failed; not yet is my prowess enough. I entered his mind to turn his thoughts yet even this is hard for me; the reason I needed to touch his cheek. It is a way to enter the mind more easily."

"You have to touch to turn a thought; so you don't always charm people?"

"Charm is hard even for one trained in its use. Should we be in fear we would use spells and pets first. Charm is a last resort."

"Yet if it had not?"

"Friends were close, worry not."

With an almost imperceptible nod to Nortee and the blacksmith at the window she sat with Jorin, "You know not the ways of my people, the ways of the enchanters?"

"No, but I want to learn all there is to know of the elves and how each of you fight."

"Why do you wish this?"

He turned to hide his face as he answered, "How can we be friends if I don't know all there is to know about you? How you fight and win so often. I want to know all there is to know of the four races of elves. Then I want to find out how each of the guild fight."

"Each of us?"

"I'll start with the wood and high elves then the river elves. I'm not sure how to get to know how the dark ones fight."

"The task would be difficult."

"I hear some of them train in your city so I'll find a way."

"It would seem your mind is set. Why is this?"

Once more he turned his head away as he replied, "If you know how your enemies fight you have a better chance of beating them."

Her fingers held his chin as she turned his head back towards her, "You believe us to be your enemies?"

He shook his head loose and started on the meat once again, "If we know how you fight then we can be of better help to you in a fight. Father's lucky he has Elesee to advise and help him and even get her people to help if it looks like he'll lose a war."

"The elves fight not so easily. War is repugnant to us and we fight only when it is needed."

"Yet you've never lost a fight. I want to be the same and win every battle!"

"Your voice is sharp, is this how it should be when friends speak with you?"

"I want to know all you know, learn all there is to know!"

"Your voice rises yet again."

He had shown his feelings too easily and calmed down, "I'm sorry, Aurorai, it's just I want to fight and win as easily as the elves seem to. I'll do it, by the Gods', I'll do it."

"Not all is as easy as it would seem. In battles many are lost and many more mourn those killed in battle. Wars cause only pain and suffering."

"And give more land so you can grow and get stronger so you can win more battles. This is what a leader of his people must do."

"There are ways other than fighting."

"Kill your enemy; leave none alive; not even the women and children. It's the way to ensure you keep their lands and your own people grow strong."

New thoughts about him sprang up in her mind, and she did not like what they were saying. Giving him an odd look she bit the apple in her hand, "To kill all, even the children, would remove them from the lands?"

"Most should never have been born!"

# Elfin Country

Walking along the wooden bridge she turned, "Seven days have I been away, Jorin, I knew not how much I missed my lands."

"The river marks the boundary of your land?"

"All of our lands are thus marked; we share the river for it belongs to none."

"My people claim all rivers belong to them."

"Rivers are free of ownership. They bring pleasure, food and water for the lands. Many wars are fought over lands rich and fertile. Never are wars fought over deserts yet even they may bear food for others."

"We don't know how to grow food in deserts and won't fight wars over them."

"We grow food in many places and feed other races not just the elves."

"I've tried some of the food, its good. I want to be like you and live in peace."

"We know not peace and I believe never will we see such times. Mother wishes it yet it can never be. I fear she strives in vain."

Scooping a handful of soil she let it slip through her fingers, "I see little difference with the land this side of the bridge to those on the other yet it feels so much the better to me."

"If Kyna's right you may lose them to the skeletons."

Crouching beside two small stones she hissed, "While breath is in my body never shall our lands belong to others! Home is to the south east yet would take many days of travel. To the west a patrol is but two hours walk and will offer a lift home. Since the incursion of the orcs many new paths are now used, and changed often."

"Then how will we find them?"

Pressing her hand into the soft clay she looked up at her, "If they know not we are here the council will speak many words to them."

Turning one of the two pointed stones on a rock she began to walk, "Friends know of the stones; the forward one points the way they have taken, the second to the sun was when they left this place, it has moved but two hours on its journey. Rangers and druids turn the stones so those who track not may find them."

Eventually she called a halt, "We wait here for them to come to us."

"We've walked two hours only, Nortee; they'll be still ahead of us."

"To surprise others you move not in a straight line for long. They will turn soon."

"Which way?"

Blowing gently at the flames she had started she added a few sticks, "It is obvious should thought be given to it."

"Any direction's good if patrolling, especially towards an enemy."

"Think, Jorin, when looking if an enemy had entered your lands and you had the setting sun to your back who would have the advantage in a fight?"

"It's obvious when explained. They'll turn east?"

"Use each and every way the land offers, it may one day save your life."

"I'll remember all you can teach me. I see why elves win all their fights."

Taking a log she placed it upright on the fire; "We make camp on the slope of a hill, a signal fire would be of little use when lit in a valley."

"There's no green wood to make smoke, what use is it?"

"Smoke may attract unwelcome attention and there are other ways to signal. Old wood burns all the brighter and will be seen for many hours walk; the hill behind hides the glow from those not on our lands. The way the fire dances up the log show friends need help; they will come to investigate."

"You're full of strange ways, Nortee."

"It is but the ways of druids."

"Father told me elves can get close to an enemy without being seen."

"It is the way grandmother first saw your father and his friends as they entered our lands, she stood ten paces from them and was seen not."

"Can you?"

"With hair as yellow as the corn, it would be hard for me."

"With a white robe we'll see you easily."

Her head dropped to one side for a moment, "Under my robe I wear the pants and top of a druid. Greetings, friend Verin."

"Ack, still your mind sees me before you do. One day I will catch you by surprise and claim my forfeit."

"The day has yet to arrive. I introduce Aurorai of the enchanters and Jorin, friend and travelling companion."

He bowed in response, "Greetings."

"You know Nortee?"

"She evaded my trackers for many hours. I look forward to her third trial."

"What's she done wrong?"

"All take the Trials of Evasion to ensure the ways and teachings of druids and rangers are in all. They must show what has been learned."

"What happens on them?"

"The first two trials we tacked her; she must show what she has learned in evading others. The next two trials she tracks two of the elite who run ahead; to show she knows how to tack as she knows how to avoid. If she can do it not I claim my forfeit."

"What's the forfeit she pays?"

"There is none to pay; an elite may ensure the tracking is hard or impossible."

"Then why has she a forfeit?"

"Verin and I have a pact for his healing of me after my first trial. He wishes to claim the forfeit and this is the way he believes he may claim such."

His body became stiffer, "We return soon. Others watch over you, rest a while."

Jorin reached for his sword, "Trouble?"

"To reach for a sword means you trust not your friends. No, Jorin, others come along the path."

"Verin and the others just disappeared into the trees."

"They are the elite trackers, what else are they to do?"

"Can any be trackers?"

Her voice filled with pride, "Father has been chosen to their group, the youngest ever to be chosen. It is my hope Verin and his party will be the ones to watch as I track the elite."

"There's more than one group?"

"Several, it is why I hold to hope father will be with those who watch me."

"Where's Aurorai?"

"She left minutes ago, Verin asked her to join them. She is to speak with our guests."

"He didn't ask her."

"There are many ways to ask without the voice. I know of who comes, the number in the group and from which direction. Aurorai saw also and heeded his commands. In our lands and forests druid and rangers command all, in the city they are as all others. How many has Verin left to watch over us?"

"I don't see any."

"Three are close; one stands not ten paces from your left."

After minutes of close scrutiny he eventually saw the ranger sat at the foot of the tree, "Looks like I have a lot to learn."

"The teachings have already begun."


Verin crouched close to the remains of the fire, "We have watched the three gnomes for days; they are not yet past the coming of age and arrive soon."

"Odd they should be so far from home, why do they travel so early in life?"

"They will speak only when Aurorai is alone with them, they have a trust for enchanters more than any. They were lost, such is obvious."

"How'd you know where they were when they were so far away?"

"We watch not only our lands, Jorin, but those bordering them when it becomes necessary. We saw them as we saw your tracks at the bridge. Three tracks we found, one heavy and two light; those of a man, high elf and wood elf. The stone of timing was moved from where it was left so a druid must be in the party. Nortee left her sign also."

"How?"

"Her handprint she left in the mud close to the stones."

"How'd you know it was her?"

"In our tracking her hand she injured, the sign of a feather shows within it."

"Only the Chosen Ones wear a feather."

"You listen not; the mark is on her hand."

Holding her hand out she let him examine the mark.

"It looks like a feather. Why did you return to the bridge?"

"Would it not be foolish to leave the path you have travelled unguarded?"

"It's more foolish to split your forces."

"If a battle were to be fought mayhap you would be right. We are tasked with patrolling to ensure none enter our lands unknown. As night draws close many gather here; more still watch all the paths."

"I see only five of you."

"You saw only those we wished you to see, it would be foolish for all to be seen. How would we protect ourselves if all were here?"

"Post guards like we do when we camp for the night."

"You place guards around the camp only, how may you see those who are still far from your camp?"

"If the guards aren't close how can they warn of danger?"

"There are many ways to warn of danger; druids and rangers use the call of birds, others use different ways to warn of danger. Your attention is always to those close to you, how can you hope to know who is friend or foe?"

"We keep a close watch."

"Yet you saw not as Aurorai was asked to follow us, or her return."

He turned round to see her sat behind him, "Can you teach me the ways?"

"Your ways are already set, a poor student you would make."

"I can learn; it's what I'm here for."

"You would ask we teach our ways to one who may become an enemy?"

"I'll never be your enemy; my people are always your friends."

"Verin, our visitors arrive in minutes."

"Thank you, Rinini. They lack not for food or water?"

"They have been tended but tire and wish to return home."

As she left Nortee nudged him, "You have spoken not to her?"

"I have not. Why is it she sees not my love for her?"

"It is you who must speak first of love, this you know."

"It is as if she is blind to the ways I try to show her. Why is this?"

"I feel you will demand she tracks no more with you; when joined in wedlock she must do as commanded. She will be happy not for she loves the hunts."

"I wish for us a child, to be as all should be."

"She must be whatever you wish her to be. Speak with her and she will set the day. Embrace changes and you will embrace wedlock; surely such is plain for you to see?"

"I may not throw away our ways, Nortee."

"I ask not you do so, only to accept our ways must alter for our good. All change their ways, if we were not to do so then our race would die; unable to compete with others it would surely be our fate. The choice of when she consents is hers alone. You must think first of her and of her desires; she wishes only happiness for both. Speak she may be with you on the hunts until she consents to be with child and she will set the day. If happiness you wish for then all you need to do is to speak with her. The male must be the first to speak; she wishes you to do so, such is obvious."

"Were the male to decide we would be joined and she be with child."

"The male sets not the day; speak with her, ask of her wishes."

"I will give thought to what you say."

Rinini pointed the way she should lead them before leaving her alone with the gnomes, their faces showed their relief.

"We are alone, speak with me and I will speak not to others."

"Mistress Aurorai, we sought only to please."

"You journey far from gnomish homelands and it is spoken you leave no word as to your direction. Those who care for you will be distressed. Why journey when still so young?"

"The feast is all but upon us, we wished only to bring the greatest of delicacies for others; meat from the lizards of the west lands."

"The rangers spoke you were far from the west lands."

"We must study the maps all the harder."

"Knowing of maps makes you not a tracker; there is much to be learned."

"We return home without the meat, for failing to do so we will be chastised."

"I believe you are to be chastised, yet for being foolish and undertaking your journey when still too young. They love you and it will happen after you are welcomed home once more."

"Rinini spoke you will take us to their camp and they will return us home come the morrow."

"When first you were seen word was sent home, all know you are safe."

"Yet we return without the meat for which we started our journey."

"The meat will be provided yet speak not from where it came. Should you be asked shake your head a little and speak 'there you will let it lay'."

"You know our way to bring to an end questions?"

"Oft I visit my friends the gnomes and have heard the saying on occasions. Rinini watched and guarded you before you entered elfin lands to ensure no harm befell you."

"We saw her not. Mayhap she will share the meat at the festival, to show our appreciation?"

"You know my people eat not meat."

"Yet you do so on occasions we hear, or to please your hosts."

"She leaves on the morrow and takes you home. She speaks of troubles in her mind and seeks out someone who may be of help to her. She would be pleased if no such foolishness were shown again. Study the ways of the gnomes, this would please her I believe."

"You speak as do others, yet we wished only to please. To return with the meats our people love."

"To be a good study would please those who love you all the more. Come, I will guide you to the campfire. On the morrow you will be home and loved once more."

"Nothing will be said of our ways?"

"I have spoken your parents are pleased you are safe and nothing will be spoken of your adventures by Rinini or the others here. They may guess you found not the meats you went for yet I believe they will speak not of it."

"Mistress Aurorai, we hunger; take us to the camp."

"A secret I share with you; easily do I get lost as do you. If I am to be lost this time a whistle will bring friends to show us the way."

# Missing

"Grandmother where is she? I had thought her to be here for my return."

"I know not where she is, she would speak nothing of her plans."

"No enchanters remain in high elf city and words she will have spoken to you. Where may she be found?"

Looking up from the large brown book she let her voice become firm, "Nortee! It is not my way to lie to those I love."

"I apologise, grandmother, I worry for her."

"She chooses not to let you know with reason. She asked I ensure you remain here until the eighth day after the meeting with the council."

"This is the eight day. I must go in search of her."

"Where would you start?"

"The uplands and its caves would be an obvious place to seek sanctuary."

"As others also thought, and have searched. Do you know not your mother so well as to realise she would not be obvious."

"Then where must I search for her?"

"You are to search not, her wishes were for you to remain here and wait."

"I cannot! She has need of me, I must find her."

"You will stay and wait as do others!"

"Grandmother...."

"Think not to push me on this, Nortee. I will suffer it not!"

"If I cannot find her...."

"Enough!"

In her life she had never known her grandmother speak with force to anyone and found it upsetting. With reluctance she sat, yet her mind began the process of thinking where her mother would choose to hide so many enchanters. She would not take them far when danger threatened her people so she would start her search close to the homelands of the high elves. Druids would have been needed to teleport so many to a place far from home and would, therefore, leave a trail to follow. If the council were to ask they would be duty bound to say where they had taken them. They must have left a few at a time.

It needed to be somewhere close with food and water. As her mind filled with maps she realised there were only six places close enough to hide so many people.

"You wish to cause problems for your mother, to have her cast out as an Undesirable?"

"No, grandmother, I wish only to find her."

"If you were to find her it would lay waste to carefully set plans. You will remain here."

"I cannot when she has need of me. I know of one who will speak of her."

"None will do so. You must wait; those were her instructions to me."

"Aurorai visits the silk shop of Myra; she decides a new robe she should have. She will speak of her whereabouts."

"You are to ask not!"

Opening the door she looked back, "I wait not whilst troubles threaten her."


"Nortee, I am surprised to see you here. Would you help in the choosing of a new silk? The dagger ripped my robe and it bothers me; a new one I will have."

"Where is mother? I must see her."

"I speak not; her instructions were firm to me."

"I would know and you will speak, now!"

Once more the words of her mentor came back to haunt her; Nortee was making the demand her mother knew she would, "You may demand all you wish, I speak not."

"Aurorai, for our friendship please, where I may find her?"

"I was instructed to speak not even if demands were made"

"We swore as sisters, does this mean so little to you?"

"It means more than you would know."

"I would see her, she needs me and I will find her."

"Greetings, Nortee. When you do so I would speak to her also."

Turning round she bowed, "Ilsto Ventrel, you know where mother is? I wish to see her."

"I do not, yet I have a few words to speak to her."

"Then mayhap we search together?"

"Nortee, he has other plans for your mother, ones you would like not."

His face grew red, "Aurorai of the enchanters if memory serves; this concerns you not. Remain silent!"

A hand spun him round; "If your thoughts are of harm to my daughter then I have a say in this."

"Grandfather, I saw you not as you entered."

"I suggest you speak not to your mother of this, she will not be best pleased. Many times she chastises you for such inattentiveness."

"Ah, Juin, I came to see you yet saw Nortee first. Where is your daughter, I would speak with her?"

"She is where you may find her not and has no wish to speak with you at this time."

"I am am elder of the council; I demand you speak of her whereabouts!"

"My duties of parentage take precedent. I speak not of this."

"I demand you speak!"

"Grandfather, I would know also."

"Remain quiet, child."

"Grandfather...."

"Enough of this! Aurorai, take her to my home and ensure she stays."

Taking Nortee by the arm she moved forward, "As is your wish."

"Leave me go, Aurorai, there are matters to finish."

"Juin has spoken and so shall it be. Is it not plain your mother wishes not for you to see her?"

"She has need of me and I shall find her!"

Juin grabbed her by the shoulders, "Foolish child! Does it not enter your head he has waited for your return knowing you would wish to see her? I stand your ways no longer. Return home or suffer my wrath!"

Seeing the situation was turning ugly Aurorai pulled at her arm once more.

"Make no threats towards me, grandfather, I will defend myself!"

"If you think I offer merely a threat then stand your ground!"

Torn between thoughts of her mother and love of her grandfather she hesitated a moment; as a hand gently pulled at her she left with Aurorai.

"Now they are no longer an issue I would speak with you, Ilsto Ventrel."

"I have little to say to you unless we speak of your daughter."

"It is of my daughter I would speak; cease your attempts to find her. You threaten her and I stand not such ways. When she returns she may consent to speak with you. Force not the issue, my temper is not without limits."

"You threaten a council member?"

"I protect my daughter."

"She places the elves in danger! It is my duty to find her and have all return to high elf city. The coming war cannot be won without their help. All must fight or we die!"

"Heed not my warning and I will have little option but to challenge you."

"So be it; on her return your challenge will be accepted."

"Never have I seen anger in him, grandmother, since I have known him."

"You have displeased him, placed yourself in needless danger and listened not as others offered advice. How is it you would expect him to be?"

"I believe he would know my thoughts, how I feel when I return and find none will speak of where mother may be found."

"Norty is our daughter; do you think he worries not for her safety? She has duties concerning her; instructions were left you fail to heed."

"I must ensure all is well, this you know."

As the door opened she bowed, "Grandfather, forgive me."

"Is your foolishness without end? Your mother's life you place in danger without thought; mine also. Was your upbringing so lax?"

"I have done nothing, would do nothing, to place you in danger."

"Yet you have done so! Norty will be pleased not and I blame her not. When she hears of your actions look not to me for help!"

"Grandfather, how is it I have placed your life in danger? I can think of no way I would do so."

Turning he walked to the bedroom door, "Then it is obvious you are incapable of thought! Come to bed, Elesee."

As the door closed she leaned forwards, "Always he wishes me a good night, grandmother, yet not this time."

Elesee rose and moved towards the bedroom, "You may use the spare room as your own, Aurorai; my grandchild forfeits her rights this night."

"Grandmother, where am I to sleep? Is it you wish for me to return home and sleep alone?"

"I care little where you sleep; words I will have with your mother when next I see her. Your upbringing is a disappointment to me. Good night, Aurorai."

As the door softly closed Nortee felt the tears run down her face.

Juin crouched in front of her, "You have slept not?"

"My mind has been tormented with thoughts. I realise how all have tried to make me see I must remain here. Can you find it within you to forgive me?"

"Had we insisted you remain here would you have done so?"

"No, grandfather, I would have left in search of her and laid ruin to plans. All were right to have me stay. Had she wished me to be with her she would have forbid not Aurorai to speak of her whereabouts. May I remain here with you?"

"You may stay and nothing will be spoken of your words or actions. She may know yet choose to ignore her thoughts if she believes the lesson has been learned."

"It had been learned, grandfather, yet it ceases not my worries."

"To worry not would show you have little love for your mother."

"Grandmother spoke my ways are not those of the elfin. Was she angry with me or is how I am seen?"

"Oft we have spoken to Norty of your upbringing yet you are her daughter and not ours. She teaches as she sees fit and...."

"Continue, grandfather."

"It is not for me to speak of. Elesee is the one to whom this falls and she will ensure her words are heard when the time comes."

"Her words will be to me? I worry, grandfather."

"There is little call to worry. Do you know not her ways to think she would speak with someone who knows not what they do? Come, wake Aurorai and we will eat."

She tried her best to smile, "Never is she one to rise early; her bed she loves too much."

## Words Of Love

"Greeting, Rinini, you have been well cared for?"

"Greeting, Norty, all have been most kind to me."

"I am surprised none were with you when you found us, druids searching travel in three's I believe."

"I had a wish to be alone when you were found."

"You were sure you would do so?"

"It is obvious when thought is given to where you would hide a guild. No city would be safe; word would soon be spoken to others so many enchanters had arrived. You would move not far from home so as to leave the city without protection and food and drink must also be available, as must a position to view the land around. Six such places exist; this is the fourth I have searched."

"I apologise no comfortable bed was afforded; and you were held against your will."

"It is not the first time I have slept on stone; had I been allowed to leave I would be duty bound to speak of your whereabouts, I had no wish to do so."

"You are cunning, Rinini."

"It is obvious there are plans, you do nothing without cause. I offer help."

"Why do you believe such an offer is needed?"

"I escorted Nortee home and you where there not to greet her. She will worry and search for you."

"She will search not, such has been assured."

"Finglas was there not to comfort her and is not here also."

"How is it you know he is not here?"

"Twice my bird calls were answered not."

"Often have I heard him speak to others in such a way though I cannot understand the calls he makes."

"Help will be needed to return all home quickly."

"You are correct in your thinking."

"There is another reason. A friendship was struck between Nortee and I. I spoke to her of the love I know and how he will approach not the subject to me. She asked I speak with you for you have suffered for love also."

"The males and their ways, never do they cease to amaze me."

"I wish him to know the love I hold yet he must speak of his love first. What am I to do?"

"The answer is easy to see."

"I smile when he is near; ensure I am chosen to be one of the three. Since I joined the group and first saw him I have tried in all ways to have him speak with me. I am at a loss."

"It would seem there is but one way to show your feelings for him."

"What way is there left? You know not the number of ways I have tried."

"My forehead touched the ground before Finglas in shame."

"I have done nothing to offend him!"

"I would be shocked had you need to do so. I suggest you need a time and a place when you are alone with him to speak of your love, yet you must also ensure he knows of your plans."

"You suggest I am the first to speak of love?"

"I do."

"I cannot do such; it is against our Lore, our beliefs."

"I was also foolish and let those ways rob me of love for many summers. Do you also wish the same?"

"I do not. I ache when he is near and shows not his love for me."

"Then speak with him."

"I must think on this."

"Cast thoughts aside. If you were to think then Lore would govern you and no words would pass your lips."

"Can such be done?"

"Let your love show the way if he is too blind to see."

"I will do so. Thank you, I must go to him."

"You will remain until the morrow, Rinini, I am sorry."

"I am at a loss, Nortee spoke your answer would be a riddle."

"Sometimes a direct path to love is best, this I learned late in my life."

"Almost two hundred summers I have now seen. Love has found me and I wish to be held by him."

"If you wish not to wait another two hundred summers do as I suggest."

# Of Pins and Fury

Glancing up from the book in the Chamber of Wisdom Icee would normally be annoyed if disturbed whilst in study but smiled as the gnome approached. Mages were not known to be friendly, even to other gnomes, a visit from one of them was unusual; in their home city it was almost unheard of.

The yellow and green of her robe had and almost hypnotic effect as she moved towards the desk, and was in stark contrast to the bright colours most gnomes wore, the mages preferring more solemn garments. Yet it was her hair she had admired since her mother introduced her long ago in wood elf city; long, black and hanging down past the middle of her back. Most gnomes, still young enough to have hair, found it grew in white tufts on their head.

Rising she bowed slightly, "Greetings."

"Greetings, Icee."

"It is not often I have the honour to speak with you, Dreth."

"Your mother and father are well?"

"They are, as I hope are you and Velrith?"

"My daughter is well and soon to be joined in wedlock to Nerid."

"As I have heard; please pass to her my happiness."

"I come with an offer I hope you will accept."

"Make the offer and the cost and I will think of it."

"I offer to instruct you in the ways of The Pin."

"I have heard not of such ways, to what do you refer?"

From just above her breast she drew a long thin pin from her robe, "Few of us now use the ways."

"For what purpose is it used?"

"Give to me your hand, palm up."

"If undue pain is caused I need not explain my reactions."

Stroking the pin along the middle finger she pierced her palm, "There is no pain?"

"You are correct."

"Close your fingers."

"I cannot."

Removing the pin she stuck it in her wrist, "Move your arm."

"Once more I cannot."

"This is the way; we have known of its uses for centuries yet few now use the ways. I offer to teach you, should you be willing?"

"Why do you make the offer and what is the cost?"

Placing the pin back in her robe she touched it, "What of the pin do you see?"

"Naught but the head and it is hard to see."

"There is more to the ways."

"I admit you have roused my curiosity."

With a flick of the wrist the pin was once more withdrawn and pushed deep into the pages of the book, "The pin is sharp and oft used as a weapon."

Pulling the pin from the book she examined it, "Longer and thinner than it would seem at first glance. I would have thought the book to have bent the pin."

"They are made for us by the dwarves, yet come at a price high to pay."

"What price is it they demanded?"

"Do you wish to learn the ways?"

"The price is not yet agreed, though I have asked."

"Through the actions of Norty my life has been saved. I have studied her and believe she would not be suitable to learn the ways of The Pin. This is why I offer to you the ways."

"Sister spoke at length of her adventure with you. There is not the need to feel a debt is owed."

"Nevertheless a debt is owed and I find no way to repay her. Each time I have offered it is politely refused. Years has this happened and my thoughts turned to other ways I may repay the debt. You will be suitable to learn the ways, and I to repay the debt."

"The ways may benefit others more; mayhap Malinna may use them to help with healing, to ease pain whilst she casts her spells?"

"They are oft used in healing yet Malinna lacks the talent to use the pins effectively. I have watched you closely and you seem to be suitable."

"I know not if I would be; how may I be tested?"

Handing her the pin she held out her arm, "Place the pin just below the skin where my finger points."

"I may hurt you."

"Think naught of it, do as I ask."

With great care she used the pin to just penetrate the skin, "You eyes show pain though your face does not."

"Try once more. Use the pin with care, pierce the skin firmly."

Again she tried, "No pain this time it seems."

"I may not move my arm from the elbow. I had thought you might be suitable to learn."

"The test I have passed?"

"I offer once more the teachings, yet I would have you speak not to any unless asked and only then to speak as little as possible."

"When may the teachings commence?"

"If you were not so deep in study...."

Closing the book with a snap she stood. I am here only to ensure questions of me are asked not by the council of elder sister; should I be home they would be asked forcibly I believe. The book is not for study, rather it is one of meats and their cooking; it may wait for another, more opportune, time."

"Welcome to the study, Icee, though few now attend."

"I am honoured yet did not know you lead the guild of mages."

"The study is for those wishing to learn the ways, as you see it is empty where once many were in attendance. Sit, I have a few books I would have you read and you must study hard. With practice you may cause pain or relief, enhance a prowess or detract from it, depending on how it is used."

"Why is it I have heard not of this?"

"Oft you have failed to notice the pin in my robe, or ask of it."

"I admit my lack of observation, it is difficult to see."

From a small drawer she took an ornate box and placed it on the desk, "The box contains several pins. Hold them and decide which is suitable for you."

Opening the box she drew one from the silk wrapper, "They are of different sizes, how may I decide the one suitable?"

"Hold each with the care you would a newborn, you will know the one which should be yours."

As the fifth needle slipped from the silk she smiled, "This feels as if it belongs to me. Lady Fortune has decided."

Taking the needle she removed an eyeglass from her pocket, as a glow around her fingers started she muttered.

"What is it you do?"

"They are soft before my spell hardens them as they should be; I need the glass to place the spell correctly. Upon completion of your twentieth test you will order a replacement."

"Still you have set no price for the learning or the replacement."

Moving swiftly she pricked Icee with the pin, "I am sorry. The spell takes time to harden the pin and the owner's blood mixes with the spell to ensure it hardens correctly. Now you are bound to the pin; take care of it."

"You had only to ask for my blood. What is the twentieth test?"

"For your twentieth test you journey to see its maker, though the price you pay will be high."

"Name the price of teaching and of the pins replacement."

"There will be no charge for the teachings. An explanation of how your mother and I met may help. She has spoken of it?"

"Always duties seemed take her when it was mentioned, as if she has no wish to speak; or a promise had been made."

Settling back in the chair her eyes closed, "You have the time for a tale?"

"To learn how you met will ensure my time is yours."

"It is so long since first we met on a winters evening, and so cold; I remember it well. An argument I had with my parents and, in an anger I had never known before, left the house. I asked another to teleport me to the lands near wood elf city, this he did. As I sat alone in the dark realisation of what I had done took me. I love the woods of your lands and thought they would comfort me; they did not. It was as if they were taunting me for my stupidity in the argument."

"What was the cause of the argument?"

"Like so many arguments I forget the cause, only my anger for they seemed not to listen to me. I admit I was scared in the forest, the trees take on different forms come the night when the mind is not calm. Each shadow was an enemy come to take my life. With the thunderstorm came rain and panic; I ran blindly until exhaustion took its toll of me and I collapsed. I had run in fear for feelings within me spoke I was followed; I screamed for them to go, to leave me alone, yet still they did not depart. In despair I cried out they come and take my life. It was then I saw a shadow cast by the moon, I was sure a demon had been summoned forth to take me for the way I had treated my parents and stood ready to accept my fate, determined to show no fear as it ate me; no fear for I am a decedent of The Riders."

"Whispers I have heard of The Riders, who are they?"

"Your family has been good to me and a promise I will make; should you make me proud of my choice of you as a student and pass the twentieth test I will speak to you the dark secret of the mages."

"I will study hard; I wish to hear this secret."

"Only upon the passing of the twentieth test I will speak of it."

"Your story intrigues me, continue please."

"When the shape drew near I saw a wood elf and felt foolish. I hurled abuse at her, more; I took a stone and threw it hard. It missed; such a trivial act is easy for an elf to dodge. I realised she must have been the one who had followed me for so long."

"Had she wished not her presence known you would have seen her not."

"Upon reflection I knew yet in my fear of the night I thought not of it. Elesee spoke 'It is not a fit night for one so young to be about in the woods'. It was then I found my running was in vain, less than one hundred paces from where I had started. Elesee took me home and lit a fire so the cold was chased from me. As the fire warmed me I also warmed to her. During the night she left, to ensure word of my safety was passed to my parents I believe. Her soft spoken words seemed to entrap me and found I could speak easily to her of the argument, and of many things on my mind. From her I obtained a promise she would speak naught of my fear and poor conduct in the woods."

"The promise has been kept; no word has been spoken of it."

"I know well the elves and their promises. When my tale was finished she asked how I felt, my reply was I felt better. She did not believe me, seeing the anger still in me she began teaching me the ways of the self. I am one with myself. For six days and nights she stayed with me and I learned much of myself, my people and the elves. In the years, which were to follow, she would instruct me away from all, as was my wish. Within I had anger unbeknown to me; it lay deep and caused me to act as I did. Elesee helped me see this anger and to control it, not to let it control me. Through her teaching I learned much of myself, and of her. The years at her side began a friendship I believe to be special. It was through this friendship she came to speak of her love for your father, of how it was different. Do I speak out of turn?"

"I know mother fell in love with father over time, not the instant she saw him as all who feel love must do. Her daughters know it was to you she spoke, you speak not out of turn."

"Over the years our friendship has remained strong, it is but one reason I offer to teach the ways of The Pin."

"There is another reason?"

"There are two. I have watched you and believe you to be suitable."

"What ways do you see?"

"As you learn there will be little need to ask."

"And the second reason you offer to teach?"

"As is the mother so is the daughter. Velrith has within her my anger. In my foolishness I tried to teach her ways I had been taught. It served only to fuel her anger towards me, to turn daughter from mother."

"I think it not foolish to teach the ways you know."

"As I at first had thought, yet I have not the skills in teaching Elesee has. One argument was unlike any before; all the ways Elesee had taught me served only to anger her at my calmness, believing I should be angry also."

"The foolishness of youth is oft spoken aloud."

"Within her the anger erupted against me, her pin she threw at me, striking above the heart. In panic she left, believing me to be dead. Elesee found me and healed my wounds; speaking nothing of my daughter's act to others. When she left I saw her not for many months though oft I called to see her she was never at home. Juin seemed not to be worried and this troubled me. Only later did I realise Elesee had taken weeks to find Velrith, to speak to her I was not dead. As she had done for me she also did for my daughter. Six months she stayed with her, teaching her, helping her control the fury burning within. From her she obtained a promise, which Velrith spoke was so hard to give, to return and speak with me. When Velrith heard she had born the Chosen Ones her mind was set to return. The anger remains yet is buried deep within; sometimes it is seen before her teaching takes control. It is strange, our anger has brought us closer together then I would have thought possible. Soon after her return to me Norty saved my life. I was able to return home, to make amends for the time we were apart; to see her grow and choose a husband."

"An interesting tale and one which opens my eyes to so much of the past my sisters and I know only a little. Much will I have to speak to them when next we meet."

"Then I am happy. All must know the paths they tread in life and the path they have travelled."

"So much is now clear to me. Thank you for the tale; it is as if my past becomes less of a blur and more into focus."

"You see now the debt owed by me to your family. Only through your family's actions have I a family and a life once more."

"Mother has spoken of her anguish over father, of not knowing which way to turn. You were the one to whom she turned, the one who would lend an ear. I know of the relief flooding through mother when she spoke to you, as we know of your answer to father when Norty returned from the dungeon. Your words sent to father eased him; my sisters and I felt the contentment he felt within himself, as the words also made mother feel all the better. No, Dreth, it is we who owe to you the debt."

# Blyth

Glancing round Icee leaned against a tree, "Many months have passed since last we visited our glade. Why would each choose to do so on the same day?"

Malinna sighed, "All will be shown in time."

"Little sister has new armour I see."

"I find the old armour heavy to wear, I asked for more fitting to my strength."

"At what cost?"

"I must replace the ore used and give a barrel of ale for each piece. I will ensure two barrels of ale are given."

"Little sister owes eighteen barrels; a goodly price to pay."

"I owe but ten barrels; the chest and arm with upper legs I wear only. The lower leg guards and boots I wear not, they encumber me. 'Tis time I felt freedom once more, though Keitun mutters much.

"You speak little, elder sister, your mind is troubled?"

"Why are all here? This troubles me. The Gods move to ....."

"Greetings, sisters, the evening is warm and pleasant."

Icee fell instantly into a defensive posture, "Who comes?"

"You saw me not, Icee, mayhap your attention was on other matters?"

"You are not as you seem; there is little to show your approach, no footprints mark the grass and no sound did you make. A robe you wear when clearly your hair shows you warrior born."

"The druid shows through the cleric in Malinna."

"Elder sister was surprised when you spoke yet knows all who come close."

"No wine dulls the thoughts of Icee."

Kneeling before her Norty whispered, "We are honoured, Blyth."

"You believe me a God?"

"I see not your mind and your voice is sweet, who else might you be?"

"Rise, it is not befitting to kneel before me."

"You are a God, all should...."

"Rise, I am unworthy. At my suggestion you were born yet I was powerless to ease the pains you were to suffer. It is I who should ask your forgiveness. I should kneel to those to whom I gave life, love and pain."

Slowly she rose.

"I come to speak of the danger threatening once more, I would offer advice before the day is upon you."

"I feel no quest to be upon us."

"I spoke naught of the quest; only of the danger which now faces my children."

"I err and ask forgiveness."

"My mind was given you as Aronath gave to Icee his gift; Trenth to Malinna gave his. Both are pleased with them yet you fail to use the gift I gave to you and this displeases me. You plan your defence against the skeletons yet it contains within it many errors, too much do you fail to see."

"I have thought of ways to defeat them, how may I know all?"

As her palm stretched forward a timer appeared in it, "I am the planner for the Gods and my mind you have been given; if I know all of what will be why is it you find the planning of a single battle so hard?. Friends have been ignored in your plans."

"Who would help I have thought not of?"

"Until the sand fills the bottom of the glass you may ask of me what you will."

"A question I have asked."

"The bitterest of enemies may also be your closest friends."

"We have many enemies, ogre, orc, gnoll, giant...."

"I speak of they who seek to return, greater friends than you suspect."

"When is it the skeletons will choose to attack?"

As the sands ceased movement her eyes lifted up, "Time I was promised, time to guide them, will I be denied not my rights....Yes....Enough! There was a bargain between us....No, never shall it be such, a deal has been struck and you will honour your part within it....Think not to betray me, Barthic; you know well my anger, cause it not to be directed to you once more."

Malinna shook a little, "The Gods argue over mortals?"

"The sand continue its journey once more, time passes quickly."

"You wish the death of your children?"

"Messenger once spoke of death to you, remember his words."

"I remember his words. Will the elves win the battle?"

"Your plans are flawed; still you fail to see those who would help you. Encompass them within and victory may yet be yours."

"I have spoken to all; no others are there to help us."

"Minutes you have left yet choose to argue and ask not questions."

"From which direction will help be seen?"

"Should you act wisely they will come to your aid from the south."

"Eldest sister would know if any would help. Speak, we must know."

Her hand touched Icee, "Above all others you know in the darkest of hearts love shines brightly. Long have they been rejected, long have they thought to seek the way back to their people. Norty knows yet once more fails to see."

With most of the sand in the bottom glass she hurried as best she dare, "How may we ensure victory?"

"When many are close there is little room to fight, less room to wield a weapon."

"How many do we face?"

"Numbers ensure not a victory, only more deaths. For each who fight nine will your enemies be. The sands have finished their journey; I may speak no more of this."

Icee sat, "Elder sister will give thoughts to your words yet no questions were answered. How may you do this to your children?"

"There are more children to me than you may know. In the days to come your sister must be stronger then she has been before. She has yet to see as she should."

"Threats I hear in your voice; though you be a God watch well your words!"

"So many years and she sees not with clear eyes; they will be opened to her."

A bolt of flame hurled from Icee, "I hear no more of your threats!"

Laughing Blyth gestured and the flames hung in mid air, crackling loudly, "Love for your sister is beyond reproach yet still she sees not what is plain to you and Malinna. Her thoughts must change. When hope for her fades her eyes may be opened."

Her voice was barely above a whisper, "Still I displease the Gods. Will there be a time I may be forgiven?"

"There is not the need of forgives, little one."

"A name I once called Nortee."

"Trenth distracts Barthic as was agreed, he sees us not so this I will speak of. Once, now long ago, you saw what none have seen before you, a glimpse to the end of your quest, a glimpse to unite all as they should be."

"I know not of a quest."

"Your quest continues."

"What was it I saw?"

"I may answer not for it would place you on the path too early in the quest."

"Yet you speak of it."

"In time your eyes will see what none of the four elves have yet seen."

"Then the fifth race of elves exists! Where may we find them? They would help their cousins of this I am sure."

"I spoke not of a fifth race, only of your eyes seeing what must be seen."

"You speak not of our cousins yet I know them to be. Speak, where may they be found?"

"If you believe them to be then continue the quest."

"The quest has been won."

"It was but a test you won."

"Love was but a test?"

"Twice love has tested you. The quest continues to its end; should you fail the hopes of many will be dashed; never will they see their brothers and sisters. Fight! Fight, more than you may know still rests on your shoulders."

"I grow weary with the weight. How may I take yet more?"

"How may you not? My words at your birth were 'the fate of the world will rely upon these children'."

"Blyth, forgive me, I try so hard."

"Cease your trying! To you I gave my gift and it is used as a dwarf would use his hammer. You fail to be subtle, fail to see all which should now be clear before you."

"Blyth...."

Leaning forward her voice become cold, "Enough of your ways I have stood! A quest is set for you, think and all will be as before. My plans were laid long before I made the elves, long before they were split asunder, long before they were thrown to the five corners. I objected then to our ways and fight to have all returned as they should be. The sisters are part of those plans; I suffer them not to be thwarted! If thought is given there is little need for so many paths to be considered."

"I know no way to do as you ask."

"Think not of the paths, rather realise what must be."

"I will place all effort into what you say."

"So soon you forget my words? *Know* what will be, place *no* effort into it."

"It will be as you wish."

"You have followed not the ways you were born to do. Thrice you have denied what must be; thrice have turned from the path set for you. I suffer your ways no longer. On your third digress I set for you a task to see as you should; even your sisters will be not as they now are."

"Punish none but me, Blyth; leave my sisters be and test me no more, long have I suffered the Gods ways."

"You suffer needlessly! It is your thoughts, which cause the suffering, not your Gods. You think yourself not forgiven? For her actions against me Icee would deserve my wrath yet still she stands at your side, as her people will stand with her in the hour of need."

"The elves stand together, now and always!"

"Still your mind is set and sees only what is in front of it! These lands about you contain more than....Barthic, it would seem Trenth was unable to keep your mind from me....A talk I am enjoying with the sister, must it end so soon? ....As was agreed....I bid them farewell and return."

With a smile to the sisters her form shimmered and was gone.

With the tears running down her face she turned to Malinna, "Still I displease the Gods yet work so hard to ensure their wishes are fulfilled."

"Blyth is right, eldest sister thinks not as is asked of her, cease your trying. Come, I have a need to show your something."


Spreading the map out on the table Malinna pointed, "Maps of how the old world was to our forebears."

Icee looked around in awe, "Never have I seen so many scrolls."

"This is the Room of Scrolls, as once was it called, I knew not of it until Grud Hearthstone spoke of it. I spend long here and still find little I may read, the language is as old as the elves themselves and I must find a way to understand them."

"You are tasked, sister, not us. Why is it you bring us here?"

Her finger circled different areas, "Elfin lands are here; this is the land of man and here the mountains of the dwarves. Here the gnomes made their home before they moved to their valley and to the west trolls took most lands yet something is missing."

"I see no lands for many people, sister."

"I have pointed to but a few, those I am able to read from the maps."

"Then how may we know what is missing?"

"The maps were made when the elves were still so young."

"They look as new."

"The eldest of the scribes draw them from older maps, they are exact in all detail. Many months I studied them before I realised and asked if mistakes were made, there were none. You know well the scribes; mistakes would be allowed not."

"Then for what do we look?"

"Show to me high elf city."

Studying the map she pointed, "I see it not yet it should be here."

"Agreed, yet something else is amiss, where are the lands of the dark elves, the lands of the river elves?"

"The maps were drawn before those lands existed?"

"Always those lands we have known. They are shown not for once all elves must have been as one!"

"Lore says such was so."

Malinna sighed, "Still you hear not the words of Blyth?"

"It seems I do not, sister."

"Her words were 'I speak of they who seek to return, greater friends than you suspect.' Think of who they may be?"

"There are none whom I have missed."

"Eldest sister sees not the obvious?"

"To you it may seem obvious. Guide me, sister, as you have always done."

"There are those who live on our southern lands we tolerate."

"None live on elfin lands, they are...."

"Enlightenment shows in your face."

"Many times you have guided us and each step was how it should be."

"Then you will seek them out?"

"I will speak to them, the time is well past for them to live alone. They are our brothers and sisters waiting to be joined with us once more. It will be as Blyth demands."

# The Undesirables

With no enchanters left in high elf city she was more careful then ever not to be seen. Any noticing her might call out and she would be set upon by the elves demanding the return of the enchanters. It was too soon to do so and she would be looked upon as a traitor and be banished if she refused. Only with the coming of darkness could she be sure she could move around unseen by her people; most would be home before twilight, these days with the enchanters missing she had heard most felt somewhat insecure.

Her meeting with Olva Minlets had proved fruitful and the next part of her plan could be put into action. She realised the inn must stay open, even though its owners were enchanters, it was the hub of the town and she could be sure the Minlets would keep her informed on the latest talk. It was also invaluable in a second sense. Olva could also start any rumours the enchanters wished. It was the reason she had risked a visit with her.
A new rumour was needed yet when she spoke of the Undesirables to Olva she had noticed her body stiffen as she tried to stop a smile and a sense of relief surging up within her. It had puzzled her but when she asked what was amiss Olva's voice had changed as she asked her to continue with the rumour she wished to start. Something had happened to Olva and she wished she could ask if she could help; it was clear Olva and her husband had little wish to speak of it.

Her mind checked the area around the inn before opening the door, only one elf was close and his mind was strange; it was obvious who he was. Closing the door of the inn behind her she stopped, it was obvious he was intent on speaking with her, "Greetings."
"You would greet an Undesirable?"
With a slight bow she smiled at him, "I greet you as I would greet all."
Sitting on the barrel she studied him. His clothes were the silver grey of an elf not of guild, unsurprisingly. The Undesirables were those who had failed to enter their guilds, for whatever reason, and cast out by the elves.

They had made a home on the forest floor seven days ride to the south and left only for provisions. The elves always supplied their needs yet most wished little to do with them. Wood elves, such as the one before her, had also been cast out and it saddened her to think her people could do this to their own kind.

His mannerisms were still those of an elf though his accent was unusual, speaking slower than most and with a hint of the darks elves mystery in his voice, something she had tried for years to imitate with little success.

"I am named Elgreth. You are the one Blyth named Norty."

"Such was my honour."

"I would speak with you."

"You may do so yet I see you care not to bow in greeting."

"To bow is a mark of respect. We are abandoned by all our people, why should we respect them? I knew on which day you would arrive, I have friends in many places."

"It seems you contradict yourself; if friends you have you are not as abandoned as you may believe."

"Mayhap abandoned by *all* is a wrong choice of words."

"Be seated, though I may offer little more than a barrel."

"Never is a seat offered, it would show friendship to us."

"I also offer friendship, to be as others towards you."

Nervously he sat, "I hear you offer friendship to all, the dark elves also."

"Many train here, and others in their city also."

"War comes."

"You have a way of stating your thoughts."

"The elves will lose."

"Such is not our destiny."

"You need help in this war."

"All who would fight with us are welcome."

"I offer the help of my people."

"We are your people."

"Such a right was forfeited the day we were cast out. There are those amongst us who would offer help."

"Your tones would suggest a deal, I am in no position to offer such to you."

"Then we have nothing further to speak of. Good day to you and may your nights be restful."

"You are further from the truth than you realise. Come to my study so we may speak freely."

"A few invite me to their chambers; I had thought you not to do so."

"I would have you meet others."

"I introduce Pose of the dark elf enchanters."

"Never have I seen a dark elf, I know not what to say, or how to greet you."

"A nod in greeting is sufficient."

Moving behind the desk she bid him to sit, "You would speak and we would listen."

"There are those amongst us who still see the elves as our people and would fight alongside them, should they ask us to do so."

"There is more to this, it is easy to see. With the death of the elves what would become of you, of your people?"

"Word spreads of your prowess of reading the body, I see it is true. Should the elves be attacked and lose then attention will turn to us and we are incapable of holding such an assault."

"By joining with us you ensure your own safety?"

"Many believe the elves will lose and the skeletons will leave; they will not. We also will be attacked and then the wood elves and the river elves, finally the dark elves would be the ones to whom their eyes turn."

"It would seem you have given thought to this, I agree with your views."

"I wish not for my people to perish, it is the reason I approach you."

"A deal you would make. Speak of it."

"We wish to be as one with our brothers and sisters. I would ask a promise from you, for us to be such."

"Such a promise is not mine to give."

"Others would listen should you speak for us."

"It is not within my power to have you return to the cities of your birth."

"We remain where we are; it is now our home. Our only wish is to be greeted as friends and protection afforded to us."

"Aid is given though you may know it not. Patrols keep watch over you, seeking to ensure you are safe."

"The patrols we have seen, they seek only to ensure we cause no trouble."

"Once I heard of enemies approaching your dwellings; they were killed before they could attack you."

"We are protected only when the elves wish it to be, not for the love of us."

"Protection is given, whichever way it is perceived."

"The elves wish us not to enter their cities; we are still distasteful."

"To enter the cities brings disquiet to those who see you; you are a reminder of their acts."

"If my people accept how may we be of help?"

"There are places where you may be of help, if enough would join with you?"

"Some have little wish to help, they fight not for those who cast them out."

"I know of the pain of being accepted not."

"Three hundred and seventeen will risk their lives, should the reward be acceptable to them."

"All in my power I will do."

"Then what is it you wish us to do?"

"I would have two things from you. On the night of the battle be on our right, three hundred paces ahead of the city limits."

"We would be alone and vulnerable, it is much to ask."

"The skeletons will have other thoughts on their minds; yours may be the safest of positions. All use a bow and this is why I need you there."

"We wish to fight, not to hide like cowards; we are elves!"

"Should all go well others would see your actions and know you are, above all, elves."

"And your second thought of us?"

"Ask those who fight with you not die to prove who you are, it is known. One promise I would have of you, if I may?"

"Ask and we will see."

"Hold not the actions of those who cast you out against those who would be a friend."

"Little friendship have we seen."

"Are not supplies always given to you, your town protected and your lives free to live as you desire?"

"We are not free to live our lives. Not free to return to the place of our birth as equals of others. In what way are we free?"

"No demands are made of you. Never have you been called to help your people. True you are Undesirables and such a call would be hard to heed, this I know."

"We are elves yet separate to others, as the river elves are separate to you."

"You are elves. As Pose is an elf and many greet her in friendship, proof is not needed more than she stands here before you unharmed by any."

"I have heard of this, the reason I sought you out."

"My thoughts had also turned to…. your people."

"To seek our help, to ask we die in your fight?"

"I wish not the death of any yet know many will die. I may grant you not the right to return home even if your wish is to do so, nor might I offer aught but a promise to use all my wits and skills to obtain your desires."

"I have spoken of the desires of my people."

"I would do all in my power to aid you."

"Then we have agreement it would seem."

"Agreements should be sealed. I offer you wine yet ask you drink quickly, we must be away before the sun sees our land."

"I would share wine with friends, with my peoples' friends."

He turned to Pose, "I have a question you will answer only with the truth."

"Your ways are new to me yet I find a demand such as this unpalatable."

"It is the way my people are; so often truth is withheld from us and we have a mind to hear only the truth. Forgive me."

"You are forgiven; ask your question."

"The dark one also have Undesirables?"

"We do not."

"Then only the wood and high elves banish their own?"

"We also find there are those who may enter not their guilds."

"Yet you banish them not."

She felt uncomfortable, "We do not. Any unable to enter their guild are.... put to death."

"You allow this!?"

"It is the way it has always been for us; to our shame this happens."

"None are banished?"

"Never have we thought of such. Only when I came here to train did I see another way for those of our people to be treated."

"Banish them and kill them not! Better a life of banishment than death."

"This I know yet I am unable to alter others thoughts at this time. When I knew of the Undesirables a thought crossed my mind yet it would be impossible for this to happen until the ways of my people are changed."

"What are your thoughts of this?"

"I have asked questions, only of the enchanters, and all seem upset a child would be killed. Those who are not yet in wedlock, or still have to bear a child, show relief when I mention others banish not those unable to enter guild. Should their young be unable to enter the guild there would be hope for them, this is the relief I see. In time my people may change the ways they have come to know and mayhap be more compassionate. We too may have our own Undesirables."

His glass rose, "To future Undesirables."

Peacemaker


"Sister would do nothing to harm our people, Ilsto Ventrel, this you know."
"She abandons us, Icee, leaving nothing in the cities but unrest and fear. Even now, a short time after the enchanters vanish fights break out amongst us. She harms us all and this you cannot deny. What are we to think?"
"I ask you think why she does this."
"It is easy to see. With our refusal to have her lead the enchanters this is the way she seeks to repay us!"
"The leadership of the enchanters is not in question and sister would seek not revenge. She wishes all to see the enchanters are a part of the elves, nothing more."
"By leading them away from the city she proves they are a part of us not."
"Do you see not? Long have they been feared, long have they been shunned by all. Each tolerates the enchanters and so few look to them as friends. It is this sister turns against. Never would she harm her people."
"She harms them now surely this you must see?"
"She wishes others to see they need the enchanters as the enchanters need them. You frequent the inn I believe?"
"I have spent many happy evenings in there, yes."
"When an enchanter enters what happens?"
"Many hope they choose not their table to sit at. If they do they finish their drinks quickly and leave."
"How is it you would feel should this happen to you?"
"Your words have a ring of truth about them, I admit to feeling somewhat .... uncomfortable in their presence."
"Yet Olva is also an enchantress and none have fears concerning her; indeed she is well liked it seems, as is her husband and daughter."
"They are ....different."
"In what way?"
"They are pleasant and speak to all."
"The enchanters speak not to any?"
"They do not. Ah, I see your words. When they sit with others they wish to speak with them yet are left alone at the table."
With a slight nod she smiled.
"If we were but to speak with them...."

"I believe the enchanters are also to blame. Oft they think themselves above others; this I have spoken of to sister and she agrees."

"I have a confession, if I may?"

"Speak as you find."

"Not all are thought of in such ways. I have seen others watching the dark elves who train here carefully. I believe many would speak with them, some even to become friends."

"Feel how an enchanter would view this; our own people would all the sooner speak with those they still feel to be an enemy rather than to their own."

"I would be most upset, this I admit."

"As I have been trying to speak. Sister wishes for this to change ...."

"Enough. I hear your words."

"Then you will speak with sister?"

"First I must thank you; my ways are those of someone wishing not to see. If the enchanters were to return would this change the minds of our people; I know not, would they not fear them or hate them all the more for their actions?"

"The skeletons attack soon."

"Hardly an answer."

"Sister would plan the fight against them with you at her side. This would be advantageous for both I believe."

"Her prowess in planning is known to many; how would this help me?"

"If others were to think you guided her in the fight would this not look good to others? Your standing amongst your people would be raised high; word is it is not all it should be."

"Norty is the one to blame for my current....standing."

"The council is to blame surely. Was it not they who refused her the leadership when all know Caspo Kwil instructed such?"

"They refused and I was left to speak their thoughts."

"They are clever. A decision they made yet you are the one to take the blame for their thoughts; no say you had in their decision. Was it not their decision to ignore the words of Caspo Kwil and refuse sister to lead the enchanters; they knew the consequences yet left you alone to face the anger."

"The decision was theirs alone; I was their voice. I agree yet trouble may be ahead if the enchanters were to return. Many will stand in the streets and turn their backs to them as a sign."

"This sister knows yet if you were to be at their head as they return to the city think of how this will reflect on you."

"Agreed, yet it would look poor for the enchanters, as if they were forced to return."

"Sister wishes you to proclaim you have convinced the enchanters to return."

"This would raise my standing in the face of others."

"They would return together, as one even if our people would turn their back to them, as you say."

"It would seem a good thought."

"What rumours abound?"

"The Undesirables wish to fight alongside us. It seems the enchanters spoke with them."

"People are happy for this to happen?"

"A few speak against this; many wish for them to join us; myself also."

"Why is this?"

"The thought must remain mine alone."

"What of other rumours?"

"You speak of the enchanters and the dark ones with them who patrol the forest to kill any skeletons who appear not where the rangers guard?"

"It is no rumour."

"When first we heard it was believed not; then rangers spoke of finding their tracks in the forest and of the dust of bones left behind."

"How did our people think?"

"They know the enchanters abandon us not; they are here to help and to kill the enemy. Many are happy."

"From where did the rumours start?"

"None know, when asked it is as if they always knew it to be true."

She was happy. Olva had played her part in the rumours so well none knew they had even started them. Her sister would be happy and proud of her and her husband. The enchanters could return home with a little more respect and friendliness; the plan was going well.

Now she had one last part to finish and she could leave. Night was fast coming and she also had a task she wished to continue; to kill any skeleton she found on their lands. A task she relished. At first Kare was unhappy she was alone in the forest with so many enemies and refused his help. When she took him with her the white bones of the skeletons shone in the moonlight; his poor night sight giving little trouble as he killed them.

"A compromise may be reached. If you were to agree to sister leading the guild it would look good for the enchanters and yourself."

"It would be against the wishes of the council."

"Is it they concerned themselves with your thoughts?"

"They did not. I agree to your conditions."

"There is but one thought now on my mind."

"Speak as you find."

"Word reaches me father is challenged by you."

"I have accepted his offer."

"Ignore the words of father and he will ignore those from you."

"A challenge is a challenge."

"Myra only knows of this, she will speak nothing, be assured."

"I forget your father's name; how may a challenge have been offered?"

"While I speak as I find, may I continue?"

His hand gestured approval.

"When first I came with sisters words I thought a long hard struggle would be the result and you to stand firm against me. I am happy you are someone who listens. Should you have a need you have but to ask."

"Then I ask now. The council have been challenged and like it not. Long has Norty spoken change must come; I ask the sisters help in ensuring the council oversteps not its mark again."

"You believe they would do so?"

"More rumours abound in the city than you may realise. Not all concern the enchanters."

"Speak of them."

"The council agreed; once the war is won Norty will be banished as an Undesirable."

"They would do this when she fights hard to ensure we survive!?"

"They have been challenged; she must realise there will be repercussions."

"If they approach her ..."

"Whilst we spoke a thought crossed my mind; I may know a way they dare approach her not. You will help me fight against their ways?"

"Gladly would we agree if it goes not against the good of all. What way do you see?"

"Many dwarves are here and a ring maker I know is with them; I speak no further on this. Now, where do I meet your sister?"

"See her at Saseens Point two days before the new moon."

# Family Feud

"I dare not, Icee."

"Not long have we been in wedlock and I would meet the parents of my husband. They attended not the ceremony."

"They have no liking for you, for any not of my people."

"If they meet me not how may I change their minds?"

"They are set in their ways. Should you enter their home they will kill you."

"Kill the one who is in wedlock to their son? I think not."

"They would kill you."

"They would kill the one who would bring a grandchild to them?"

He was stunned, "You are with child?"

"Should I wish for us a child first would I speak with you."

"I know not if I am happy or sad. Happy you are not yet with child for you spoke naught of it to me; sad you are not with child."

She felt her heart melt once more; he always had a way with words, "When this war is won then shall we speak of a child."

"Then I fight all the harder!"

"Your wish is for a child?"

"When first we joined in love the thought crossed my mind; almost did I ask you consent."

Once more her heart melted, "Then when the war is won I shall consent."

"I would join in love with you this very moment."

"We are in the forest to kill skeletons, not to join in love."

"Let them stand and wait."

Giggling she pushed him off her, "Later. What the score?"

"My count is twenty nine; your count but four behind."

Pulling him down she pointed, "Then a deal I make with you. Should my score best yours this night you take me to your parents come the dawn."

"Still you need five to best me; if I kill no other this night."

"So sure of your prowess you refuse to make the deal?"

"Think not to tease me to have your way, wife. My score is the better and never will you beat me."

Entering the house he nodded, "Greetings. I hope the day sees both well?"

Liss jumped to her feet, "You know our thoughts yet still you bring *her* to our home!"

"She is my wife; her right is to enter our home."

"She has no rights in this house!"

"I would have you greet her as you would greet me."

"Never shall this be! Take her from here never to return!"

"It is my home also. I invite her in."

Taking her by the arm he ushered her past his parents, "You are home, Icee; be seated."

"You bring us disgrace with her presence."

"I bring none, mother. You know of love; why is it you find it hard to accept I also know of love?"

"They will challenge her; kill her the moment she is seen in the city."

"I count six who approached to challenge her; all withdrew the challenge."

"Why would they do such? Her kind is allowed not in the city."

"Yet enchanters enter often. Sit, mother, and I will explain."

Sitting she glared at Icee, ensuring she knew her thoughts.

"When we entered the city, through the third passage, day had just broken yet six necromancers waited as we entered the southern square."

"How is it they knew you to be there and not kill *her* on sight?"

"We know not how they knew. One spoke we were welcome."

"I believe this not."

"It was how I speak. As we walked along the east wall a shadow knight saw her and ran towards us."

"The city guards; why is it he killed her not?"

"The guard knew Icee by name and greeted her."

"What madness is this? He should have killed her instantly."

"Her name is Jennka. She had been in high elf city many days waiting to speak with the council; I know not of what was spoken."

"She knew her? How is this possible?"

Icee saw a chance to speak, "We fought...."

Liss glared at her, "No permission has been given to speak!"

"I respect your wishes and custom."

Suddenly Liss felt a little less anger towards Icee. If she knew a shadow knight, guardians of the city, she may not be as she seemed.

Why such a guard would visit high elf city she had no idea but if Icee knew her and the necromancers then she could be more powerful than she seemed.

Her voice was strained as she nodded, "Icee."

Without a word Icee nodded in return.

"My son has taught you to nod in greeting. There may well be something within you to save. Continue, Kare."

"Jennka led the way to our home yet one saw us and challenged Icee. The necromancers formed a ring around us and Jennka drew her sword speaking to make way for a guard. This she did."

"You may have been injured in the challenge; I care not if Icee was injured."

"As we continued I heard the wizard begin to cast a spell and turned to protect my wife. There was no one to be seen."

"He merely teleported away."

"No, mother, I know well enough the sound of teleportation; he cast not the spell. It was then I noticed the necromancers had turned not; it was as if they knew there would be no danger. Others challenged us on the way yet all backed away soon after. It was only when we arrived home I counted thirty necromancers around us."

"Never have I heard such."

"Before I could speak they turned and left; no word spoken by them."

She turned to Icee, "Permission is given to speak. You are not as you seem. How is it you know the necromancers and why is it they protect you?"

"I know them not nor why they offered protection."

"None like the necromancers; they are an abomination!"

"Before I met your son I was travelling the path to the mountains ...."

Kare interrupted, "It is where I first saw her."

"I knew not the path would lead to Kare, for which I thank the Gods. On the path ahead was a necromancer. Never have I fought one such as him yet it is not my way to refuse a fight. As I stood there he sat and gestured I eat of his food. This I did and when all was finished he nodded and turned on his side to sleep."

"You spoke not?"

"I knew not the language as I do now, he knew none of mine."

"They are strange people and this is unlike them. Always they kill the enemy on sight; I have seen it often."

"Mayhap he thought me not an enemy?"

"Speaking of food I hunger. Food you will have; this offer I make."

"I may only remain a day. Soon my people's enemy will attack. I must kill all I may before the day arrives."

"I have patrolled the woods with her, mother. Last night alone my score was forty eight."

With all revealed to her she had new thoughts of Icee yet could not be seen to back down, "Mayhap you are not the enemy you seem yet still you are welcome not in this house."

Without being seen by anyone else his father had smiled at him. He knew his father only too well. He could have commanded his wife to greet her in friendship yet knew it would never work. His mother had set ways, but changed them if she may be proved wrong; although it rarely happened. His father had signalled he approved of Icee and the smile was returned.

"Your mother will prepare food for your return and will instruct Icee in the way you prefer such."

He watched his mother's eyes widen in dismay yet rose from her chair and walk, somewhat haughty to the kitchen, a bewildered Icee following behind.

"I need not food, mother; plenty there is in high elf city."

"To be fed well....*she* must learn your needs, learn *our* ways."

He sat and lowered his voice, "A dangerous game you play bringing her here."

"Icee insisted, father; as I also knew the day must come."

"I like her, Kare; she has courage and seems unafraid of the looks given by your mother. Some I have learned, to my cost, to ignore not."

"She is not as others, father. I feel if I were to command her against her wishes she would ignore me."

"This you will speak not to another. On the day of your joining she would leave not her room, refusing my commands to attend the wedlock. So much she wished to be with you yet she is a proud female. The tears shed were of missing the wedlock, not those of shame for who you joined with."

# Strategy

"Saseens Point is a strange place you choose for a meeting, Norty."

"Ilsto Ventrel, should a meeting be held elsewhere then word would surely reach the council. You wish them not to be present I believe?"

"I do not. Icee spoke you are willing to return with the enchanters. When will this be?"

"There are plans to be made, this is the more important; the skeletons will attack soon."

"We know not when this will be."

"Surely it is obvious?"

"To know would mean you are part of their plans."

"A jest I hear in your voice, it is good to hear such. When would you plan an attack?"

"On a day when a celebration is to be; we would be at our most vulnerable."

"None are close and they will be aware we know of them. They must attack soon before they believe we may offer battle."

"All will fight, all defend our lands; all will give their lives in protection."

"As I have spoken, should we fight we shall lose. Many agree to join in the fight against them. Help we must have yet we should join not in battle."

"You have spoken to others, to ask they join in battle?"

"Many agree yet we should fight not."

"Only in fighting may we win. You ask we let them enter our cities with none to offer a challenge."

"Should we fight them we will surely lose, too strong they are for us to win."

"You would surrender not; plans you will have."

"In a battle we should give not an advantage to our foe; this we would give should we place our hopes on one battle."

"Speak of your plans."

"Blyth has spoken to me there will be nine for each of our number. Their numbers must be few before they reach high elf city."

"I agree."

"Effort must be placed to ensure they are slowed at all times whilst our defences are built."

"You would place walls around our city, to have them enclosed as do man?"

"To leave them open would invite the enemy into our city. We know from where they will attack; only in this do we have an advantage."

"No walls! On this I will hear no more. Never in our history has high elf city been walled."

"Never has it been threatened as it is now. Walls alone will ensure they attack as we wish and to give places from where we may also attack."

"We are not man, they fight from behind walls."

Fighting down the reply she knew to argue would pointless. She must make him realise in other ways. "All you speak is true yet I believe a compromise may be made. A wall may not be permanent."

"I agree. Thoughts spring to mind as to the way it may be achieved."

"Then the way to harass them must be discussed."

"You believe they must be slowed?"

"Little time do we have to plan, less to ensure all preparations are made. They must give us the time and this they will do not unless we force them."

"How may we force an enemy to give us time to prepare against them?"

"Whisper Valley must be full of rangers and druids. Whilst they remain there is little chance for them to attack."

"If they do we would lose so many of our people."

"They will attack not until the rangers leave."

"This makes sense."

"It is known where their tracks first appeared in our lands and it is from there they will begin their march to high elf city. They must be harassed all the way by our people and others. To slow them is our only hope."

"Who would join with us?"

"Man has offered help in our fight."

"I hate the thought of man entering our lands in such numbers. Well may they turn against us if the skeletons are defeated. We would be few in number and unable to resist them."

"I agree yet we would be powerful enough to hold them behind walls."

"The walls are not just for defence against the skeletons. I see your thoughts on this."

"I believe man would attack us not yet a belief is not enough. We must be prepared for everything which may happen."

"Who else would join us?"

"The dark elves wish to fight also."

"I am unsure. For them to enter our city...."

"Oft do they enter."

"Enchanters only."

"It is they who would fight. Many offer to join us as friends; more than I had hoped."

"I begin to see the way you would gain the friendship and trust of our people."

"It should have to be gained not. Trust should be there for all our people."

"I agree."

"I include in these thoughts the Undesirables. They too are our people."

"They are banished; no longer are they elves."

"Elves they were born and forever will be elves."

"They fail their guilds."

"In truth their guilds fail them. Do others banish their own from their lands when they find they cannot do as others? A task is found for those who cannot be what their parents wish for them. We only banish our people and do so for we are afraid of them."

"We fear nothing!"

"We fear our own; those we consider different to us. Are we so proud we deem ourselves perfect and will have naught to with those we consider below us?"

"We cannot live with them, this you know."

"Yet live with them we do; they are banished not from our lands. There is still within us the hope they may one day return to us. We are elfin kind, never should there be hatred within us and I believe it is there not. We fear the Undesirables yet realise any of our people may be one; even ourselves when we are born. This fear lives in the hearts of all until accepted by the guild to which we were born. Should there be hatred we would put to death any who enter not a guild."

"You have a wish for me to speak to the council and have them return?"

"They have not the wish to return, only to be greeted as friends."

"I must ask you speak not of my next words."

"Naught will be spoken."

"A son and a daughter have I."

She nodded in understanding.

"Neither entered their guild and this burns within me constantly. No, speak not and let me say this. A son was first born and failed to enter the guild. Many years later a daughter we had and she refused to train to enter the guild speaking if we would banish our son she will find and follow him. The next day we awoke to find her gone."

"I may only imagine how you feel."

"Oft they return to our home and the look upon my wife's face is such a sight to see. She glows when they are near and we sit and eat at the table as others would do. Always they leave before the sun sees our land; they wish not to cause us embarrassment."

"You would feel embarrassed?"

"I feel proud of them! It matters little to me they are Undesirables. They are, above all else, my children!"

"I also had such a fear in me when Nortee was born. I knew not if she would have mana within her or if her mind would leave her body. I know not if I could have banished her and wish not to think of such."

"Last snow fall I asked Lilika, my daughter, if she would enter the guild. The mana she has within her and I feel she would pass the tests. Her head she shook and spoke she had little wish to join; her home is now with the Undesirables and would always be so. Long have I thought it is our shame we banish our children; I knew not others thought this way."

"In truth I believe many of our people fain a dislike of the Undesirables so they appear not to be different to others."

"Ideas come to mind and mayhap we think of a plan to have all see the other as they should be seen. If the Undesirables wish to remain in their home town this I think is not a problem. If our cities were to welcome them whenever they entered it would be less of a problem I feel."

"A discussion for a day when the war is won. One I would gladly speak of with you."

"Speak your thoughts of the battles; of how we may win."

"So much work is there to do. They must be harassed from the moment they are seen until the moment of the final battle. Blyth speaks ...."

"Blyth guides you, this is known by all, yet never did I know she speaks with you. How is she; is she as beautiful as her voice? You know not how I have wished to see her since she spoke to all in the forest on the day of your birth. I ask forgiveness for my words. She has spoken of how we may win?"

"She spoke to me yet said so little. Whilst we have been away from our home chance I have had to ponder her words. Nine skeletons for each defender she spoke."

"The odds stack well against us."

"The reason they must be harassed all the way to high elf city. Never could we win the fight in a single battle. All our people must fight; the young and all able to cast."

"Placing the young ones in a battle would be hard for all."

"Yet we must do so. We can afford not any to remain away."

"Word has been sent to all the lands for elves to come home and defend their lands. Many I have seen who have entered not the cities in many years."

Handing him a scroll she agreed, "It is good to know. The scroll shows the path from where the skeletons will attack to high elf city and the places best suited to harass them."

Offering another scroll she continued, "A plan of high elf city. Marked on the scroll are the places walls should be built. Windows may be placed to our advantage to face Whisper Valley. Each advantage we gain may mean less die in the final battle."

"You have thoughts to our losses?"

"One death is too many."

"You answer not."

"Many will die of this I am sure; each death will be a loss to families. I believe mayhap a third of our people; most deaths would be among the wood elves. It is they who must fight first; and to the very walls of high elf city."

"I see the way you plan. Many traps are marked on the map and it is they who must spring the traps."

"The first battle must confuse the enemy. Only those able to teleport must enter the first fight. We must have the enemy believe we may enter and leave the fight as we wish."

"To have them believe we are more powerful then they first thought?"

"To have the enemy become nervous is a way to lose less of our people in battle."

"And of the others who enter the fight with us?"

"Mounted men only must be used. Those on foot may be unable to avoid the skeletons when it becomes time to leave a fight."

"You speak of the race of man?"

"I do. They alone have the horses needed for such a fight. Yet here my fears surface and cause worry."

"If you have planned so long this fight why are there fears?"

"It is the only time in my life I wish to have followed mother on her ambassador duties."

"All know you have no love of man; why speak such?"

"I have asked they fight the way I have planned and the king nodded only his agreement. It is my fear he will listen not and lose so many men and return home. Should this happen he may well lose us in the final battle."

"He may not be asked to change his mind?"

"To ask would show we trust them not. One other speaks they will attack the way they love; this also is a worry for me."

"Of whom do you speak?"

"The dwarves love a fight; if their enemy is more in number than them they love the fight all the more. I feel mayhap half of those who would fight for us are in the city. Finglas speaks he sees many in the forests of our lands and many skeleton dusts. They have split their numbers; some to fight to protect the city and others to fight the skeletons in the forests. Should such happen they will lose many of their numbers."

"I would worry not for them. Fights they may love but they also love life and will throw it not away so easily."

"You are correct; I have seen this in Keitun so often."

# The Return

One hundred druids and rangers cast their teleport spell and they left the ruins of the old city; with them they took the enchanters to the druid rings close to wood elf city.

Ilsto Ventrel walked towards Norty, "Never have I thought this possible; I welcome the sight of so many enchanters around me."

"It is to be hoped others feel the same. We thank you for arranging our home coming."

"It is arranged not how you would think."

"What is it you plan, Ilsto Ventrel?"

"All who brought you here are sworn to secrecy. None in the city know you are returning."

"I believed we agreed it was to be spoken to all."

"It may give others time to think of your return and, mayhap, decide to turn their backs to you when you enter the city."

"My thoughts are they would have time to think and be pleased we return. In this way they will have not the time to think; to feel as do you."

"Each knows the enchanters are powerful and needed in battle. It is the thought of how powerful you are which turns their thoughts I believe."

"Each guild is powerful and fights the way they know best. Were we to be matched against a warrior we would have less chance of survival than if we were against another caster of spells."

"All know this yet it is thought not of. Come, we have a walk and few will see us as we travel."

"How so?"

"War is coming and few leave the confines of the city. Many others now join us. Dwarves by the hundred are there."

"I am surprised not they are the first; dearly they love a fight. A suggestion I make. If we were to walk down Whisper Valley it may look as if we have fought the skeletons."

"My thoughts also; the rangers will lead and I would ask questions."

"Ask."

It was in almost silence they watched the enchanters walking towards the city; the crowed becoming greater as the word spread. From every vantage point the watched; and most had but one thought on their minds. It had taken centuries but at last they had thought of their roles in life, their places within the elfin communities, and the way they should be to all elves.

When the enchanters left there had been disquiet, almost hatred, the enchanters had left the city when they were needed the most. Those drinking at the inn at first cursed the enchanters yet over as little as a few days the cursing had almost stopped, to change to words of how the coming war would fare without them.

None had realised when their thoughts had started to change; yet change they did. None knew as Olva and her husband served drink and food it was they who had started the whispers. Those approaching the bar heard but a few words of conversation between them, they had ceased the conversation mid sentence to serve. In this way the elves had taken back to their table the merest hint of the enchanters. They would speculate over the words heard by the inn's owners and slowly the whispers gained ground; and slowly thoughts changed. It was with relief they saw their enchanters walking the last few step to the city's boundary and they held but one thought and as the enchanters past, most of them bowed.

Bemused, the dwarves watched the spectacle; unknowing why the elves bowed and what had happened the last few weeks. Becoming quickly bored with the procession they returned to the inn and their favourite pastime, drinking.

Ensuring Aurorai was at her side before they reached the city she beckoned her closer, "Aurorai, never have I been so pleased. Your parents ensure our homecoming a happy one. You have missed them and they will have missed their daughter. Go to them and take with you my thank you to them."
Turning quickly Aurorai moved towards her parents, a voice stopping her. "Walk, Aurorai Minlets, walk."
Without looking back she smiled to herself and ensured her walk was one of poise and calm.
Reaching her parents she bowed in respect, knowing so many were watching, before embracing them. Even here amongst the jubilation her mentor ensured she was an enchantress; not quite scalding her for thinking of running yet with the softness of voice used in, almost, praise.

## Preparations For War

Ilsto Ventrel stopped shouting orders as she approached; it was time for a rest from the planning and testing of the defences. As the wall slid back into place against the outermost building facing Whisper Valley he felt pleased. Only a few months ago he would never have dreamt of a wall in high elf city yet now he was pleased to see it. It would, he hoped, save many lives.

With a slight bow he excused himself, "I must sit, Norty, times are hard to me and I tire."

"It is understandable. The planning goes well, more is accomplished than I had thought possible in such a short time."

"Five walls of stone; never would I have believed it may happen in our city yet I see why it must be so."

"They may be locked once in position?"

His hand gestured, "The left wall swings out to meet the right and they lock in position with a bar. We use locks rarely and I feel they are not as strong as others would make them."

"Strong enough it is hoped. What of the other preparations?"

Once more he gestured, "The highest of the buildings facing Whisper Valley now have a window from which spells may be cast or arrows loosed. New hills left and right overlook the valley from where we may take yet more lives."

"Each day as I awoke I saw as they were constructed yet they seem as if they have been there for all time and not as new."

"The wood elves we have to thank for their time and effort. I admit they look as if Blyth herself planted them as she made our lands."

"They work hard here and in Whisper Valley also. So many surprises we have for our enemies."

"Yet one surprise still eludes me."

"All was spoken as you helped in the planning; what is it you know not?"

"Never was the role of the enchanters mentioned and I wonder why this is? All know where they must be, where they will fight. Nothing of the role of the enchanters has been spoken."

"We are to be behind the walls to aid in the fighting. This you know."

"Seek not to dismiss me so easily; I would know how the enchanters fight our enemy."

"We fight for the city as do others."

"I speak not of the battle for the city; it is well known how the enchanters fight. In all the talks of plans and traps you would evade the question when I asked what part the enchanters will take in the battles."

"Plans we have yet they are set not in stone. In the to-and-fro of battle we must be free to fight as we are needed. Six plans we have to fight as the situation demands."

"I ask you speak of the plans."

"The enchanters fight not but help friends in battle. This is the role of the enchanter yet we are not helpless in a fight. In this battle we try another way, one used not for five generations."

"You speak of the war against the giants. The enchanters, so it is said, fought as one to the left flank of the giants. They took many lives."

"And lost so many also."

"If I recall the teachings; the enchanters broke and fled. It is hoped they will repeat not those days."

"We broke from the battle after heavy losses to us yet in...."

"Then your minds were used to enter those of our own people! It is since this war we began to trust not the enchanters."

"In *our* teachings it is spoken we did so to show to others we needed help and to instruct our people what was needed. Others saw it not the way it was meant. It is the way we are and no harm was done to others yet I see the way in which it was taken. Long have we lived with the thoughts others trust is not. We *will* amend for the day; we *will* show we may be trusted; the enchanters *will* fight and turn *not* from this war!"

In his three hundred and twelve years he had never heard a single enchanter speak with such determination and force. He could only watch as Norty turned and, almost, hurried away from him. The enchanters were going to fight once more on their own. Never had they fought directly since those days; now they aided others in their fights. A brief feeling of sympathy momentarily flashed across his mind for the skeletons.

Pacing the floor she found her anger growing and it seemed she could do little to prevent it, "Still they press the old war with the giants to us, to have us feel shame and remind us of failing, Jenay."

"If you anger reason will be taken from you and all will suffer death at the hands of the skeletons. Calmness you say to us all; do as you instruct us."

"Should the enemy come within two thousand paces of the city and look to win this battle then the enchanters will form and add to their ranks! We will show the elves the real meaning of war! The real meaning of the enchanter!"

"If any of our people live to see it, Leader."

# A Shout in Whisper Valley

"It begins, Norty, they appear in Whisper Valley in untold numbers only two days after the rangers and druids left the valley. At the moment of sunset they came."

"It is to be hoped we see the sunrise. You know your duties."

"As word reaches us as to their progress I will ensure you know. It is to be hoped our plans succeed."

"You remember my words as to the fight?"

"I remember only too clearly."

"Nothing changes. Should we win still shall we lose. I know not the Gods plans yet see little in the way they wish to slaughter their children. The elfin race will die."

"We need yet more to fight with us; none wish to do so."

"To keep them engaged is the only way, Jenay. Gaps there are where none should there be. We must attack and retreat; it is the only way we may stand a hope when we must engage them in the final battle."

From their vantage point in the trees and behind cover druids and rangers watched as the skeletons emerged through a large black disc hovering just above the ground. Twelve abreast they began a slow but purposeful walk down the valley towards high elf city.

By the time the first ranks had drawn level the hidden druids they knew they were vastly outnumbered yet none had thoughts of not entering the fight. They would fight for their lands, dying proudly should the need arise. On a single blast of a horn those on the left stood and cast their deadly spells, and gaping holes appeared along the ranks of the enemy. Thrice they cast with deadly results before the enemy moved to engage, yet from the treetops a rain of arrows harassed their movements. The still hidden rangers on the right cast to cause havoc, their spells of a higher level bringing down the skeletons in even greater numbers than their counterparts.

For a while there was confusion as the skeletons tried desperately to fend off the attacks from both sides. Then the skeleton's ranks broke as they split their forces to meet this deadly threat, and the rangers took full advantage. Logs stacked on the slopes were loosed to begin the decent towards the skeletons; hitting the constructed earthen ramps they became massive trunks of airborne destruction, striking the enemy and smashing them aside as if they were paper.

Twenty minutes after the start of the battle the skeletons had gained no ground yet the druids and rangers numbers were reducing; the horn sounded once more for all to retreat, they would be needed later in the fight.

From high in the trees Verin looked to were Rinini had been placed for the battle, and saw she was not there. His eyes searched the trees around her hiding place and saw others casting their spells to vanish from sight and a sick feeling took his heart. Forcing his eyes downwards to the ground he looked for her once more. The sight made him heave as he fought the feelings down in his stomach; the skeletons were hacking at the bodies of fallen elves, throwing limb after limb to once side. If she had been slain he would never know which was her. With an oath of vengeance his spell took him away.

"The initial fight is over, Norty, yet still they come."
"How many did we lose?"
"The count is eighty."
"And the skeletons losses?"
"We believe over six hundred."
"Too few, Jenay, less than eight for each of us we lost, we cannot afford such losses for so few we kill."
"Finglas is not amongst the dead?"
"He is in my head so is safe; though I feel anger in him as never before."
"He has thrice more to fight before the skeletons reach our city."
"Thrice? Should he fight them one hundred times thrice I feel there would still be anger within him."
"I have heard much of the first battle. I am thankful I am elfin and have not the need to fight our druids and rangers."

At the sound of the second horn Lasic knew no rousing words or actions would be needed, the gnomes owed a debt and the time to repay had arrived. He could hear the heavy footsteps of the enemy as they approached down the valley; they were still hidden from the skeletons, but not for long. His voice rose for all to hear, "Our time to help the elves approaches. Once, whilst still in our old city on the hilltop, they alone came to aid us, they alone headed our call for help. Millennia we have waited patiently to repay our debt. The time is upon us, the enemy approaches; not just the enemy of the elves but ours also. Make no mistake! With the defeat of the elves their eyes will turn to other victims. Mayhap not to us in the next year but they will turn our way. It cannot be allowed! Alone we would succumb, as the elves will do this day should our duty not be done. Defend the elves and their lands as you would your own. For each of the enemy we destroy we ensure the debt is repaid and others will think once again before looking to take elfin or gnomish lands. Only upon the signal do we withdraw. Fight as gnomes; fight to show we repay what is owed. The time to repay the debt is at hand!"

"Norty, the gnomes now attack and fight with a fury which has to be seen."
"They are needed, Jenay. It was arranged they attack as the druids and rangers withdrew, we must keep them engaged as long as is possible. The more they lose the less we lose when the final battle comes."
"They fight as if it is their lands they defend."
"It is one and the same thing, Jenay. Do we know of losses?"
"Word is they are heavy, I worry for them."
"I have fought alongside of them, they can be single minded when the mood takes them. They will withdraw before too many die and make all haste to be in the next position alongside the rangers before returning to the city."

The orange mana flare arched into the sky to signal the gnomes to cast their teleportation spell and leave the battle; yet most ignored the signal. It was if they were of one thought, one purpose; still they continued to cast their deadly spells. Each cast reduced the enemy yet their numbers were reducing also. As a second mana flare glowed brightly in the night sky they cast once more to disappear. Leaving behind uncounted numbers of gnomish dead, but thousands of skeletons would fight no other wars.

A full hour had been wasted as the skeletons began to reform their ranks and begin the march once more. They had barely moved one hundred paces when from the rocks and earthen mounds screaming hordes of dwarves descended upon them. Battle axes and war hammers smashed through the ranks of the surprised skeletons. Within thirty minutes over a thousand skeletal bones lay lifeless on the grass and the dwarves suddenly seemed to tire of the battle and withdrew. Those foolish enough to give chase were rounded on and slaughtered, and then the dwarves walked slowly away.

They reformed once more to begin their march; their orders specific, attack the city! At the signal to commence their march rang out five hundred spells ripped into the reformed ranks. Dwarf clerics hurled death at the skeletons. As they turned to face the new threat the dwarves who had seemingly walked away turned and attacked them from the rear.

Attacked on both flanks the skeletons numbers were reduced heavily by spells and weapons. The clerics ceased their casting and joined the melee as only they could. Trained to perfection they took the lives of thousands of skeletons before suddenly turning and running from the battle. Within a minute there was no dwarf to be seen.

"The dwarves, Jenay, what of them?"
"Many died, Norty, yet took with them over four thousand of the enemy. Their losses have been reported not to us."
"They are a proud people and will speak not of their losses. Now my worry begins; they may march over one hour and we have none to attack. They will believe we have used all our forces and stopped them not. It will give to them a confidence victory will be theirs."

The rise of the land offered an excellent view of the skeletons as they continued their slow walk. Word had reached her they had reformed to the all too familiar twelve abreast and had closed ranks, to form an almost impregnable column as pike men formed the outer guard. They had learned. Hidden behind the rise Feleth smiled inwardly at the thought, most dreaded the necromancers, yet so few understood them. To others they dealt in death, to command the un-dead to do their bidding.
So much of what others thought was untrue. They let them believe their thoughts, yet most of the fears concerning necromancers were wrong. They took those slain in battle and turned them against their enemies to aid them in the fight. To let others believe they commanded the dead to harm the living had worked well for them for countless centuries.
Now she and others of the guild had new thoughts. At first the thoughts had troubled her, made her feel as ill as if she had taken a glass of wine. Years ago

140

she had submitted to the new thoughts entering her head and challenged for leadership of the guild; such were her convictions. The fight was both hard and costly. Close friends had offered their lives, to have her kill them so she could use their bodies in the fight. It had taken the loss of four friends to win, and she still missed them, only Josli had not been sacrificed in the battle. Yet she had her revenge, ensuring the old leader died in agony.

"Feleth, others approach; man comes this way."

"I know not who are the worse; man or skeleton."

"Man is the worse; they offer only a slow and painful death, after they would use all females. At the hands of the skeletons it would be quick."

"Yet this time they may be put to use. Where do they attack?"

"To the north; a few minutes of running only."

"Then we join them in the fight."

"No, Leader, they will attack us as they have always done."

"Their thoughts will be on other matters, Josli. In the heat of the battle they will be happy to accept help, even if it is from those they hate. Who leads and what are the numbers?"

"The king leads mayhap two thousand men. Five hundred Paladins ride less than five minutes behind."

"Then our task shall be all the easier, the paladins hate the un-dead as do we and will fight with greater fury."

"It is to be hoped they hate them more than they hate us."

"Tell all my command. If they see but one man in need they are to give aid, no matter the cost."

"You would sacrifice our own over the lives of our enemy?"

"The plans we have discussed over the years will be all the easier if others were to think differently of us."

Her head gave a sharp nod, "The command will be given."

"Have all move within a hundred paces of them and remain hidden until they attack. If any are seen I will see it as betrayal."

With the skeletons passing just below them the king raised his hand, and over two thousand mounted soldiers spurred their horses to charge at the enemy, sweeping into them as a boulder would smash open a door. With swords slashing they cut and hacked at the skeletons, using their horses to trample hundreds under hooves as the skeletons tried in vain to fend off the onslaught. The skeletons withdrew, and man charged after them, into a well conceived trap.

From the rear of the skeletons pike bearers buried the ends of the shafts in the ground, and the moon glistened on the already blood stained weapons. Those fleeing as if in fear rounded to the rear of the pikes and yet more pike men appeared to both sides of the mounted soldiers. From behind them scores of doubled handed sword wielding skeletons circled round and began to close the avenue of escape, they would push the enemy onto the pikes.

Unseen by the ranks of horsemen fighting for their lives the skeletons had laid iron chains midway between the swordsmen and those carrying the pikes. When they charged the chains would be pulled hard at the last moment to the height of the horses' knees. The enemy would be unhorsed; easy kills. Man must have thought them stupid; they had fought mounted foes before.

Seeing the trap the king waved his arm in a circular motion before pointing to the east, it was time to ride hard through the thinnest section of the trap, but he knew many of his men would die in the attempt. He needed help from the paladins but as yet they were still too far away; he realised he had attacked too early. He had to fight his way towards them, and his only hope of help.

Their battle plans had been decided before they rode to help the elves, riding in to slaughter them in countless thousands. This way they loved to kill, to enter the battle and fight till all the enemy were dead. He has decided to ignore the way Norty wanted him to fight. He had fought in many battles and only in one point did he agree with her, the enemy must be stopped.
If any were left alive then all lands would be unsafe from them. The best way to win was not to give the enemy any respite.

He knew better ways to fight than an elf who had fought in only one battle. Now he saw what she had asked of him; his men would die needlessly because of his eagerness, and his thoughts turned to the elf he had loved so long, and would never see again. He whispered his goodbyes to Elesee.

Fighting hard his sword took the head of a skeleton as he saw the danger too late, a pike was headed his way and there was nothing he could do to avoid it. Yet the pike missed him and entered the rib cage of the skeleton on the back of his horse, to be twisted and removed once again. Then it was lifted and swung in an arc, the broad blade along its edge slicing into the ranks of fellow warriors.

Unable to believe the skeleton had turned on his own he looked around, power blasts were erupting amid the ranks of those blocking the way east; he could not believe necromancers were helping him, they were loathed not only by his kind but by their own also. The necromancer spells were carving great swathes amongst a common enemy; and they were taking control of hundreds of skeletons making them fight amongst themselves. He and his men were being offered a chance of escape; and his paladins were headed at a fast gallop directly for him. With his men and the paladins joining with the necromancers the task would be all the easier.

His voice rang out, "Fight toward the blue skins; they seek to help us!"
In the mist of battle they heard his voice and turned to obey his command. An opening was appearing in the enemy as the necromancers took so many of their lives. Hoping it was not a trap they fought towards the necromancers and hopes of living through the battle.

Feleth was happy, the necromancers had new aspirations and this could do nothing but help them. The battle was not part of the plans laid down so carefully over the years, but she would take any action she thought would help in achieving their aims.

Man hated the dark elves more than most of the races in the world, this would show they meant to change those thoughts, and show others how wrong they were about them. She had sought out the king to ensure he survived the fight, taking the most powerful in the guild a little south of the main fight as she saw the trap into which the men had fallen

The king would be surrounded by his men, to ensure he was safe, and then move east towards the thinnest part of the enemy. But from her vantage point she saw the new threat he could not, skeletal archers were running along the eastern flank. He would be leading his men into the deadliest part of the battle, a hail of arrows, and to their deaths. There was only one section where escape would be possible, south of the east flank.

She hoped the paladins riding close behind would see her intentions and act accordingly.

Necromancer and proud of her long heritage Feleth had been taught how to fight death all her life; this battle was just as all the others she had fought. Yet she had never imagined she would one day be fighting to save the lives of those who despised her kind. Her spell had taken hold of the skeleton about to take the life of the king, took him and made him attack his skeletal brothers. Yet would the king realise they were trying to help and not attack them as they approached?

Her companions cast and the skeletons to the south of the men collapsed, and gaps began to appear in their ranks faster than they could be filled. More spells erupted and finally a way clear was open for escape, yet still the king and his men were unable to fight their way clear.
"He must be saved, form the ring and fight towards him!"

At her command eighty necromancers formed around her, a circle large and offering protection to any in its centre. Two hundred fighting on the east saw the move they had used so many times in battle and turned their attention to the skeletal archers now taking up position and engaged them. With their spells shattering bone to dust they watched as the paladins raced into the rear of the archers ensuring bows could not be used at close quarters. Under such a combined attack hundreds of the skeletons died.

Astounded the necromancers would help them the king began to wonder if this was some elaborate plan, to trick him and take him prisoner. Yet the more the circle of necromancers shrank as their numbers depleted the surer he became they meant to help him.
"Give aid to those who help us! Join them and fight together!"

High in the trees a druid watched; almost unable to believe his eyes as he saw necromancer and man fight towards each other, to eventually join and fight as if they had done many times before. Watched as necromancers gave their lives protecting those who hated them. Watched as the necromancers outside of the trap cast spells and gaps opened in the ranks of the enemy, allowing those trapped inside an avenue of escape. Watched as paladin joined with necromancer, fighting together to ensure those in the centre of the battle would escape certain death. Watched the battle disengage and those still remaining live to fight again. His head shook, this was one story he wanted to tell others himself.

"I never thought my life would be saved by your kind. May I know the name of our saviour?"

"Feleth I am named. Where now do you go?"

"To harass and kill the enemy; do you join us?"

"We were asked not if aid we would give. It is we who decided help must be given by us so they may survive. We would be welcome not and will return home. Take care in future battles if you wish to survive."

"I saw the sacrifices you made; you lost many people today trying to save us. One day, the Gods willing, we may repay the debt."

Feleth nodded, "No debt is owed, none will be asked in return."

For the first time in known history man and dark elf parted from a battle with none looking back, each knowing they would not be attacked when their backs were turned.

"The necromancer fought the skeletons, Norty, and gave aid to man. The druid speaks they fought not each other but joined in battle against a common foe. Never would I have believed it. Do they show aid to us or is there something we know not?"

"I am unsure, Jenay. Oft have I seen them yet never have they approached me or shown signs of friendship or of hate. Mayhap this is a way they wish show us something. Time will explain their ways; if the elves live to see such."

"We will live, it must be so. Blyth would cause not her children to fade from the land."

"The necromancers know not the help they have given. We are indebted to them; they acted when the time was right and when there would be a gap in the harassing of the enemy. How is it they knew where to attack, where we were not present and the way to inflict such damage?"

"The druid spoke many thousands of skeletons perished and hundreds of necromancers. The fight saved man, it is spoken they lost but three hundred mounted soldiers."

"Yet still so many die. If only it were different."

Anyone walking along Whisper Valley to high elf city they would not have noticed, or at least ignored, what appeared to be avenues amongst the trees. The gaps in the trees were only several paces wide but over one hundred long; fifty avenues on either side. Had any taken the time to stop and look they would be confused as to the purpose of such a gap. Too thin to be a firebreak and a firebreak should run the total length of the trees, these did not. The skeletons, however, would soon know the purpose.

Marching past the avenues the skeletons gave them little thought; they were more concerned with the rangers formed in front of them. At two hundred paces they called a halt, and for bowmen to take the forward point. The bowmen had little chance to fight; hardly had they reached their allotted position and the rangers cast their deadly spells, and the bowmen began to fall. Out of range of the skeletons poor bows the rangers cast over and over and yet more fell to them.

He was getting angry. No orders had been given for bowmen to move forward and the line had stopped once more. It would take ages to have his men move forward as a single unit. Yelling aloud he commanded the line to resume its march.

The rangers cast again and began to walk backwards, casting as they went and more of the enemy fell. As their mana was used they saved a little for their teleport spell; they would be needed in another fight soon. Now the rangers used their bows to deadly effect, killing hundreds as they continued to move backward.

The skeletons should have investigated the one hundred avenues for it held a great danger to them. At the end of the avenues hidden mages moved and cast their long range spells up between the gaps in the trees. Two spells raced along between the trees of each deadly path; to erupt amongst the enemy with devastating effect.

Once more the skeletons stopped their march as they considered what to do against this new form of attack. It was unknown to them. Until now each attack on them had been direct; and answered the same way, by brute force. By the time they had decided on a plan the mages had cast five more spells each, and they lost more to them. Arrows loosed at the enemy were useless against them. To travel the length of the path they needed to shoot them high into the air; there they hit the braches of trees before they were halfway to the targets. It left but one option open to them. They knew they would lose more to the mages as they charged them but loses would be acceptable. Not to deal with them would leave them open to continued attacks and the loss of countless more; it could not be allowed.

To see them charging along the narrow path almost made the mages laugh; if it were nothing more than practice fighting. Their spells smashed into the skeletons, brushing the first few aside easy; and mortally wounding those behind. Yet it was not all of the plan to have a few of the enemy leave the others behind and come to their deaths. In the tree tops druid cast their spells and the skeletons charge faulted, then stopped as they all died.

It would cost the lives of many more skeletons to deal with this new threat yet deal with it they must. At a signal scores of skeletons charged down the paths, to be met with mage and druid spells. Yet for every skeleton lost another took its place as, slowly, they gained ground on the enemy.

Their spells could not keep so many at bay for long and they knew it. Casting so often the mages mana was running low, as were the druids. As the skeletons reached the tress the druids final spells were cast and all disappeared from sight; to leave behind a depleted and confused enemy.

"The avenues, Norty, so well it went we lost but two druids and a mage."
"The trap was not at my suggestion, Jenay. A ranger spoke of such ways to me and I agreed it was good. To lose so few is heart warming. What of skeletal loses?"
"Over two thousand it is thought."
"Would it could be such all the time, if only...."
The three shorts blasts from the horn made her stand, "They approach the pits, Jenay."
"All we may spare who use a bow are ready. One hundred and seventy ranks of twelve will play their part."
"Pike men still form the front ranks?"
"Have no fear; Nortee will follow orders whilst with the archers."
"I know well her feelings for our lands; she will ignore orders if she feels so inclined. She is headstrong; too much she fails to see when her mind is set. Would I could change her mind."
"I have noticed her ways in training, three are instructed she heeds all commands given."

"It is little wonder you are the strength on which I lean."

"Think not it is I who gave the instruction."

"Then who did so?"

Without a word she turned and walked away, she had duties to attend.

Nervously Nortee rubbed her stomach, the feelings churned inside, making her feel sick. She longed for her robe; somehow it offered more comfort than the tunic and pants she wore but it was in her home; she cursed. This was her first war, and the lives of the elves and their lands hinged on the battle. With the sound of the enemy drawing closer she followed the command to string their bows. In the ground fifteen arrows stood ready, on her hip a full quiver of thirty. She had promised herself not to move until all had found a target; or she died trying.

The ranger at her left turned, "There seems little point waiting for formal introductions before a battle. I am Jerit, Lady Nortee; remember your teachings and all will be well."

Through her feelings his voice seemed soothing, "Sickness takes my stomach, Jerit; I am more than a little afraid. You think me a fool?"

"Before a battle only a fool is not afraid. Mark your target and let training guide your aim."

"Each arrow shall find a target, none shall boast they fought us and lived."

From the rear his voice carried loud and clear, "Mark your target by your rank and position. One arrow to each target; those on our flanks will deal will any who survive."

Mentally she checked, 'six rows back, fourth on the left.'

"String your arrows!"

There was little need to watch what she was doing, her grandmother taught her the bow and it was second nature to her now. As the arrow slipped into the string she saw her enemy clearly, eight hundred paces away.

'Come to me, my enemy; feel the fury in me as an arrow finds you.'

"Hold steady, Lady Nortee, be proud this day."

"Why does he give not the order to shoot? They are within range! Instruct me to kill them, please."

"For us they are yet those behind will find their arrows fall short. We must waste no arrows, all must find a target."

"I move not till all my arrows are loosed."

"You are here to obey commands!"

"A hatred burns in me as never before."

"To win this fight we act as one or lose the war. The orders you will follow!"

"I am better than the sixth rank, I should be further back."

"You wish to be further away from our enemy?"

"I wish to kill them, nothing more."

"Then you are lucky, in the sixth rank you are nearer to them."

She laughed, "Thank you, Jerit, your wit relaxes me."

"Which was your last test of the bow?"

"Four I have taken."

"When you take your seventh it is I who will instruct you."

"Draw!"

Her bow came up as her right arm pulled hard on the string, her hand resting on her cheek. She was pleased; on passing her fourth test Yestre Highleaf had made the bow for her. He was by far the master bowyer. It was better balanced than the one she had used before yet took more pull on the string.

It mattered little to her, its range was better and in this war it meant she could kill more of the enemy whilst they were still some distance away. It pleased her.

"Shoot!"

Her arrow found its mark; with satisfaction she saw the skeleton collapse.

"Hold your arrows!"

She muttered, "I wish to kill them, give the order."

"Shoot!"

Before the arrow had found its mark another was being strung, "I like not to shoot so slow, to have arrows remain in the ground unused."

"Shoot!"

"If they realise our tactics they will outflank us; we would have no arrows to fight with. Your mother planned the fight, under the guidance of the rangers, trust to her."

"Shoot!"

"We would cast to bring them down."

"Shoot!"

"Are you so blind you see there are those not yet of age, not yet gifted with mana?"

"Shoot!"

"We would protect them as they withdraw."

"Shoot!"

"Then so many would die in vain; you have much to learn."

"Shoot!"

Jerit gasped, "The fools! Do they not see what it is we try to do?"

Her eyes were drawn to the top of the hill left of the valley; seventeen hundred mounted soldiers were charging the skeletons.

"The king and his men. Have they learned not it is foolhardy to charge the skeletons?"

"I have heard as those here speak if not for the necromancers there would be so few to attack them, so few to give aid to us."

As she watched the pikes were rammed into the ground, their deadly blades facing the enemy bearing down on them. With paces to spare the horses veered and ran along the ranks of the skeletons to smash into the swordsmen beyond the pikes. An instant later they retreated up the hill, with the enemy in pursuit.

"It would seem they learn, Jerit."

"The ranks are now broken, the pits will trap but a few of those we would wish to kill."

"Pits would trap but a few, Jerit. When the first fall into them the others would stop or walk around them."

"You think we have done not this before? The ground is well prepared and will collapse only when hundreds are upon them. Deep in the earth spikes ensures those who fall will raise not again."

"I know of the pits and the spikes yet not they would collapse with the weight of so many."

"Your mother plans the way; it is we who know how to construct such traps."

"First twelve ranks only. Three arrows; harass those who give chase."

"It would seem they learn quickly; their plan was to draw off a number and kill them where it is much the safer."

At the sight of a red cloak moving in the breeze she pointed, "Paladins wait in readiness and guard their flank."

It was as if those chasing did not see, or did not care, a deadly enemy lay in wait; atop of the hill paladins spurred their horses and gave chase.

The commanders voice rang clear again, "Forward fifty paces!"

As Nortee reached to retrieve the arrows still in the ground Jerit stopped her, "No, now is the time for movement and not standing. The arrows will be for later, and much needed."

Stopping after fifty paces she turned, "I fail to understand this, Jerit."

"All will become clear. To fight another battle you must learn from the first."

"Three arrows only; form your skirmish lines!"

"I know not what is expected."

"We break ranks to spread out and select our own targets to anger the enemy; to draw them to us. As their numbers reduce listen to the horn for guidance. Three arrows only, remember the words."

This was the way she preferred to fight, allowed to choose her targets, and knew which they would be; any skeleton threatening her friend. Kyna and the paladins had engaged the skeletons drawn off by the king at the top of the hill. The rest of the skeletons would not move forward again until the threat had been eliminated. With her fourth arrow notched she heard the horn sound three short blasts, and drew back on the bow.

"Fool! Place your own life in danger if you must yet not those of others. Back into ranks and prepare to give your life so others may live!"

"Norty, bowmen have broken from the skeleton ranks and have gained ground behind our archers. They are surrounded and have little chance."

"What of the king and the paladins?"

"They leave thousands of the enemy dead yet ride fast to the east. It seems they leave the fight as instructed and will arrive shortly. There they will strike again yet without aid our archers' chances to live are slim."

Her eyes lifted up, "Blyth, be a mother to your children once more. Send help to save them; save your children I beg of you."

As they faced the skeletal bowmen she whispered, "A dual of archers; never had I thought to die this way, Jerit."

"You gain your wish, Lady Nortee; you are no longer in the first six ranks but the sixth from the rear. We die facing them and hold our ground to the last. Retreat would show the enemy their fate as we fall into the pits dug by us."

"Why do those to our rear not attack? It is the way others would fight."

"I know not the true reason but believe they have suffered greater loss than they would like in the battles. We are but one hour from the city and bowmen would be of little use within the town. They sacrifice them yet if it seems we are to win the dual those to our rear will attack. Listen for the sound of the long horn; then turn to face those at our rear before we die."

"I had hoped to live my five hundred years."

"We are the lucky ones."

"How so?"

"We meet the Gods before so many others."

"Never have I known another to see only good in what is to happen to them."

"What other way is there to be?"

"At least in death I will meet the one who gave to my family our...."

"They attack!"

Watching the black cloud of arrows she laughed, "Archers they are not, they will fall short by twenty paces."

"Our bows are the better and will strike true."

"Mark your target by rank and number. Shoot."

She gasped as rows of the enemy were smashed aside as if a gigantic hand has swept over them.

"They are nearer, Nortee, so our broad bladed arrows have greater effect."

Stringing another arrow she nodded, "I know well the sting of an arrow."

"Keep their bowmen out of range. Shoot as your target is in range!"

Stringing the fourth arrow she noted her voice sounded a little strained, "We may only keep them at bay whilst arrows remain, Jerit."

"So soon are you ready to let your life slip through your fingers?"

"I die knowing I helped my people yet wished to die an enchantress death, not one as meaningless as an archer."

"All fight as they know; each plan was considered, each way we fight is to harm the enemy more than they would harm us. We delay them for reasons; do you see an enchanter here?"

"No high elves attend; they are not fond of the bow."

"Here all are trained archers for it is needed. To split our forces, to ask others to do as we, would bring harm to them. We are here to engage not in direct battle but to harass them, ensure so many reach not the city. This is the role of the archer, belittle them not."

Stringing the next arrow she muttered, "I wounded him only; I will not be as careless this time. I mean not to belittle any, forgive me."

"Make each arrow count; ensure they pay a high price for your life."

Instantly she reached for an arrow in the quiver, "The twisted heads on these will ensure they die. It is time war arrows were used."

"You looked not for an arrow in the ground, Lady Nortee."

"I was chastised on my third test of the bow for not counting the arrows I had used. I reached for one when none were left in the ground. Such will happen not again."

"I believe you may take other tests of the bow, Lady Nortee. Your counting is as your aim, true."

"Our people to the front fall as their bowmen come in range; we too will die soon I believe."

"Yet you spoke you would die an enchanters death."

"Such will be not my fate it seems."

"You die not on this battlefield, Lady Nortee."

"Whilst I live I will run not; I will shame not my parents, my people."

"You would die taking more of the enemy with you?"

"With no arrows how may I take more lives but as an enchantress?"

"So new to battle yet I believe you will see more. Listen as you fight, do you hear them not?"

Hardly daring to believe her eyes she watched the paladins ride into the unprotected rear of the surprised bowmen. With horses smashing them under hoof and swords taking their toll the skeletons began to break and run; into the waiting arrows of the elves.

"With no swords they are defenceless, Jerit."

"If you were but to use your eyes you would see we have no swords either. Why make a gift to the enemy of weapons better than theirs?"

With the paladins rapidly approaching four long blasts sounded on the horn.

"They offer a ride home; it seems this day you will speak not to the one you wish to see."

"I will run not! Three more arrows have I left for the enemy!"

"Question not the saving of your life and ride to fight the final battle."

"I will run not! I have promised so to myself."

"Sometimes a promise is best broken if your life is saved."

"I am taught as all are; a promise is never to be broken. I break it not!"

He pulled the arrows from her quiver, "As I break not my word. You have no arrows; the promise to yourself is kept."

"To whom did you give your word, Jerit, to whom?"

His arrow found an enemy who had strayed too close, "Ride, Lady Nortee, I need no help to return."

"See me in high elf city; we have a score to settle."

"In the mist of battle you would have us fight amongst ourselves?"

"The score will be settled, should we both live."

"I intend not to die, yet the enemy will fall not into the traps set for them unless they are teased. This is now my duty."

As a hand reached down to offer help in mounting the horse she looked up, into the smiling face of Kyna.

"Yet the paladins rode after their king, Jenay."
"The enemy who chased him were soon put to the sword. Kyna speaks she knows not why yet took her paladins in a great arc to come behind the bowmen. She knew not they were there."
"Mayhap my prayer has been answered. What of our losses?"
"It is most surprising; we count ninety dead and sixty wounded. Many have left the field of battle; few only remain to ensure the traps are used."

His voice rang clear once more, "Reform your ranks to forty!"
With little waste of effort the elves formed to forty abreast. Only those skilled in the ways of war had remained, ensuring the others had left the battle. Now they were prepared to give their lives to win the war.
"Volley fire!"
Five hundred and thirty eight archers drew back on their bows and death rained down on the skeletons stood waiting for orders.
"Outer markers keep them in formation!"
The last five on both the left and right of the elfin ranks knew the order, to keep any straying from the main column. Those who did break were rewarded with an arrow to strike them down.

Fifteen minutes later the plan began to work and the harassed and annoyed skeletons charged those causing so much death amongst them. Wild screams filled the air as the headlong rush took them towards the enemy, and over the traps so carefully laid. With over two hundred on the first trap it collapsed, and two hundred skeletons fell to their deaths.
A triumphant voice called out, "Leave this place! They will find other traps to enjoy!"
Almost five hundred spells were cast and the elves disappeared.

The delay caused by so many skirmishes was unacceptable. They needed to be in high elf city and the battle won then return to the disc before the sun rose. They were almost at the city yet more than half the night had passed them by. It was not imperative they return to the disc before sunrise.
If they could not return they would seek shelter in the rooms in high elf city, once any opening had been boarded up.

They needed to ensure victory before the sun rose and battle plans were changed yet again. Orders were given to stop for nothing, whatever the losses. Keep moving forward, ever forward until the city was visible below them. Once the city was below them they would stop and consolidate their forces, there would be few elves, or other races, left to protect the city, their losses must be high with all they had killed.

He cursed the way they had been delayed; too may hit and run tactics had taken so many lives but he knew the elves must be almost alone and terrified now. Man had not been seen for most of the night and not a single dwarf had dared to show himself. They must have left the fight to the elves and for daring to defy him he would ensure any race helping the elves would be amongst the first to be wiped from the world. All was not yet lost; the city was not too far from them and the end of this war was close, yet it was only the beginning. Other wars were needed to wipe the scourge of skin wears from all the lands.

# Traitors

The look on her face as she approached spoke of the progress of the enemy, "What news, Jenay?"

"They fell into five of our traps, many have been slain."

"Yet not enough."

"More traps they have yet to pass."

"Yet not enough to even the odds. How far are they from us?"

"Mayhap three thousand paces with only two traps left. Many asked if they could harass the enemy more, to lay in wait and cast to kill them as they pass."

"I knew naught of this!"

"It is obvious your thoughts on this were...."

"How many have done this, what losses!?"

"Many asked and many asked not yet did so. Word is we have lost mayhap over one hundred."

"How may they be so ...."

"Leader calm yourself. You thought not this would happen?"

"My instructions were clear! We can ill afford the losses these foolish actions bring."

"I admit I would have done this were my duties not set out before me. The thought of others on our lands, of them defiling this beautiful place, of building walls, sickens my heart as I had thought not possible."

"I knew not of your thoughts."

"Leader, all feel as do I. For others to be on our lands sickens us; our lands must be free for us to be as we wish. The command was issued several times. It would seem it was ignored."

"Well I know the feelings yet we must control our thoughts. For each death there is less chance the elves will survive."

"No more will fight in such a way, the enemy is too close."

"What numbers?"

"Far too many is all I know."

"The last line of defence is ready?"

"All enchanters are ready to fight, to die for elfin kind."

"No more deaths, we can ill afford to lose more, so often I say this."

"The walls are in position and our allies ready. All are safely in the city and ready who must be. Casters take all the highest posts and archers ready themselves behind the walls and the new made earthen mounts. The final battle approaches."

"The horsemen of man?"

"They are in position also and ready for war. They move not until the horn sounds, this is now assured."

"So many died needlessly before the lesson was learned; why is it they listen not?"

"They are a proud people and believe they know the way to fight. Mayhap in fights to come they will listen well."

"I like not to think of more battles yet know within my life so many more will be fought."

"Not for many years it is hoped. None who have fought may think their losses so little they may start another war."

"I need ask not of the enchanters?"

"All are ready though I feel they are more than a little eager."

"They are split and organised as instructed?"

Her look was more than any words could convey.

"Forgive me, Jenay."

"Much is on your mind; there is little need to ask for forgiveness."

"Our people will believe not their eyes."

"This is a plan you care little for. It is to be hoped it goes well."

"Our best will be in great danger once our deception is revealed."

"This they understand. Not one has asked to remain in the city. So proud I am of them."

"And the dark elves?"

"Their best have asked they join; three hundred and fifty six including Pose."

"Little do I want her to join them yet she alone knows how to ensure those with her will do as commanded. Return to your position and ensure I am informed on all matters."

"As you command, yet I wonder what our people will believe when the enchanters join the ranks of the skeletons."

# The First

After millennia of waiting his army was within one thousand paces of high elf city. Each and every one of his skeletons hated all elves yet hated the necromancers with venom few of skin could imagine. It was they who had called them back from the afterlife to inhabit cold bones. He was the first, but not the last. Where the necromancers had obtained the bones he had no idea, and did not care. They had tried for over one hundred years to give life to the bones he now inhabited. They had cast spell after spell to summon a spirit and time after time they had failed.

Then he was in the bones and unable to move, even a finger, powerless as he watched the necromancer casting to bring life to the bones. They did not know they has succeeded, he was unable to voice his feelings. Each spell they used brought pain coursing through him and with each cast he hated them more.

Finally they had grown tired of their believed failure and discarded him to the room he was to call home for so long. Yet the necromancers continued to try and bring forth life and have it inhabit the bones. Once in a while they would discard the bones in the same room as he lay, and something strange began to happen.

The more the discarded bones began to pile in the room the stronger he felt till he found he could move. At first it was just a finger, but it was movement. Then he found he could speak and encouraged the others in the late hours while the necromancers slept. Very slowly he found others could speak and they discussed the pains they had endured. Over time his movements became stronger until he could, finally, stand. Then the others followed him, one at a time, to stand shoulder to shoulder with him.

When the necromancers tossed a new skeleton into the room they would be inert until they left and he found the extra life-force gave movement to others in the room until they could stand and speak.
They began to call him The First and plans were hatched. Revenge was the key; they would kill the necromancers for the abuse they had suffered. As plans developed they began to encompass more than revenge against the necromancer, it was to be against all elves.

Soon thousands upon thousands of skeletons packed the rooms in the lower depths of the city and their plans were steadily formed. The time was at hand for their revenge to be started. In a next few nights the elves would wish they had never tried to give life, it was only the Gods right to do so.

The moon was just a crescent in the sky when they crept from the rooms to which they had been banished. The dark elves had poor eyesight at night and they knew of it. With The First leading them they ascended the steps to the guild hall and found it peaceful and quiet. It would not remain so for long. With swords looted from the armoury they were drawn in readiness to attack the necromancers as they slept, and the slaughter would be great.

Their eyesight may be poor but the dark elves had keen ears. They awoke and their spells and weapons began to take their toll of the skeletons but the numbers were too many. The necromancers were forced to into the streets of the city and the skeletons began to kill any who ventured forth to help them. Dark elves were killed in the streets, killed in their homes, killed in their beds, their losses beyond imagination.

With the breaking of the day the skeletons rallied and headed for the depths of the city and the citizens sealed the entrances with stone, mortar and spells. Then the elves turned against the necromancers, it was they who had brought the skeletons into the city and caused the slaughter. At first the others shunned the necromancers; turning their backs on them as they passed by, yet soon it turned to hatred. Through the centuries, which were to follow, the necromancers turned away from their fellow elves and were always alone; never asking or receiving help, yet always trying new ways to give life to, and control, the skeletons.

Soon after the necromancers found a new spell to control the skeletons yet it had a consequence they had not envisioned. Life and bone were sucked from their prison into a void so black nothing could be seen.

Over countless millennia others joined them in the void and the plans they had so carefully laid were in ruin. There could be no revenge while they were trapped, and time was meaningless there.

In despair they cried out to be free of their prison and a split in the void began; gradually it opened until it was wide enough for them to pass through. Another form of frustration took those who had left the void. No elves were found, they were no longer in dark elf city, and their anger knew new heights.

The trolls were close by and the hatred for flesh had grown too strong for them to resist. The few who had left the void attacked the trolls and the battle raged most of the night. With the dawn came defeat. Not at the hands of the trolls but with rising of the sun. As the warm light of the sun touched them they turned to dust and were blown away on the breeze. It was a lesson they would never forget. Scouting parties would scour the lands close to the opening for signs of life. All attacks would start as the sun set and they would return to the void before it rose once more.

Over time the split had returned, but never often and never in the same place. Once it opened close to a city in which man dwelled, and they had attacked again. The slaughter had been great. Most of the city's inhabitants were dead or had run away and they thought it a victory. Yet it had served as a lesson for those who lived in skin.

Each race had devised new ways of dealing with the skeletons; man being the more successful in dealing with the un-dead. Over years they had turned to the Gods and were shown the way to defeat their enemy; and so were born a new type of man. They were faithful to the Gods, strong of arm and sharp of eye; the paladin had come into the world; their duty to return the life within the skeletons to their resting places with the Gods. They were deadly to the skeletons. Faith and a broadsword took its toll of the skeletons; they were fast becoming the scourge of the un-dead.

The time spent in the void was not misused. They found a way to partially control the opening of the void, and when it would open.
With each opening they would attack a race, and the dead swelled their ranks yet more with each raid.

The dwarves suffered the least casualties; they had heard of the paladins work against the un-dead and had trained their own kind for such an attack. The clerics were devoted to their Gods, their very worship giving them the extra strength, faith and fighting skill needed to kill the un-dead. Spells were found to banish the life inhabiting the bones; it made it all the harder for the skeletons to archive the easy victories to which they had become used.

160

Now most of the races knew the skeletons way of attacking, suddenly and with the setting of the sun. They had organised lookouts and alarms throughout the known world. Yet the people of these lands did not know secrets the skeletons knew, or of how they had set in motion the destruction of other races.

The ape-like creatures of another place were too low in intelligence so they had set them on the path of havoc towards the elfin races. They would become the only skins the skeletons would ever trust. Yet when all the elfin races were cleansed from the land the ape-likes would be the next killed.

The First grew stronger with the passage of time and each new skeleton entering the void. Now he could almost control where and when the next opening would occur. His trials and mistakes he kept hidden from all but a few, those who had been with him the longest. Five times he had failed to open the void close to dark elf city but his army must never know the truth.

Then it opened to fresh air and green forests with a stream gently flowing down the slope. In anger he sent scouts out to search the land but they never returned. The eighth time he sent older friends out and they returned with great news. An elfin city was close at hand, undefended by walls or lookouts. They had seen the enemy and returned without incident to report to him.

Once more they were in elfin lands and he was overjoyed. High elves gave little thought to making their city safe; they would launch a new attack and kill the elves before they knew of the danger.
No one saw the black disc, it was almost impossible to see at night and in the daylight it faded from view. There could be no chance of being seen, they only moved during the night and they could plan the best way of approaching the city to place great fear in any seeing them, and make the killing ever more pleasant.

Then he found the elves had somehow become aware of his skeletal army. Although frustrated he changed his plans somewhat. Whilst the elves kept watch for when the attack would begin he recalled his scouts. The time would come when the elves would cease their watching. The time to retreat to the void and wait had arrived. The time they would have to wait was negligible compared to the millennia they had waited. To be sure he knew when the elves ceased their watching he sent out scouts but so few ever returned. He worried little as the losses he suffered; and it ensured he knew the elves were still vigilant. One day they would grow weary of watching and the day would not be far away. Then he would strike!

How the high elves had persuaded so many other races to fight for them he did not know, and cared even less. Every race protecting the elves would also be cleansed from the lands. When all were dead he would turn to the rest of those who lived in skins. Each would die to their great numbers and, eventually, there would be none of skin to be found in the world. His task would be over, only skeletons would live in the lands, and in a peace none had ever known before.

## Outflanked


A little over nine hundred paces and the accursed elves' city would be theirs for the taking. No quarter would be given, no elf spared; old and young, male and female would be slaughtered as they rid the world of the elves. They would ensure they paid the highest of prices; the losses in the fight had been great, far heavier than planned. They had not expected the elves to fight so hard for their lives or for so many other races to join in the fight to help them, but they would have revenge. As the elves died there would be more skeletons to swell their numbers for the next attack, on the river elves.

Then they would fight the dark elves and those who had made them; the necromancers. Above all others they must die yet they had a plan to deal with the most hated of all the elves, a plan to ensure they died in the most exquisite pain ever devised.

With spear raised The First began to signal the final attack, all he had to do was point the spear towards the city and the battle would be over in a few hours. Then they would spread throughout the land in search of any who had tried to hide, or wait for the next night to bless the land before seeking them out. They knew not all the elves were in the city; some had been seen as they advanced. There would be others not on the lands, those who had run away in fear. They would know real fear as they tortured them beyond their wildest nightmares.

The sound of marching feet made him turn his head to the right, and knew victory would be theirs. Five hundred skeletons with double handed swords were marching one hundred paces from their lines. Reinforcements were always welcome, and these would come in handy, they could attack the flank and split the elves' forces. But he found it odd he had not ordered these reinforcements.
Then the marching stopped as the front ranks drew level with the main column and another sound of marching replaced the stillness in the air.

To the left another four hundred skeletons were marching and stopped as they also drew level.

For a while The First was confused, this was not in the battle plans. It did not matter, a greater army was poised to attack; the elves would be slaughtered, as would those who helped defend their city.

Then the skeletons turned to face the main column and confusion took him once more; their fingers glowing as they began to cast spells. All around the reinforcements grey clouds of smoke covered them and when it cleared almost a thousand enchanters stood facing the enemy. Once more fingers began to glow and shock waves of the spells ripped into the main ranks as the skeletons were cut down were they stood.

Four times the spells were cast before he recovered and yelled for the enchanters to be attacked. Then the glow around their fingers changed colour as the enchanters cast once more and fur balls were let loose on the enemy. Sharp teeth and claws ripping at them, gouging and killing; wanting only death.

Yet all did not go well for the attackers, the few remaining bowmen loosed the charges from their bows and the enchanters began to fall to the arrows. Those closest to the bowmen were less protected, even their shields of living glass crumbled under the onslaught.

A final cast and flames and ice assaulted the skeletons, adding to the carnage their pets were wreaking. Then the enchanters started to leave the battle area, fewer in number than those who had first marched along the ranks of the enemy, but leaving over five thousand five hundred less to attack their city. Now they had to return to the city, their task not yet complete.

It would take time for the skeletons to regroup, to form the all too familiar line and renew the attack. By then the enchanters would be in high elf city, they had not yet finished with the skeletons. The next part of the plan involved the enchanters once more. They were needed to slow down the skeletons whilst the forces gathered for the final battle.
It was the problem with owning the largest of all the lands each of the races claimed, it took time to traverse the vast area. Yet it was the least of the problems the elves faced. The enchanters needed to infuriate the skeletons beyond reason, to make the anger in them boil over so they saw little of the trap into which they were being lead. The only possible

way was for the skeletons to fight amongst themselves, to make them unsure of who was friend, who was foe. Once they were beyond reason they would charge headlong towards high elf city and into the trap Norty had conceived.

For the races watching in high elf city it was a sight never before seen. The enchanters were always sedate, always walking with carefully timed steps. It was a part of the way they were, to be in a hurry they considered unseemly. The watchers knew the final battle was upon them but still they stood in awe at what they witnessed, and knew the final battle was to be hard. It would take time for the enchanters to reach their next fighting position and only one option remained to them.
The enchanters were running!

## Heavy Losses

Over one thousand six hundred high elf enchanters stood to block the path of the advancing skeletal army, their numbers swelled to two thousand by the dark elves standing shoulder to shoulder with them. Not often in their history had so many stood side by side to fight a battle, and never with dark elves as friends. They would stand and fight although they knew the losses would be heavy.

Their way was to fight behind friends, to give support and aid in battle. Enchanters were there to give their mana to friends running low on mana; to slow enemies and to enhance the speed of friends. This was the enchanters' main task yet they were more than just support. Only they and the mages could summon pets out of the very air around them and have them fight. Still it was not all they could do, as the skeletons were to find out very soon.

As the skeletons finally overcame the enchanters' pets a single hand was raised. Spells were cast and shields of living glass formed around each enchanter. The hand was brought down and two thousand pets surged forward to attack the enemy. They knew it would never be enough the stop the hoards yet every moment they could delay them the greater was the chance for the survival of the elfin race. Not all friends had yet arrived.

The pets clashed with the enemy, screaming balls of fur and claw slashing them; cutting through them and in the process slashed and hacked to pieces by the swords of the enemy. Each pet furious someone had dared to attack their master, each pet wanted only to kill, to serve before it returned to the dust from which it had been summoned.
Ranks of the enemy fell to them, thousands falling beneath their frenzied attack before the skeletons finally gained the upper hand.

Once more skeletal bowmen, useless against the pets, had moved forward to take positions on each side of the ranks. With arrows loosed a shower of death rained down on the unprotected enchanters.
At the very edge of the arrows range few struck the defenders and most bounced harmlessly off the living glass shields; yet the range would narrow as the pets died and the advance began once again.

The hand was raised again, and less than two thousand spells began to take their toll on the ranks moving forward once more. Time after time the spells sent the skeletons to their makers yet still the gap between enemy and defenders continued to narrow, slowly, inexorably.

Now the deaths amongst the enchanters began to mount as the bowmen found their arrows more effective. Yet the enchanters were aptly named. Powerful minds raced across the gap to the enemy, to enchant them, to turn them against friend.

Among the skeletons panic reigned as they fought amongst themselves; none able to tell friend from foe. Archers turned their bows on the pike men; sword was met with sword as the battle raged. As one skeletal enemy fell the enchanters found another mind to control, to turn it against yet another foe. It was all the enchanters could do to keep control. Such might of mind had its strain on them, as a heavy sword would strain the wielder, and many collapsed under the force of will needed.

The command to retreat behind the walls had been ignored several times yet now it was heeded; ensuring the skeletons were still fighting amongst themselves as they slipped quietly away, taking with them the bodies of fallen friends.

As the skeletons finally defeated those who turned against them they continued their slow march to the elfin city yet no enemy was to be seen, even the bodies of those who had died under the rain of arrows had been removed from the battle field. Yet left behind were witness's to the slaughter; countless piles of bones who had once thought invading elfin lands, to kill all of elfin kind, would be a easy task.

With a heavy heart she watched as Jenay approached, the look on her face speaking of the news she was bringing. The question in her mind was easy yet the words choked in her throat as she asked, "How many, Jenay, what losses have we suffered?"

"Far heavier then was planned; the enchanters were ordered away several times yet disobeyed. They wished to kill the enemy, to show to all the enchanters fight and will never run, never turn their backs on their people."

"How many have we lost?"

"Almost four hundred of ours, one hundred the dark elves have lost."

"They were fewer on the field of battle; their loss is all the greater."

"Those who return speak the dark elves ensured they were in the front of the fighting. It speaks well of them."

"Of the skeletons, how many are there left to attack us?"

"It is thought still over forty thousand."

"The odds grow better yet still we fight three to one. Casters and archers are our hope now, Jenay. Within hours the elves live or die."

Dreth stood with the mages, an anger slowly brewing inside of her. The mages had not fought with the gnomes, for a few reasons. They held no love for gnomes not of mage born. They had tormented the mages for untold generations; called them 'The Riders' as an insult yet it had an effect on the gnomes they could not have foreseen. The mages took it as a compliment, infuriating the gnomes as they smiled when the insult was used.

Another reason was more obvious. The mages fought not as the other gnomes. Their spells were used for long range crippling, to slow down their enemy so other spells could be used to kill them. It was a technique they used to full advantage. Crippling the enemy to a slow crawl they could run away, as fast as their small legs would allow, then to turn and cast yet again. In this way they usually won a fight.

The way of fighting had led other races to call the mages cowards. They were akin to the enchanters; the spells given to a mage to kill an enemy with ease were few. Yet in one respect they were so different to the enchanters. Where the enchanters used pets as a first defence the mages used them as a last resort. The mana used to summon their twin swords from the air around them left very little mana to fight with. When the mages summoned the twin swords they acted as did the enchanters pets; they would attack any who threatened their masters.

Pets would not be used this fight. As the skeletons came into view they cast their spells carefully, aiming not at the front ranks but those behind them. As the enemy dropped, crippled, those behind trampled over the bodies.

In the highest tower Norty watched the latest delaying tactic, "Blyth was correct, Jenay, and I see her meaning!"

"Of what did she speak?"

"She spoke Icee would stand with her people and I see now her people. She stands with the gnomes to encourage them and to ensure they leave the field of battle when the time is right."

# Final Battle

At last he had rid himself of the pets the enchanters had leased on his army and his temper knew no bounds. The accursed elves were cowardly; they used pets to fight their battles or took the minds of friends and have them fight in their place. They were as the necromancers, afraid to join in battle, afraid to fight with sword, to have others fight in their stead.

His thoughts turned to the latest battle with the mages. They at least fought a battle without using pets or controlling the minds of their enemies. When they fought they were within range of the bowmen and a few mages had been killed but he wondered why a single elfin wizard was with them, casting to help the mages and causing so many deaths among his warriors. He respected the mages and wizards but now new orders were issued, 'kill all but take the enchanters alive; they will suffer as will the necromancers.'

Three hundred paces now separated them from the city and the first of the victories would be theirs. The killings would serve two purposes; to kill all elves and to act as a lesson to the rest of the lands. The other races would hear of the slaughter this day and tremble before the skeletons, to wonder when they would be attacked, to die as easily as the elves had died. It would make other victories all the easier.

Finally his spear lowered and pointed towards the city and the attack began. Swords beat on shields, the noise deafening the defenders as the attackers slowly walked towards them in time to the beating. Then they stopped the marching but the beating remained. Suddenly all noise stopped and the defenders waited with baited breath. Screams filled the air as the skeletons howled like dogs; before charging headlong towards the city.

From the path of the skeletons the enchanters moved to the rear of the defenders as if in fear, yet it was part of the plan. Behind them over one hundred gnome mages cast their spell, but not those of killing. They cast crippling spells to slow the front lines of the attackers; and those behind stumbled over them.

As more spells crashed into the enemy confusion reigned as they tried to move round fallen comrades, or over them.

Yet again the attackers had been slowed so the enchanters could escape and give yet more time for the trap to be completed. Above all else the path to the defenders must now be left clear, the skeletons must have easy access to the defenders, it was imperative.

It was too easy, far too easy, he knew it yet the headlong rush could not be stopped, its momentum far too massive. Something was wrong; the elves had fought far too hard to just give up now, they were planning something, but what? Why were they not casting to kill more as they charged, it was the obvious thing to do, to cut down the attackers numbers in the vain hope of victory.

Then the front ranks hit the thinly spread defenders as a battering ram would hit the keep of a castle. The line held, but only just. More skeletons ploughed into the rear of the others and the pressure on the defender grew, and they were slowly pushed back as losses mounted with each passing second.

From her vantage point Norty gave a sharp nod and the elf next to her took a long breath to blow into the large horn protruding from the window. The very city seemed to move as walls swung out left, right and centre of the attackers. From behind them casters of all races let loose their spells to push the skeletons, to funnel them towards the warrior defenders.
From either side of the path the skeletons had run to the city the ground began to move as large shields covered with earth pushed their way to the surface to reveal yet more warriors eager for the fight. Most of the warriors who had joined the fight for elves had not entered the battle; they would have been slaughtered by such overwhelming numbers.

They had dug their hiding places and waited only for the sound of the horn. Now they were to enter the battle they had waited for so long and were thirsting for blood, each knowing to lose this battle was not only to lose the fight for elfin lands but the fight for all life. With shields locked together they advanced to close the sides of the trap.

A second blast echoed around the city and ever more warriors seemed to grow from the ground and advance ready to take the place of any who fell in battle.

It was the part Norty liked the most in all her schemes. Emerging from the ground it seemed as if the earth was giving birth to warriors to protect the elfin city. The effect on the skeletons was all she had hoped; they clearly had the same thoughts and, momentarily, paused in their attack.

Yet the trap was not complete. From behind the hill where the skeletons had advanced came the sound of hooves and over one thousand mounted soldiers and paladins followed their king as they charged towards the rear of their enemy.

He saw the trap into which he had been drawn and cursed. All the fighting to high elf city had been designed to slow his progress whilst the trap had been set. To the rear a small chance of survival offered itself before the riders could seal the only avenue of escape; but he soon dismissed it as he saw mounted paladins riding with their king. Paladins were a fear to him; their faith seemed to lend a better cutting edge to their swords and swiftness to their movements, only they could kill so many of his men with seemingly little effort. His only hope now lay in numbers; he still had the advantage in this respect and intended to use it. The weakest part of the trap was the wall of defenders in front of the city, if he could push them back, break the wall, he could enter the city and still win the battle.

Norty knew the skeletons would realise the trap all too quickly and push the defenders in a desperate attempt to gain open ground and wreck havoc as the defenders would have to enter the city through the narrow gaps between the buildings, giving the skeletons an advantage. The gaps had been made small deliberately at her insistence. When it was explained how easy it would be for an attacking force to enter the city almost unopposed she had met little resistance yet knew the attacking army were instrumental in winning her argument. Before they knew of this imminent danger the elves would never have listened had she pleaded her case to make anyone attacking have to fight hard to enter the city.
Now it had been almost too easy to convince them. A few had raised objections speaking an enemy would need to travel the length of their lands before attacking the city leaving ample time to kill them or to evacuate the city should it become necessary. With the opening of the black disc so close to the city they had dropped all objections to fortify their homes.

The elves were still set in their ways; they would have nothing to do with walls out of keeping with the looks of the city. A compromise had been reached; the walls were of wood and stone but able to swing out of the way in times of peace, to become almost part of the buildings, invisible as to their real meaning, yet be easy to place in position should an attack be evident.

Now the last part of her plans dropped easily into place. From behind the new walls dwarf and elfin warriors rushed the aid of those fighting for their very lives. They pushed back at the enemy, holding them but only just and the pressure was building against them.

Relief came to their aid; from the rooftops of the buildings archers took their toll of the enemy; black war arrows smashing bone as a knife would rip through paper. Joining them were the casters, their powerful spells turning bones to dust. Behind them enchanters sent yet more pets to fight the enemy before giving their mana to caters in need.

To the right the defenders could see the Undesirables join the fight with bows and sword as if they were repaying a debt, or had to prove who they were, elves!
Finally the mounted soldiers sealed the rear of the trap, their hooves taking the lives of skeletons as the swords of their riders took a greater number as they pushed them into a smaller and tighter trap.

The skeletons found it hard to move, to raise sword and fight; they were too tightly packed to offer much resistance. The defenders were not so contained. Shields pressed the skeletons ever closer together while swords thrust through the small gaps in between to take life after life. Swords were taking lives yet could not compare to the casters' spells; thousands of spells were erupting amongst the skeletons.
As numbers dwindled the defenders pressed the remaining into a smaller and smaller band. Spells took the lives of their enemy ever faster in such conditions; it was too much for the skeletons. As the casters' mana drained with each spell the enchanters gave to them their mana so they could cast ever more spell. The enchanters' final part of the battle; to aid their fellow elves and friends.

His plans had been laid so carefully over the centuries and were now in ruins. His army was being decimated before his eyes and there was nothing he could do about it. He had been defeated by an enemy who had out-thought him from the moment he had emerged from the void. Each and every attack had been designed to wear down the overwhelming number he possessed, to make it easier for them to trap him. He had led them to destruction and once more hatred stirred within him. Somehow he would find a way to return and repay not only the necromancers but all those who wore skin. Now he had even more reasons, and even more hatred towards the elves.

The arrow found him and he wanted to scream as it buried deep into his shoulder to shatter the joint; his right arm, along with his sword, fell to the ground. He could show no fear, no pain, just urge the remnants of a once proud army to continue the fight, though he knew they had lost.

They were on her land and killing her people; she would never allow it, not while a breath remained in her body. Seven had fallen to her bow and another six to her spells yet still the hatred for them in her had not been sated, and would never be while one of them lived.

"Nortee, they fall so fast. Your mother's plans work well. They are so pressed together they cannot fight back."
Drawing back on the bow once more she released yet another arrow, "Mother spoke little to me of her plans yet I see how well she thinks. Few would have thought of such a way to reduce the numbers of our enemy."
Casting yet again Aurorai felt pleasure sweeping over her as another fell to her spell, "None would think to invade our lands when they hear of such a victory."
"Many fight with us, Aurorai. Many see we have need of others to win victories."
"This fight we win. Let your mother worry as to when alliances are made and broken."
"Ack, only did I take his arm from his shoulder. I will ask grandmother to instruct me more in the way of the bow."

To the right of Aurorai, not fifty paces, an Undesirable dressed in black used her bow to great effect, yet chose her targets well; any skeleton facing the two lone friends on her left. She had watched as they left the main group of casters high on the mound of earth to stand alone midway between them and the Undesirables. It was not the safest of positions should the defenders fail. She wanted to protect them so any enemy who looked as if they may break out of the trap she chose to kill.

"We win, Norty, we win! They are all but defeated."
"Yet at such a cost, Jenay. Would I could plan as Blyth spoke. Mayhap we would have lost fewer of our people or of others."
"Reproach not yourself. Was it not your plans which saved our people, your plans which ensured victory?"
"Still there are hundreds left to fight and the sun finally rises to see our victory."

The sun creeping over the hills finally made him realise defeat was inevitable. Those of his army still remaining were turning to dust as the rays of the rising sun touched them. He had failed in his bid to rid the world of the elves, failed in his bid to rid the world of the plague of the skin wearers, failed in his bid to take his army to safety when he realised defeat was inevitable.

He was not the last to die but he saw most of the army crumbling in the warming rays of the sun before an arrow removed his head from his shoulders.

Lowering her bow Nortee almost screamed "They are dead! We win, Aurorai!"
"Had I the time to cast one more spell, to have them pay for daring to tread upon our lands."
"Well I know the feeling yet always will I remember my last arrow took the head of one of them before the sun came to our aid. Come, Aurorai, there will be celebrating then I have an account to finish."

As Nortee walked away she did not see the look as Aurorai glared at the smoke arising from the remains of the skeletons or hear her mutter the words, "First the skeletons then all who would ...."
Shaking her head violently she dismissed the dark thoughts rising in her head, 'Not you, Aurorai, this is not you. Is it something ails you?"
"Come, Aurorai, I wish wine at your mother's inn and will drink many bottles."
"Wine you shall have, Nortee, and it is I who will ensure you drink your fill."

"Jenay, everywhere have I looked and can find her not."

"She was here but a few hours ago, Finglas. She asked I ensure the wounded enchanters were well cared for. She spoke Malinna asked to tend the wounded."

"I have spoken with her yet she seemed distracted; too many wounded has she tended and I feel the task tires her."

"Icee will know of her whereabouts; she joins others in the inn."

"Icee would visit an inn? Truly times are changed."


"Icee, Icee, awake."

Her eyes opened but recognition did not follow.

"Icee; you are drunk!"

"Who?"

"Leave her be, Finglas, only two she has drunk."

"Aurorai, I believe this not; Icee is drunk in your inn? Never does she drink wine. For her to be slumped in a chair is unbecoming of her."

"One she drunk and then was teased by Kare until she drank another. Mother insists she sleeps in my bed till she awakes."

"Thank you, Aurorai. This I would never have believed. Where is my wife?"

"I know not. The top room of the tower to the right of the west wall is where she has been all the night. Have you asked for her there?"

"With the rising of the sun and our victory all began to celebrate; none know where she went. Where is Nortee she will know?"

A slight blush caught her cheeks, "She sleeps."

"Speak, Aurorai."

The blush deepened, "She drank wine and I brought to her a special one."

"A special one?"

"Understand; she was high in spirits and becoming....excited."

"What did she drink?"

"A potion of sleep I gave her."

"Where does she lay?"

"In my room; worry not she will sleep for many hours, until the excitement dies away somewhat."

"Your room will be full to breaking, Aurorai. Why did you make her sleep?"

"As she drank she spoke often of an account she must settle. I liked not the way she spoke; it is clear anger was in her eyes."


Ensuring Icee was more comfortable in bed he turned to leave, "Thank you, Aurorai."

"I will ensure Kare feels the sharpness of my tongue for his actions."

"Icee will also ensure this when she awakes."

"Wait. If I had such responsibilities as Norty has to bear I too would need some time alone, a time to think."

"Where would you wish to do this?"

For moment she thought, "Home, home is where I would choose."

Frustration was beginning to show in his face; she was not at home, 'Norty where are you? I worry for you.'

Leaving the house he looked down and examined the grass, newly broken leaves, their sap glinting in the sun, lead away towards the river. With a smile he realised where she would be.

Swimming to the waterfall he surfaced close to her, "My wayward wife."

"I am sorry if I have caused you to worry, husband."

"Why hide yourself away, there is much celebrating to be had."

"I need a time alone, to think."

"You wish me to leave?"

"I do and I do not."

"Why sit here under the waterfall?"

"I find it washes away thoughts."

"You are troubled?"

"I am sad."

"Why so?"

"So many lives ended this day; each life lost was due to me."

"No, through you many a life has been saved."

"So many, Finglas, so many we lost this day. Would I could plan so much the better. Through the failing in my planning many lives were lost who may have been saved."

"Through your plans many a life has been saved who would have been lost."

"Elf, dwarf, gnome, man and many more have died to protect us. Pose was wounded also."

"I heard of this and sought her out. When last I saw her she was tending others though her arm was strapped tight to her chest. Malinna spoke she was concerned not with herself but with others wounded in the city."

"In truth I believe her heart was never dark."

"It is a large heart. Now come, we must return to high elf city."

"Return, I will follow soon."

Pulling his legs underneath him he sat as the water cascaded across him.

She knew he was being stubborn but after minutes of silence she turned to him, "You are refusing to return?"

"I wait with my wife until she is ready to make the journey with me."

"I may sit here the day through."

"Then I will remain here with you."

"Husband, you are infuriating."

"Wife, I know this."

"It seems I must return."

"It seems you must. After your eyes are dried I would suggest."

"You see the tears in them?"

Standing he held his hand out to her, "All the water flowing in the Great Waterfall of Sahera could hide not the tears you shed. Come, return with me and dry the tears; the day is sad yet there is much to celebrate."

Letting herself be pulled into his arms the tears dried as he kissed her, "I am ready. Mayhap it is foolish to think in a war we would lose none of our people."


"There seems little room in the inn this night, Finglas. Many celebrate the victory."

"A table is always free for my leader."

Turning round she saw Aurorai smiling at her, "Thank you, Aurorai. Not yet have I spoken with your parents and must thank them."

"Not this night, leader, they are busy and it is I who serves you the wine and ale for Finglas. The table in the corner I have ensured remains free."

"You knew I would return?"

"Long have I served here and many times have I served you. Your habits are known to me; it is why the table you prefer is free."

"I knew not my habits were obvious."

"To be a good innkeeper you should know your customers. Come, I will escort you to the table. Word has been sent to Pose, she will join you soon."


"Never have I seen you drink four wines within the hour."

"Should I not do so I may lay awake through the night and worry."

"Aurorai ensured Nortee sleeps; I may ask her for one of her special drinks."

"I will sleep."

"Yet not for some time it seems, Pose comes."

"So many of my people lost to us also yet something I see this night makes me so proud."

"Your people are looked on as friends; I see many here and all enjoy the company of your people. Many drinks flow freely."

"It is good to see."

Finglas touched her arm, "I am angry you are hurt. How did this happen?"

"An arrow struck yet no bone is broken. Worry not."

Lifting a glass she toasted, "To friends unable to attend and to friends able to celebrate."

Finglas called out, "Aurorai; more drinks if you would."

Within minutes their glasses were refilled.

"Aurorai, so few drink ale yet it is served to me endlessly."

"There are friends to this inn and there are special friends to this inn. Mother ensures special friends have their needs fulfilled."

Before he could speak Aurorai walked away.

# The Accounting

Entering the Rooms of Prayer she headed towards him, "The time is now, Jerit. Two days have I waited and I wait no more."

"I am in prayer, Nortee; you know well I should be disturbed not."

"The Gods may wait! I have a need to speak with you."

"I am in prayer for those slain, was your upbringing so poor?"

"My upbringing was as it should be, to bring to account those who wrong me!"

Reluctantly he rose, "I will ask the Gods you are forgiven for my withholding prayers. Speak."

"You know of what I would ask, I demand you speak!"

"I will speak naught of it."

"A promise you have made?"

"I have not."

"Then speak to me."

"Oft there are times when no promise is spoken yet the other knows it is as if one had been voiced."

"Who is it who believes this?"

"I am not free to speak."

"I demand you speak!"

"From his quiver he held out the arrows, "I return what are yours."

Snatching the arrows she threw them to one side, "It is not the arrows which matter, this you know. Insult me not!"

"I have returned those taken, there is little more I may do."

"You may speak! If you fail to do so then the challenge I will make!"

"Of what use is there to save your life to have it taken in the challenge?"

"Speak, or enter the arena with me if you dare!"

"Too long have I kept the Gods waiting; I must return to prayer."

As he knelt her spell hit him, the pain on his face telling her of the damage done, "The Gods will wait, I will not! Speak!"

"I may not."

Before she could cast again a hand clamped firm around her wrist, "Desist!"

"Leave me go, Rinini!"

"I had thought you grown, you prove me wrong."

"He refuses to speak as to whom asked my life be spared in the battle."

"As is his right."

"It is mine to know who spoke with him!"

"All you need is to realise someone loves you enough to ensure your life is spared in the battle, should it be possible."

"Then you answer my question; mother would ensure I survive!"

"Is your mind so dull? To show favour to you in this war would bring her only disrespect, and the loss of all who would follow her. Had she done such she would have sent you not with the archers."

"I would know who asked, you know not the shame I feel."

"For you to be loved brings only feelings of shame?"

"Twist not my words, Rinini."

"Should Jerit speak what would be your actions?"

"It...would depend on who asked."

"So your anger may suit whoever asked?"

Her mouth moved for a moment.

"Your actions are those of a child! You attack and harm one who ensures your life is given not needlessly yet would change your actions to the one who asked? Is this the action of an adult?"

"I wish only...."

"You wish nothing! You believe your pride has been hurt yet it is not such. There are those who would ensure you follow orders given so not to waste the lives of others needlessly. Your ways are known to many! In battle you would give your life without thought, and mayhap end lives who try to help, to show the way. It was not your life which was thought of but those who would give theirs to help a *child*."

"Rinini...."

"Silence! You bring disrespect to the Gods when you fight in their place of worship; you harm another without thought. Be gone whilst I tend to Jerit and think if this is to be reported, and to whom."

"Rinini ....."

"Be gone I say!"

Turning she walked slowly away.

## Against Their Wishes

Ilsto Ventrel sat once more in the great hall and looked slightly down and to the right; once more eight high elves sat and tried to look impassive, and failed. Even they could not maintain their calmness ten days after the war had finished, smirks were exchanged between them and, he thought, they were about him.

To his left five wood elves sat and talked excitedly, there should have been eight; the same number as the high elves, yet one had died in the war and Herth had left the council after a disagreement with him. The other council member had not been seen since the war began.

Secretly he admired Herth, he was one of the few to speak his mind and not let the others members decide on all actions. He admitted to himself he missed him.

This time when he looked towards the elves sat in front of him in the great hall they were subdued; the war seemed to have drained them of energy. It was how he preferred it, for now; he would ensure they were stirred up before they left the hall.

Unlike the last time when he stuck his gavel he was happy; this time all the enchanters were in attendance and the one who would to be their leader could not refuse, "The inauguration will commence."

The noise in the room died from a murmur to silence.

"Not long ago we gathered in this hall for a leader to be chosen for the enchanters. All know they left with no leader appointed by the council yet had chosen Norty to lead them. All enchanters now attend this ceremony and the council has once more chosen a leader for them. The council's first choice of Dolat of the enchanters to lead the guild will never be; all know he gave his life protecting his people. I ask Resil of the enchanters to stand before the council."

He was amused as the enchanters cast glances to each other, how could they not know another would be chose to lead them?

With somewhat more than a little trepidation Resil stood.

"Resil, the council has duly selected you to lead the enchanters."

"I thank the council for their faith in me. Norty leads as was the will of Caspo Kwil."

"You refuse the leadership of the guild of enchanters?"

"We have our leader, another should not be chosen."

It was more for show he slowly shook his head, "The council is most disappointed and once more Norty is mentioned to lead the enchanters."
The time had arrived and he was prepared, "Norty of the enchanters I bid you stand before this council."
Standing she bowed before them.
"Norty of the enchanters, when last you stood before us few enchanters were at your side. Against the will of the council your guild chose you to lead them before you walked out of the hall. Is it you have regrets on your actions?"
"I have none."
"The council insists you lead them not."
"All know the council's thoughts."
"However, there is one whose mind has changed. As leader of the council I ask you accept leadership of the enchanters."

The silence was at last broken as a murmur ran round those sitting in the hall. The elves sitting on either side of him stood, they wanted to speak yet Lore stated they may only stand and wait to be asked to voice their thoughts. He had no intention of asking them.
"Speak up, Norty of the enchanters; I heard not your answer!"
"I accept the leadership of the enchanters."
"I bid you come stand before me."
"It seems others would speak first on this choice."
"They may sit; none here wish to hear their voices."

Standing before him she bowed.
"Your left arm, if you would?"
Her left arm reached out and rested on the bench before him.
"I present to Norty of the enchanters the twin gems of leadership to be worn on her sleeve. I ask she wears them with pride and lead her guild along the true path, the new path all here see she must walk."
Carefully he pinned the twin gems on her sleeve.
As she turned to retake her seat he stopped her, "Stay your ground, Leader Norty of the enchanters."
She looked at him unsure of what he wanted to say.
"I see before me some two hundred dark elves. When last I was here I spoke Pose was unwelcome in this hall."
All eyes turned to Pose.
"I offer to Pose my apology and ask she forgive me."

Standing Pose gave a slow nod, "There is little need to apologise."

"Then Pose of the enchanters I bid you stand before me."

As Pose walked towards him he continued, "I had thought ill of the dark elves, as so many here have also done. It became clear to me as I watched the battle their true feelings. In the mist of battle the dark ones stood shoulder to shoulder with us though their losses mounted. We could ask no truer friends. Pose, I ask you forgive my earlier thoughts."

"They are forgiven."

"Hold before me your left arm."

Nervously she placed her left arm on the bench.

"I asked a dwarf attending the battle for a special favour, this he granted. It has never been known in our history for two to lead a guild yet I would break with tradition. The dwarf made for me a pin and gem of leadership."

He paused as another murmur ran around those sitting in the hall, "To Pose I offer a single gem and pin of leadership made by the dwarf. To wear it on her sleeve so all will know she is second in command of *both the guild*s."

He was unsure of the murmurs and looks on the faces of those before him in the hall. Most were incredulous a second leader was appointed and to wear a pin. It was usually left to the guild leader who they wished as a second.

His hand signalled for silence, "I am in error it would seem, I speak of two guilds when there is but one. The dark enchanters are our friends and I welcome the joining of the guilds. There will be but one guild. If any disagree I ask they show their thoughts."

Most enchanters remained seated but ninety five stood and left the hall; many of the elves within the hall following them. They had shown their thoughts as tradition dictated.

"It would seem there are those amongst us who accept not the dark ones as friends; it is my hope their thoughts will change. Norty, Pose, you may leave and begin your reign of leadership. May it be long and the guild prospers."

Turning to him both bowed low before turning to the other and, in a very un-guild leader way, hugged the other.

Now he had to defend the decision for Norty, and Pose, to lead the guild, "The enchanters have left the hall and I believe many may object to my actions. I ask they stand so their voices may be heard."

Each of the council stood and he had to decide who was to be heard first, "It would seem my decision was popular not with the council. Before I ask each to voice their thoughts I ask those in the hall show their thoughts." Most in the hall stood and turned their backs to the council.

He was overjoyed. The elves knew Norty had devised the plans to defeat the enemy and now the council could see the thoughts of those before them. The power of the council had waned; if he could have them voice thoughts against Norty or his actions it would show to those in the hall the true ways of the council. He had spoken they must be changed, stopped from making the rules as they saw fit. To speak now against him or Norty would show they had little regards for the thoughts of other. He had asked them to stand before asking those in the hall to show their thoughts; he had trapped them as they had done to him.

"Councilman Herat, your voice I would hear first."

Herat knew the trap he had fallen into. They had discussed the problem of Norty so long ago and decided he would be the one all would blame if their plans failed, in either refusing Norty the leadership, in her taking it by force or by default.

Nervously he started, "I thank you for the privilege of speaking first. When the problem....of the leadership of the enchanters....was first known to us...."

Ilsto Ventrel sat back, a smug look on his face. Herat was not speaking as he normally did, his words were quiet and he often paused to try to rethink them. It was obvious to all in attendance he was trying rapidly to find the words needed to look as if he had always agreed to Norty taking leadership.

## Locked Doors

It was something rarely seen in high elf city, a locked room. Outside the door stood two captains of the guard swords drawn to hang loosely at their side ready for instant use. All knew of their prowess and few would choose to challenge them. Close by were two powerful enchanters; their eyes alert yet nervousness showed uneasily on their faces. Even to the casual observer it would leave no doubt in the mind as to their purpose. No one would dream of entering the room yet tradition decreed the room to be guarded.

Few meetings were ever secret in the city and, before the day was little more than a few hours old, rumours had begun to circulate. The dark elves were to be barred from the city; the dark elves did not like Norty as the leader of both the guilds. The dark elves had challenged Norty; the joining of the dark elves and the high elves had proved unsuccessful. It seemed all the rumours flowed along the same path; the fault was due to the dark elves.

The enchanters had defended the dark elves saying they gave their lives in the fight with the skeletons and wished to be friends with all the elves; yet still the rumours spread unchecked.

The sanctum was used only rarely, when absolute secrecy was necessary or when a guild needed a place of sanctuary to study a new spell. The enchanters had not used the room in over two hundred years.

Even the enchanters knew little of the facts, each had been dismissed from training as soon as they attended at first light and instructed to return home with all due haste; with rumours so rife in the city it would ensure their minds would not concentrate.

Almost six hundred paces from the locked door Aurorai sat at a table in her mother's inn, "Worry not, Nortee, your mother does nothing to endanger her or others. It is not her way as well you know."

"She speaks not of what will take place in the room yet I know she worries. Late in the night two dark elf enchanters, high ranking it is believed entered the city to speak with mother and Pose. It is unlike them; always they ensure those who journey here are known to us."

"I have heard the dark elves are not happy your mother leads the guilds and wish Pose to do so. Many believe they are here to offer a challenge."

"Rumours trouble me not. Should they wish to offer a challenge they would do so on home ground where they would feel all the safer. The battle against the skeletons should leave little doubt in others minds; they are our friends and would never offer a challenge to a leader. Mother's lack of trust upsets me; why would she speak not with me?"

Glancing at the two high elves standing shoulder to shoulder with her highest ranking dark elves Pose nodded before turning her attention to the figure on the bed, "You are relaxed, Norty?"

"I am nervous yet not overly so."

"For any pain I may cause, I am truly sorry."

"I hold you to your promise. Should my mind be harmed you know your duties."

"They are known to me. I will enter your mind with the greatest of care. Resist me not even a little and, by the Gods will, both you and I will have a mind after our experiment."

"Nortee is still linked with me; she has left not the city as instructed. She will have heard rumours; I would have words with her later this day."

"I have tried to convince her to leave the city, to no avail."

Slipping the stiletto from its sheath she handed it to Jenay, "If my mind is to be lost ensure my death is quick."

"It will be quick and painless, my friend. Trust to Pose, she would harm you not."

"I am prepared."

"Resist me not and help me find what I search for. All thought must cease while I do as I must."

It was the first time Pose had entered her friend's mind. In training together neither could enter the others mind, their wills equal. Each thrust had been parried by the other, each subtle attack met with resistance or impenetrable wall. Now there was no resistance, no walls blocked her carefully chosen path, and Norty was helping her, guiding her along the path leading into her mind.

Occasionally a thought would hurl past, fleeting as dust on the wind; some to cease almost before they began and she knew, instinctively, Norty was struggling to keep her thoughts under control. In the youngest of enchanters the path into the mind was broad, to become narrower as they progressed in understanding, narrower as they began to control their own mind.

186

In Norty Pose had found no way in, no path on which to tread. Now her mind was open as she had seen none before. She stood not on a path but, it seemed to her, in the middle of a great meadow with no wall to be seen in any direction, she could move freely wherever she wished.

Momentarily she did not know which way to turn, as if she had entered the mind of a newborn, it was almost blank, so peaceful in its existence. Her mind heard the voice, 'move towards the hills, they beckon to you.'

Nortee shook her head as if something had made a noise near her ears, "The linking with mother grows weak."

"How may it be weak?"

"It is as if she sleeps; no thoughts flow in her mind."

"You see her thoughts?"

"I do not; when she sleeps the linking grows weaker as thoughts cease. When she trains against Pose she fights her hardest and the link grows stronger."

"I would like not to be the enemy of either. When they train me I feel their minds, so powerful, yet I know they use only a little against me."

She leaned a little closer as her voice lowered, "I know not if I should speak of this. Pose and your mother train me how to enter a clear mind. Why is this so?"

"I know not, she has spoken nothing of such ways to me."

Finally she stopped to rest, she had journeyed into a mind far deeper than she had even done before and it worried her, 'where is it, why do I do see it not? The old scrolls speak of the thought; it should be here.'

The voice belonged to Norty, but it was as if it were carried on the wind, 'mayhap the thought is near the surface, it is there I think you must search.'

Standing she nodded, 'I will do so yet I begin to tire.'

'I will help; force myself see what you wish.'

'open your eyes, see what we wish to see.'

'they are open, Pose.'

Pose moved swiftly back to the entrance to her mind and searched again. Thoughts were few yet one seemed to evade her gaze, 'what are you, the one I seek?'

Once more a thought passed her but she ignored it, the thought was of dry lips. Norty was becoming thirsty.

'you! Cease your movement! You are the one, this I know.'

The thought was gone once more, to vanish as if never existing, 'cease your ways, I stand them no longer! Face me if you dare?'
The thought seemed to freeze at her command and she took the thought. Then once more the voice of Norty echoed around, somehow excited yet at the same time scared, 'I see! I see!'

"Mother is in stress, Aurorai, I must go to her!"
"It will be allowed not, Nortee, her instructions were clear; none are to enter the building for any reason. None will allow you to pass."
"She is my mother and none would dare bar the way. I will see her."
"You must go not!"

Racing down the hall fifty paces separated her from the room her mother was in. Outside the door were the ones who would stop her, if she gave them the slightest chance, and she was not prepared to do so. The enchanters must be eliminated first, they were the more dangerous; the guards she would deal with after. Her head lowered slightly as she began to let her mind reach for the nearest enchanter, and darkness took her as an unseen force closed her mind and she fell to the floor.

"You are well, my friend?"
"Thank you Pose, yes. We found what we seek!"
"Then we know enough, the old teachings are true. More will we see as we try again."
"To cease thought is harder than I had realised, I tire so."
"Sleep a while; Nortee will be in our study when you awake. She came as expected."
"I felt not her approach; all effort was taken in concentration. Sleep also; the wait may serve to have her think, though I doubt she will do so."

"Pose, for hours I have waited in the study and I ask yet again, why does she see me not?"
Pose looked from the scroll, "First she speaks with Aurorai."
"Why speak to her when her daughter waits so anxiously to see her?"
Once more she looked up and back to the scroll.
"Pose, please, I ask you speak."
Shaking her head she did not look up from the scroll.
The door opening made her stand and move to embrace her mother.
"Stay your ground, child; remain seated!"

"Mother...."

"I grow evermore weary of your ways! I spoke with you, asked you return home and you fail to listen to me; failed as Pose also asked you return. I gave instructions none were to enter the building, none did so; *except my daughter!*"

"Mother, it was with reason."

"Silence! You will speak no more until instructed! Twice within the month you have brought the enchanters into disrespect and I stand this no more. If I may not have my daughter follow instructions given to her then how may I ask others to do so? Stand!"

Shakily she stood.

"Nortee of the enchanters, from this moment until the passing of the new moon you are refused training with the enchanters. You may speak, if such is your wish, yet be careful of the words you choose."

"I see not why I should be punished for the love I hold for my mother."

"I see your words are unthought-of! Six new moons should you be barred from us, three for each of the disrespects you bring to this guild, I bar you for one only. If you see not why you are punished after this time I feel all hope for you is lost. Leave; you may return to our study once before the new moon. It is my hope you will see the reason to return and of what to speak. You may leave."

Watching Nortee leave Pose sighed, "I understand the punishment yet feel your words somewhat harsh."

"It must be so. The punishment is light; my words have hurt her more than the suspension. Nortee must realise the danger she places both the guild and herself in with her lack of thought."

"I feel you are too strict with her."

"I feel I am not strict enough. So hard have I tried with her; I train her hardest of any, as well you do also, yet I feel it is not enough."

"We train her to fight and to live only."

"As she should be so taught yet I feel you have left words unspoken. In what way do I fail?"

"I accuse you not of failing."

"In what is it I am lacking? As a friend I ask you speak, guide me please."

"I have no child of my own and cannot speak of what you ask. Mayhap you should seek guidance from another mother?"

"Who could guide me?"

"This you must decide yourself."

"I believe I know why I must be so harsh with her. It is the fault of myself she is as she is yet cannot think of what it is I have done. I have failed her, Pose. She is unlike any and allowances I have made yet still I know I have failed. How may I find the way to teach her? If I fail to see where I have erred to who do I to turn for advice, for help?"

"Elesee is knowledgeable in so many ways."

"Mother has spoken often to me Nortee is not how she should be yet not why she is as she is. If she knows not then how may I know? I worry, Pose, I worry."


"Drink the wine, Nortee. It will soothe you. This is used only for special occasions."

Taking a sip of the wine she sighed, "Never has mother spoken such to me. I agree punishment is needed for my lack of thought with Jerit. I have upset her yet the fight with him was not why she spoke such to me."

"Take another drink, a sip is too little to have you relax."

Taking a long drink she felt herself relax, "She spoke I should answer her and I wish I knew the words she would hear."

"You know them not?"

"I do not. To whom should I turn for advice?"

"I know not yet there is a way I may help my friend."

She could feel herself getting drowsy, "How may you help?"

"Finish the wine and sleep; on the morrow you may have a clear mind and turn to the one who would know."

"I wish not to sleep!"

"Finish the wine."

Suddenly it became clear, "You drink not?"

"As I spoke, the wine is for special occasions."

Her mind was becoming cloudy, "What is the occasion?"

"You must sleep, your mother ordered such."

"Mother orders sleep? How? The drink...is a sleep potion?"

Catching her as she slipped into unconsciousness she called, "She sleeps, father, take her to my room. Norty wished for me to do this and I see why she does so; I hope my friend also sees."

Sweeping her up in his arms he carried her to his daughter's room, "It is my wish also yet I believe she knows to whom she should turn."

# The Spark

"I am confused; I wished only to ensure she was safe, all was well with her. I have been forbidden to train yet mind it not; it is her voice which upset me, she spoke so harsh. Why would she speak such to me, grandmother?"

"I have duties to tend, Nortee. Juin returns from travels with friends by the evening and should expect our home to be ready to entertain them. You believe I should put this aside so you may ask foolish questions?"

"If an answer is unknown the question is never foolish!"

"Should you wish me to ask you to leave you have but to continue with the voice you use."

Her voice softened, "I apologise, grandmother. Why do so many treat me as a child? Long since have I passed the coming of age, I am full grown."

"Think back two days; why did your mother ask Aurorai to ensure you slept?"

"All yesterday I have thought of this and asked Aurorai why mother asked her to do this to me. She spoke not the reason though I feel she knows the answer."

"The answer is obvious to all but my granddaughter it would seem."

"Speak, grandmother. I wish to know why she is this way to me. You know not how upset I am."

"We have sat and eaten while you spoke the words of your mother and asked yet more foolish questions; eight have I heard, five of which never should have been asked. How is it you see not your mother's wishes?"

"The reason I asked to speak with you, I see not what she wishes from me. Long have I thought while I lay in the bed of Aurorai; now it seems strange she came to see me not when I awoke."

Picking a few sticks from the container Elesee looked back to her granddaughter, "Aurorai saw you not so you may think of your mother's words; it seems to me you lack the ability. Oft your mother has spoken of a spark within you, and to where this may lead. Since your friendship with Aurorai blossomed she now speaks of who follows your spark. Hetyial of the dark elves is oft seen at your side; do you begin to see your mother's worries?"

"Aurorai is a friend since first we met; both felt we may be the best of friends. Hetyial is of my age and new to our ways; she seeks words of instruction and teaches me her language in return. Am I to be denied friendship?"

"Once more foolish questions are asked and I see the frustration my daughter suffers; she brings this upon herself. Oft have I spoken your upbringing was not as it should be yet little notice she has taken it would seem."

"Mother and father work hard to ensure all is known to me; for me to be the enchantress as I was born to be; the druid I will be."

She handed her the bundle of sticks, "Break them for me."

Straining for a moment she shook her head, "I cannot break them."

Taking three sticks she broke each as she whispered names, "Nortee; Aurorai; Hetyial. Break the remaining sticks."

Straining she managed to break them, "I begin to see; I must ensure friends stay together."

"Your mother's lack of teaching shows ever deeper and I worry. Still your first words are of yourself; your thoughts stray not beyond those around you. Think, Nortee, think of the whole and then your place within it."

"I see not what you try so hard to show me."

Elesee sighed, "When the enchanters were summoned for a new leader to be chosen for them why were you sent to the lands of man?"

"Mother insisted I visit the land of man with you; this you know."

"Why was this?"

"Caspo Kwil had voiced mother was to lead the enchanters on his death. She wished me not to see her embarrassment when she was refused."

"Once more the foolish child I hear. You would have stood and given voice to your thoughts."

"Mother believes this of me?"

"Do you believe this of yourself?"

After a moment's thought she nodded, "I would have defended mother's right to lead; given voice to my thoughts and mayhap shamed her. This I now see."

"Giving voice without permission would show your lack of control and discipline; it would bring shame to you and not your mother. This is the reason I was asked to take you to the land of man. Do you understand of what I speak?"

"I understand, grandmother."

"Yet other actions speak ill of you. Jerit you attacked in the Rooms of Prayer and caused harm. Only Rinini saw this and was duty bound to speak to the council yet spoke to your mother only."

"I knew not you knew of this; I admit some surprise. Rinini and I have a liking for each other. I am thankful she spoke only to mother."

"Even through pain Jerit refused to speak. His ways are as they should be."

"Jerit would speak not of the promise he gave, this is against all I hold dear."

"No promise was made so no promise could be broken."

"Yet he...."

"Think of his words to you; he spoke no promise was made. I asked Jerit to ensure you caused the deaths of no others, no promise was given; it was an understanding between friends."

"You, grandmother? Is it you think so little of me you ask others to ensure I was to be kept safe?"

"Still you listen not. I asked four they ensure you caused not the death of others; think and understand your place in the scheme of the elves."

She could feel the tears starting and could no nothing to stop them, "Others know my ways and I feel ashamed of the way they think of me. You were correct to ask, grandmother; my actions may have caused the death of others. I am sorry such steps were needed."

"My granddaughter pleases me, she sees of what I speak."

"I try hard, grandmother."

"Then while you think let us continue. You entered the sanctum where the study of new ways and spells are learned for the first time. It was against all instructions given. In so doing you placed the life of your mother and the others in great danger. Explain this to me."

"When the linking with mother became weak I believed she had need of me. I did this through love of her."

"The truth you may hide from others if you feel you must. To hide the truth from yourself is to lie to yourself. This is not the way of our people. Is this the way you would be?"

Hanging her head she corrected herself, her father would be angry if he saw her actions, "Mother has spoken not of what was to be studied in the sanctum and to go to her with a weak excuse may have let me see a little of what they study. I was curious, this I admit. It was wrong; I see the way I have been and the foolish actions I justified as love."

"I am happy; there is still hope for my granddaughter, she begins to see. If it is your wish I will instruct in the ways my daughter has so fleetingly taught you."

"As I lay thinking I knew of but one I could turn to for advice. I ask you teach me; above all I wish mother to be proud of me."

"Do you fail to see how proud she is of you? This all see in so many ways."

"I know her love for me."

"A question I now have for you. Why did Aurorai ensure you slept?"

"Mother asked her to do so. She would do all mother asks of her."

"Now I hear a foolish answer. Evade not the question, Nortee."

Her eyes lowered as she spoke aloud her thoughts, "To ensure I returned not to the guild? She wished me not to see her. No, this is untrue."

"Not often does my granddaughter speak her troubled thoughts. Speaking aloud is oft a way to clear the head."

"I know not why mother asked Aurorai to do such to me. No harm was meant, this I know."

"She would harm not her daughter. What would you have done had sleep been withheld from you?"

"With thought I would have angered; sought out mother and spoken as harsh to her as she had to me. Now I see why she spoke to Aurorai before she would see me."

"Sleep ensures calmness come the morrow. Aurorai knew why your mother asked her and agreed. If she had thought it may harm you she would have refused, she is a true friend. The sticks you still hold, speak of them as they should be, see the whole."

"I need instruction, I see not of what you speak."

Collecting more sticks she tried to break them, struggling hard as she tried.

"What is it you try to do, grandmother?"

Elesee put the sticks to one side and placed the broken sticks on the table, her finger flicking them apart one at a time, "First the enchanters then others must follow; guard; warrior; ranger...."

"I see of what you speak; when all stand together they may not be broken or split asunder. Through my actions I may cause a rift in the enchanters and then the breaking of other guilds. How could I be so thoughtless? I feel sick, grandmother."

"You begin to see the whole?"

"Lore says should one guild fail then all elves will perish. If my actions were to break the enchanters I would be the cause of the death of my people; I wish it not. Grandmother, teach me as I should have been taught."

"It is a price you may find hard yet I believe you will prosper."

"Name the cost to me; any price I pay to save my people I do so gladly."

"Return to high elf city and speak with your mother; apologise for your ways, for your lack of understanding. Knowing her she will ask you return to the guild to train once more."

"I see the error of my ways, this I will speak of to her."

"She spoke to you only with Pose, not in front of the guild as she should have done, as Lore demands; she wished not for you be seen as a problem to others. You will speak you will stand before the enchanters and accept punishment of ten new moons for you were wrong."

"Mother should bar me not for so long."

"This I know. Within the space of ten new moons you may begin to grasp a little of the teachings you have missed; if you mark well my words and act upon them."

"I see the cost I must bear."

"It is but part of the cost. Your mother has left instruction on elfin ways too long; teachings should have commenced before your fifth year and understanding would be yours before you came of age. Your mind is not so set it may not be changed. On your return we speak of the child, the spark, within you."

"I will return; the child must be banished."

"Banished? No, Nortee."

"Then the child in me causes not the problems?"

"The child should be in all of us; even your grandfather still has within him a child I love, a child I see as we have fun together. When the weight born by your mother as she guides the guilds is hard to bear I hold her in my arms to comfort her and ensure she has the strength to continue once more. At these times the child in your mother is shown to me; never is there such a feeling in the heart of a mother when it happens, it bonds them together in a way only they may know. Even the brave, the leaders, need to know there is a place for them; a place where love and comfort may be found."

"With your help, grandmother, I would find these feelings also. If I may I will return in three days when grandfather returns to the land of the river elves."

"Three days are a long time for you to do this."

"I must speak with Aurorai and Hetyial I will be not able to see them for duties take me."

"You seek to lie to them?"

Her voice became softer, "I seek to ensure they know not how I am."

"Speak the reason you are to remain away, Nortee. Are they not friends?"

"They are the best of friends, grandmother. I will speak the reasons. On my return grandfather will be gone and our talks and training may begin without him seeing I am not as I should be."

"You think he sees not the way you are? He says little yet worries much. We have spoken of this and it is the reason he visits others so one day you may speak with me. He will continue to do so until he sees all is as it should be."

Throwing her arms around her she whispered, "Long ago mother spoke words to me she had spoken to father of you."

Returning the hug she asked, "What words?"

"Mother spoke you were wise and hoped one day to be as wise as you. You are not just wise, grandmother, you are the wisest of all people."

# A New Beginning

Finglas squeezed her, "Always your plans come true. The enchanters are stronger now the dark ones join with us, to become as one once again."

She yawned; tiredness was taking hold of her no matter how hard she fought it, "Not just the enchanters, as other guilds see how we prosper thoughts they will have of how they may also join with the dark elves so they will grow yet stronger."

"Now you lead them with Pose you have great powers to wield. I see the way Pose glances often to her sleeve; never have I seen her so happy."

"I care not for power. The elves were losing their fight to stay alive in this world. So many other races fight for lands belonging to us, with each passing year a new war starts and yet more elves die in battles to protect one side or the other. We are unlike other races; only two children are born to us, even to the river elves. Others, like man, may have many. It takes us so much longer to recover our losses after a war. It is time we lived in peace, and it is to this end I strive yet I know peace will never be. If the elves are to live and grow strong we must take part in no more wars. Let others have their wars and ask not the elves to join them in their fight."

"Wars serve only to kill."

"Still I worry; our lands are safer for the joining with the dark enchanters for few now would think to attack either of us. Yet we are not safe for so much land remains to be patrolled. Wars will still be when you and I are long dead and sit with the Gods; only in war may we truly know peace."

"Ack, more riddles and I grow too tired to think of answers."

"With the joining of the dark elves we are stronger and our flank protected, yet we are still open to attack. We need friends to call upon who would have others think yet again before attacking us. We need not alliances to cover our borders for they show we are weak. I fail to see from where we may find such help."

"The river elves are friends."

"Yet they have mated with man, to whom would they turn if another war between elves and man was to start?"

"They could choose man or us."

"So they are not friends to whom we could turn with confidence. We need another to whom we can be sure, yet where could such be found?"

"Sleep now, tomorrow we talk."

She was tired and unable to fight any longer, as she lay in his arms sleep took her, and in her sleep she began to dream. The world around her shimmered and faded, leaving nothing but a void of darkness. There was no sense of time, unable to move or speak yet somehow knowing danger lay in wait for her. Her mind recalled her mother's dream of the protectors on the day she and her sisters were conceived, and a fear came over her. Her greatest dread was for the Gods to grant her a child as she and her sisters had been to their mother, to fight a quest and possibly die in the attempt to win it for them.

It was impossible to stop the Gods if they demanded she should be the mother of a new Chosen One, but she knew she would never let it happen. She would die; kill herself, before she would give in to them. Her child would not be born for the Gods to play with as she had been. Resolve took her and her mind she screamed at them, 'No, it will not be, never will I bear a child for your pleasure!'

Lights flashed brightly in front of her, moving round and behind, she could no longer see them but felt them they prodded, feeling and testing her. Cold took her, so numbing she wanted to shiver, yet could not. Her body was no longer part of her, only her mind existed.

'Now want do you ask of me, have I not done all you wished, all you demanded? Leave me; I have done all for you.'

The cold turned warm, warm to hot, then to unbearable heat. She did not know if she was sweating or not, the heat she could feel, but not how her body was reacting to it.

'Messenger, let them not do this to me. I have done all they asked, they may ask no more. I beg you speak with them, tell of how I feel.'

The feelings in her body began to return, slowly, as once more she could feel her feet, her legs, and then the feelings stopped. Worry began again, why just parts of her and not the whole? Her fingers came to life, her hands and arms felt as if pins were dancing along them, around her body and down her legs, disappearing as they left her toes.

A new feeling took her, there was something on her back, cold at first but warming slowly as the heat from her body melted with it, and she realised she was laying on a bed of soft sheets.

Straining she tried to open her eyes, but nothing happened, they refused to obey her, remaining steadfastly closed. She was paralysed, unable to lift a finger or open her mouth to call for assistance.

Fear began to take control of her, to whisper in the darkness of dreads yet to come. She fought them down, recalling her mother's teaching of the self; it was hard work but banished them from her mind. 'Thank you, mother, your teachings save your daughter once more.'

Resignation took her as she let herself relax, yet unsure if her body had done so. She would use her mind to see what was around her, to try to make sense of the strange noises. There were minds all around her, yet somehow different from any she had seen before, covered by a fine veil as if to hide the thoughts not only from them but also from her. Most were in a state of sleep, yet she was confused, the minds were above, below and all around.

The odd mind was awake and one was approaching her, a fear began to take hold; if they should attack she was unable to defend herself, and there was no sign of the paralysis leaving her. Would her mind be enough to defend herself?

It was then she heard the voice, undoubtedly female, but she did not know the language or any of the strange sounds assaulting her ears. Unable to know if this female had challenged her to a fight and for what reason; she hoped there would be no struggle, no fight for supremacy.

Her mind was somehow weak from the paralysis, too weak to use against a foe. Her mind was powerful, able to throw another from her with ease; yet now it felt as if it belonged to a child, to an enchanter new to the ways of the mind and unable to use it. What the female asked of her she had no idea.

"Who the heck are you and where in Heavens name did you come from?"

**Next: Norty, The Love of Man.**